Chapter 1

Sophia's fight was not  w
months since the diag ıg
more we can do for y ⅃o
now is keep her com .rn
off the life support.' ᴅɪ ɪ ɑ... ᴜ ... nd
sincere. He was obviously well practised at delivering
bad news, but this was of little consolation to Amos. He
tried to concentrate on Dr Patel's words, but they were
alien and surreal. He strained when the doctor tried
explaining it to him again, but it was no use. The words
sounded muffled and distant, with no real substance or
meaning. They were individual entities existing in their
own universe with no relevance to each other. He shook
his head and moaned, then slumped in the chair beside
his wife's bed. The chair groaned slightly under his
weight. It was oversized and uncomfortable, despite its
thick padding. The wooden armrests felt oddly cold in the
warmth of the room. Amos thought it odd that he would
notice these details at that moment yet struggle to
understand the doctor's words. He was supposed to be
present and focused on his wife. He was supposed to be
caring and worried, but all he could think of was how
uncomfortable that chair felt. *The mind takes you to
strange places when you are hiding from the truth.*

The doctor offered his condolences one last time and
left Amos alone in the room with his comatose wife. He
pulled the uncomfortable chair closer to Sophia's bedside
and took her hand in his. The feel of her warm, smooth
skin grounded him and brought him back to the present.
Her touch soothed him the way it always did and helped

him relax. He checked his watch again — 5 pm. *Where was Mary? I called her hours ago. She should be here; she knows I struggle to focus when I'm tired,* he thought. He had spent the last five days and nights at the hospice and hadn't slept much. He needed Mary to listen to the doctors and translate for him like Sophia used to. A warm rush of blood flooded his face. He had been an engineer in a past life, an education that was paid for by the army decades ago. He had built bridges, designed great big things, and created wonderous, complex infrastructure all over the world. An expert in demolitions and explosives, his skills had been in high demand since leaving the army. That was all before the incident. Now he needed his daughter to explain to him why his wife wouldn't wake up. Amos leaned close and pressed his face into the back of Sophia's hand, hugged it as tight as he dared, and closed his eyes.

He was asleep for almost two hours when the room door swung open, and Mary barged in, being obnoxiously loud and waving her hands aggressively at the person on the other end of the phone. She was dressed in a fake fur coat and thick, black-framed sunglasses with diamonds in the upper edges. *She looks like one of those social media influencers,* Amos thought, w*ith too much money and no self-respect.*

'Alright,' she barked into the phone. 'I said I'll be there, OK? I need to go now.' She stuffed the phone into her pocket and turned to her father.

'Where have you been? I phoned you over 6 hours ago,' Amos snapped, checking his watch.

'Don't start, Dad, I've been busy.'

'Busy doing what, Peanut? You don't have a job.'

'Just because I don't have a job doesn't mean I am not

BEAST AND BURDEN

Lee Adam

First published in 2024 by Blossom Spring Publishing
Beast and Burden Copyright © 2024 Lee Adam
ISBN 978-1-0686195-0-2
E: admin@blossomspringpublishing.com
W: www.blossomspringpublishing.com

For Paige
Without you, this would not have been possible

He had died once before, but this time was different. This time, it was final. His head lay cradled on her lap as his breathing slowed. His once broad, strong frame felt weak and limp in her arms now. Her hand pressed tighter onto his wound to try and stem the flow, but it was no use. The thick blood oozed, mixed with heavy rain, and washed into the gutter. With the last of his strength, he raised his hand and wiped away her tears, and he smiled.

He was ready now.
Ready to die.
For her.

busy. And stop calling me Peanut. I hate that name; it's so childish.'

'I've called you Peanut since you were a baby,' he replied.

'Yes, and I hate it, so please stop. Nobody else calls me that.' Mary slammed herself onto the chair on the opposite side of the bed. Her fake fur coat hung loosely from her shoulders. The phone vibrated once in her pocket. Not a phone call, Amos guessed, but a message. He watched as she pulled the phone from her pocket, and her fingers danced across the screen, typing a reply.

'Aren't you even going to ask how your mother is?' he asked through gritted teeth. There was a long pause before she glanced up from her phone.

'Well? What did the doctor say then?' she said, before returning her eyes to the phone.

'Could you please put the phone away and try to show some respect for the woman who gave birth to you?' He could no longer hide his indignation. This moment deserved her attention. Sophia deserved her attention.

'Oh my God, Dad, what?' she snapped, taking her sunglasses off and waving them in the air. 'How am I being disrespectful? She isn't even awake, so what do you want me to do? Eh?'

'Just put the phone away, please, and could you go find the doctor? He tried explaining your Mum's condition, but I was too tired, and I couldn't take in what he was saying.' The anger was gone from his voice and was replaced with pleading. Mary's arms fell, and her brow furrowed. Amos saw guilt and pity flash in his daughter's eyes. He turned his head, hiding from her gaze.

'OK, Dad.' She put the phone back into the pocket of

her coat, put her sunglasses back on, and quietly left the room. Amos turned back to his sleeping wife and took her hand again.

'I know you asked me to be patient with her, and I'm trying, Sophia. I'm trying to be understanding, but it's hard when she's being like this. She won't talk to me. And I know what you would say. You'd say that I don't listen to her when she does, but I just can't understand what she's saying half the time. I don't know if it's a generational thing or not. I mean, how much can a fifty-three-year-old man and a twenty-three-year-old girl have in common anyway? She's lazy, aimless, and disrespectful, and I don't know where she gets it from. She's stubborn too, just like you.' He glanced at the door nervously, suddenly aware he was speaking louder than he probably should. 'I love her with everything I am, Soph, but I just can't get through to her. She just won't listen. I'm not asking her to change who she is. I just want her to use some of the brains I know she has. I just want her to think and make good choices for a change. I don't know; maybe we're just too different. I just want to connect with her, but I don't know how.' Guilt now washed over him. 'There, I said it. I don't know how to love her.' The jagged words stabbed him deep, and he swallowed hard.

The door opened, and Mary shuffled slowly in, her feet dragging as she walked. She quietly closed the door and kneeled in front of him at the bedside. Mascara-stained tears dripped from under her sunglasses as she sniffed hard. She opened her mouth to speak, but nothing came out. Amos pulled her close, wrapping his arms around his daughter as tight as he could. He did not allow himself to cry. There would be time to weep later. Time to be weak and wallow in self-pity, but right now, in this room, Mary needed him. His little girl was scared and in pain, and she needed his strength.

She was going to need him more than either of them knew.

Chapter 2

The sun rose early on Glasgow's Marie Curie hospice, and long, bony shadows from the trees in the car park stretched towards Amos and Mary as they stepped out into the cold. The smell of fresh rolls from the hospice's café lingered in the air, but he had lost his appetite, and he suspected Mary felt the same. Neither of them had slept the whole night. They had sat at Sophia's bedside, talking to her, saying their goodbyes, and telling her they loved her for the last time. *This was not how it was supposed to end, she was supposed to be at home with me,* he thought, as the image of his wife on her death bed flashed in his mind; The harsh glow of the hospice's artificial lights had turned Sophia's skin unnaturally pale, the glare of the white sheets giving her an unhealthy, ghostly complexion. He closed his eyes and thought back to the good old days, before the illness. Her skin was the colour of honey, warm and silky to the touch. Her angelic laugh was light, playful, and infectious, and her gentle eyes were deep, swirling pools of green with a small fleck of brown in the upper corner of her right eye. A small mole tucked itself behind her nose under the right eye and only served to highlight her natural allure. A passion for running had kept her figure trim and athletic. Slender without being frail. Her long, muscular legs had made her slightly taller than average. She had been a wonderful combination of stubborn, funny, strong-willed, and brave. This is the image he would keep. This is what he would think of to replace the image of the frail woman he saw in the bed. Keeping this image in his mind wouldn't be difficult as Mary shared all the same features, minus the mole.

They walked slowly and silently across the car park. His Audi was parked at the far corner under a small, naked tree. Amos climbed into the driver's side while Mary slumped into the passenger's side. The March frost was thick on the silver Audi and glistened in the low sun. The cold nipped at them both, but neither of them had the energy to shiver or complain. They just sat in silence and let the car's heater defrost the windshield.

'I love you,' Amos finally said, because he had to say something.

'I love you too,' Mary replied, her voice breaking a little. Amos fumbled in the pocket of the driver's door for the packet of tissues he kept there and handed one to her. 'Here, Peanut, your make-up is running.' A sad laugh escaped from her dry lips, and she dried her eyes, wiping away the make-up that was hiding the bruise on her right cheek, just below her eye. 'What happened to your face?' Amos asked. He reached out to touch his daughter's cheek, but she quickly turned her face away.

'It's nothing, can we just go?' she said, and put her sunglasses back on, failing to hide the bruise.

'What do you mean "nothing"? It's clearly not nothing.' He turned in his seat to face her; fear and anger now occupied the space where numbness was moments before, and he could do little to hide it. 'Was it him? Did he do this? That's it. We're going to the police right now.'

'Dad, no, please! I said it was nothing, please don't go to the police. I just want to go home and get some sleep.' It was useless arguing with her, and he knew it. She was as stubborn as her mother. Sophia was the only one who could get Mary to open up, and he didn't have the strength to fight with her right now. He turned his

7

attention to the road, pulled slowly out of the car park, and headed north.

Mary watched in silence as the world passed by her window. She possessed a level of natural beauty that was matched only by her mother but was now unique. Her persistent use of excessive make-up was entirely unnecessary, as Amos had often said. This was more than just the distorted opinion of one prideful father. Her beauty had received comments from everyone since she was a baby. A friend of a friend once asked if he could do a photo shoot with Mary when she was a child, with the promise that she would be on the cover of some magazine Amos had never heard of. Both Sophia and Amos had refused. They had seen the effects of this type of thing all too often. They just wanted their daughter to have a normal, happy childhood, a decision Mary still holds a grudge against to this day. She pulled her long brown hair down across her face, where the bruise was exposed. The leather of the steering wheel groaned as Amos twisted it in his hands, turning his knuckles white. He was concentrating hard on the road ahead when Mary's pocket started blaring a song he didn't recognise. As far as he could make out, it was a female rapper asking someone to touch the dangly thing in the back of her throat. It sounded far too crude for his taste. Mary quickly looked at her phone, silenced it, and put it back in her pocket. The Audi crossed the river Kelvin a little after 7 am, Amos turned west, and shortly after, he pushed the button next to the overhead light to open the driveway gate.

Bearsden had one of the lowest crime rates in Glasgow, and Anderson Street had the lowest crime rate in Bearsden. The large, luxurious houses here had names instead of door numbers and six-foot walls marking their perimeter. The Audi's tyres rolled slowly over the loose gravel driveway and stopped inside the two-car garage, which only ever housed one car. The garage's interior door opened into a large, spacious kitchen with a centre island. Its white cupboard doors contrasted with its black marble worktop. The black and white theme carried on around the rest of the room and gave the kitchen a clean, clinical feel. Ceiling-to-floor windows with large patio doors that looked onto the back garden flooded the room with bright, natural morning light. Mary entered ahead of Amos, and he watched her kneel and give their golden retriever a long, lingering hug.

'Hi Sandy, have you been a good boy?' she asked, while rubbing the dog's back. Sandy wagged his tail excitedly then shook himself free. Mary rubbed her eyes and yawned as she stood.

'Why don't you go for a nap?' Amos said. 'It's been a hard night for us both.' Mary's pocket burst to life again with the same vulgar song he heard in the car. She snatched it from her pocket and walked to the hallway.

'What?' Amos heard her say, 'No! My mother has just... Look, I'm done, OK? I'm not doing this anymore. I'm done.' There was a pause. 'I said no; it's over. I don't care. I can't do this anymore.' Another long pause. 'Not my problem; I'm out.' With that, she hung up and walked back to the kitchen with her head hung low, slid her phone onto the island worktop, and turned to her father. The inner corners of her eyebrows rose, coming together in the middle. 'Dad, can I stay here for a while?'

'Of course, Peanut. You don't even need to ask.' He walked around the island and hugged her tight. After a minute, he broke the hug and held her at arm's length. He stared at her for another long moment, enjoying the connection. 'You're just as beautiful as your mother,' he said, brushing her hair from her face. 'Your bedroom is just the way you left it. Why don't you go for a shower and have a nap, then we'll get some lunch when you wake up?' He pulled her closer again and kissed her gently on the forehead. Mary wiped a tear away with her palm and made her way upstairs.

Amos walked to the patio and pulled the heavy sliding doors apart. Sandy rushed for the trees that lined the garden wall, as a blast of icy air flooded into the room, sending a shiver through him for the first time that morning. The phone vibrated on the island. Amos dashed for the phone and snatched it from the worktop before the song could start. He stood silently listening for any evidence that Mary had heard the vibrating and was making her way back down, but heard nothing. The caller ID showed only the letter B, but he knew who it was. It was the same man who gave his daughter the bruise on her face. The same man who stole his Peanut from him and robbed her of her potential and innocence and who was told minutes ago that this relationship was over. Amos answered.

'She said it's over. Now leave her alone.'

'Put her on the phone now,' the voice hissed.

'I said leave her alone. Phone this number again, and I'll call the police. Stay away. I'm warning you.'

'Warning me?' B scoffed, '*You* are warning *me*? Listen, old man, I really don't care if your wife just died; Mary is mine. Tell her she has two hours to get back here or else.' The phone went silent.

Amos scowled at the phone as his hand tightened around it. Finally, he loosened his grip and tossed it back onto the worktop.

He walked to the staircase, gripped the banister, and began to climb, but he froze on the first step. This would be the first time he would sleep in his bed without his wife for as long as he could remember. He turned and headed to his study instead, where his comfortable reclining chair awaited. The ceiling-to-floor windows, which lined the kitchen, continued into the study and gave it a large, open feel. The armchair was positioned so that it looked out across the garden, which ran along the back and north side of the house. The sun poured into the room and gently warmed it. The heat of the room and comfort of the old leather armchair conspired against him and lured him into a much-needed sleep.

Maybe it was because he hadn't slept much in days, or maybe it was because he was emotionally drained, but whatever the reason, he was in the grip of a deep sleep when two shotgun blasts destroyed the hinges on the front door, thirty minutes after the deadline given by B. The explosions threw Amos from his chair, and he rushed towards the sound at the front of the house. He only made it as far as the doorway of the study when a large, rough hand clamped around his throat and gripped tight.

'Hey, old man. Remember me?' said the larger of the two intruders that now stood in the hallway. 'Get the girl.' he barked at his accomplice. The smaller goon stomped for the stairs that ran parallel with the hallway. Sandy, the golden retriever, emerged from the kitchen with his teeth bared and charged at the intruder who was choking his owner. With his free hand, the gorilla-sized man quickly whipped a pistol from the chest strap inside his jacket, pointed it at the lunging animal, and pulled the trigger. A deafening crack made Amos's ears ring. The dog lay motionless in a pool of blood on the hall floor.

'Sandy!' Amos shouted. He tried to struggle free, but huge muscles in the intruder's forearms tensed and tightened the grip around Amos's throat. 'What do you want?' Amos choked.

'We only came for the girl,' the gorilla replied, putting the gun back in its holster. The danger was real, that point had been made. There was no need to keep waving the gun around. 'We have no orders to hurt you, but we also don't have any orders not to. Do you understand? I'd rather not hurt you, so please don't give me a reason.' The man's voice was deep and smooth, with an air of calm and confidence.

'What are you talking about? Orders from who?'

'You know who; please don't act stupid, Mr Fisher. We both know you're smarter than that. Now, Mr B is not a very patient man. He asked you nicely to return what's his, and he doesn't like asking twice.' If not for the vice-like grip on his throat and the very real threat of violence, Amos might have mistaken the man's tone as polite. Given the circumstances, though, his mild manner only added to his menace.

'Where are you taking her? I won't let you do this; I'll phone the police,' Amos choked.

'Yes, Mr B said something about your little threat. He wasn't impressed. Let's just say it'd be better for Mary if you didn't. Mr B has plans for your daughter. She's his own personal mockingbird, you might say, and killing a mockingbird would be a sin.'

Muffled screams echoed from upstairs. The smaller goon had Mary slumped over his shoulder; her wrists and ankles were bound with cable ties, and her mouth was taped shut. She seemed weightless to him. Amos watched on as Mary kicked and tried to scream when she saw the larger man with his hand around her father's neck.

'Shut up,' barked the smaller guy as he gripped the handrail tightly, taking one careful step at a time. The gorilla turned his head to assess his accomplice's progress, his hand still gripping tight around Amos's throat. Amos saw this lapse in concentration and took his chance. He wedged his foot against the corner of the door frame for leverage and pushed as hard as he could, hoping to catch the beast off balance. This only rocked the large man back, however, and infuriated him. The big guy swung his free hand and caught Amos hard on his chin.

Everything went black.

Chapter 3

The vulgar song echoed loudly through the hall as the phone rattled against the worktop. It rang long enough to stir Amos awake, then stopped.

Silence again.

Pain radiated from his jaw up through his head. Slowly, he peeled himself from the floor and rested his back on the door frame of the study. He sat stunned on the floor. One minute. Two minutes. His eyes glazed over as he stared at the hole in the wall where the door once was. The door lay on the floor among the shattered splinters of the door frame that had held it in place. A cold wind blew through the house, and a shiver shook him back to the present moment. Slowly, Amos stumbled to his feet and grimaced, holding his head with one hand and using the other to steady himself on the wall. The phone kicked into life again, with the rapper asking to be choked. He shuffled awkwardly towards the noise, avoiding the puddle of blood that pooled around the lifeless dog, and picked up the phone.

'Mary? Is that you?' he groaned.

'No, it's Beth. Where's Mary?' a voice asked, sounding rushed and panicked.

'They took her, I don't know where. I need to call the police.'

'No, don't. It'll be worse for her if you do. She'll be safe for now. Sort of. I hope.'

'What? Who is this? How do you know Mary? Where is she?'

'I'm the only friend you have right now and your best bet of getting your daughter back alive. OK, they took

Mary, but you still have her phone. That's good; that gives us leverage. You have to get out of there, though; it's not safe. Once they realise you have her phone, they'll be back. I can meet you, but you must bring the phone with you, do you understand?'

'What? No, I don't. Why do you need her phone? What's going on here? Who are you?'

'I don't have time to explain right now. All you need to know is that you need to get out of there now. Do you have a pen and paper?' Amos scrabbled in a drawer, found a pen and a scrap of paper, and scribbled down the address that Beth gave him and hung up.

Amos stood still for a long moment, staring dazed and empty into the middle distance.

The silence of the room was deafening.

Two whole minutes passed before reality crashed back in, and his training took over. *Time to get moving, soldier,* he thought. *You need to be prepared. Proper preparation and planning prevents piss-poor performance. You are a Royal Engineer. You are a Sapper.* His jaw tightened and his fists clenched as he took off down the hall. He took the stairs two at a time. The pain in his head hadn't subsided, and he still felt groggy from the large intruder's blow, but he couldn't slow down.

There was no time.

At the back of his wardrobe, he found relics from the old days. The olive-green T-shirt, woolly pullover with dark olive-green shoulder patches, and dark cargo trousers were much more suited for what lay ahead than the jeans and T-shirt combo he was currently sporting. The steel toe-capped boots and black waterproof jacket completed the look. The phone fit snugly in the zip

15

pocket on the left breast of the jacket. Lastly, in the drawer of the bedside table, he took out the small black rectangular box with Smith & Wesson written on the side. Inside was the SWBG2TS tactical knife that Sophia had given him for his 50th birthday. The 4.4-inch, high-carbon black oxide, Tanto serrated blade folded neatly into a black, textured handle. With one smooth movement, he slid the blade free and, with his fingers nestled nicely in the ridges of the handle, inspected the knife closely. The blade had no knicks or dents and was still as sharp as the day it left the factory. The blood lines were clean, and the window breaker at the handle's base was undamaged. Carefully, he folded the blade back into the handle, slipped it into one of the narrower pockets of the cargo trousers, and charged back downstairs.

Grabbing the car keys from the kitchen worktop, he darted for the garage through the same door he had used to enter only hours earlier. Hopefully, the goons hadn't shot the tyres of his car after knocking him out. They hadn't. He backed the car out of the garage and turned around in the driveway. Loose gravel from the driveway was kicked up as the car lunged towards the gate. He glanced at the address he had written down earlier and entered it into the car's satnav. He turned left as instructed and gunned the engine. A wail of police sirens sounded in the distance; they were getting closer. It was better that he was gone before they arrived and put Mary in even more danger.

Chapter 4

The car's built-in satnav led Amos to the Clyde Boatyard in Clydebank. It was only 15 minutes from the luxurious gated community in Bearsden, yet worlds apart. The crime rate in this part of Scotland's largest city jumped tenfold, and the average life expectancy fell dramatically. This particular boatyard had seen more than its fair share of late-night exchanges between questionable characters and was even the final resting place for a few of them. Amos stopped at the eight-foot tall, barbed wire fence that separated the boatyard from the road. Scattered barren trees lined the fence, hiding the yard and its warehouses from the road, which ran parallel to the north-east. The only entrance was through a large double gate, which was held permanently open by rusted hinges. The open gate was probably more suited for quick getaways than to entice uninvited guests. To the left of the gate, one of the few patches of grass left in the industrial area was littered with an old fridge that lay on its side and the remains of some flat-packed furniture scattered around it. A patch of gravelled land opposite the rusted gates was used as a makeshift car park, which currently hosted only one car. All four tyres of the car were flat, and the windows had been smashed. Amos guessed it had been there a while, abandoned by its owner and destroyed by bored local kids looking to fill their time with whatever little excitement they could find.

Large water-filled potholes in the dirt road slowed his approach as he drove carefully through the gate. The satnav announced that he had arrived at his destination when he pulled up outside an abandoned single-storey warehouse on the left of the dirt track. The once-white façade of the building had discoloured over time and was splattered randomly with graffiti. A small, dark Kia Picanto was parked outside. *Not the usual car of choice for crime bosses or drug dealers*, Amos thought. *Beth's*, he hoped. He drove slowly past and parked the Audi behind a smaller warehouse, twenty yards farther along the track. Amos pulled Mary's phone from his pocket and stared at its blank screen for a moment before stashing it in the glove compartment.

Slipping out of the car, Amos crept around the back of the smaller warehouse. Avoiding the gravel path, he quickly made his way across the patch of grass that separated the two buildings and ducked behind the rear of the graffitied building. A quick perimeter check confirmed there were no other cars and no backdoor exit. *One way in, one way out. No surprises.* The wide shutter at the front of the building was rusted shut and looked like it hadn't been used in years. It had probably been used when large machinery was towed in and out of the warehouse way back when. The small wooden door to its left lay ajar. It groaned slightly when he tugged on it, and a female voice echoed in the empty space inside. He stopped and listened carefully for another voice to reply, but none came. *A phone call*, he thought. The voice was clipped but amplified by the stone walls and slanted tin roof. Amos inched his head carefully inside the door and saw the origin of the voice. She stood twenty feet from the door, facing away from the entrance. The tin roof was supported by two rows of six concrete columns. Each column looked roughly two feet by two feet and was spaced evenly every forty feet or so along the length of the warehouse. The woman turned and walked towards the rear of the building, then stopped when she reached the second pair of columns. Amos crept in and hid behind the first column.

'I don't know,' she said. 'He should be here by now.' She paused, listening to the voice on the phone. 'I told him to bring it. You'll know as soon as I have it.' Another pause. 'Yes, I know the girl is not a priority; the phone is.' Another pause. 'He may be useful.' Another pause. 'You don't know that. He's her father, for Christ's sake.' Another pause. 'No. This is my call, and if there's any blowback, then I'll deal with it.' With that, she ended the call and stuffed the phone into the pocket of her coat. A frustrated sigh filled the empty space as she raised her eyes to the roof.

'Who are you and where is my daughter?' Amos asked, as he stepped from behind the column.

'Jesus. You frightened the life out of me,' the woman said, jumping around to look at him.

'Who are you and where is my daughter?' he asked again. His voice boomed in the empty building.

'Like I said on the phone, my name is Beth. I'm a friend of Mary's. Now, did you bring the phone?'

'I want to know where my daughter is first.'

'She is safe for now, but I need the phone to keep her that way. Now, please, where is it?' she pleaded.

'Why? What's so important about the phone?'

'Something Mr B wants is on it, and I can use it to get Mary back safely.'

'Who are you? Are you with the police?'

'Listen, Amos, I don't have time to explain everything, you're just going to have to trust me.'

'Trust you?' Amos shouted. 'I don't know you. I don't know what is going on. This morning, two maniacs broke into my house, kidnapped my daughter, killed my dog, and left me unconscious on the floor. I'm now standing in a warehouse, talking to a woman I've never met, who is telling me my daughter is in danger unless I hand over a phone. You won't tell me who you are, who you work for, or what is on the phone. So, forgive me if I'm not in a trusting mood. You need to explain exactly what is going on here. Now.' he demanded.

Beth sighed heavily. 'Mary is mixed up with some bad people. She's in a lot of trouble, and I'm trying to help.'

'Where is she?'

'I don't know.'

'Then how do you know she's safe?'

'Mr B needs her. He needs what is on that phone. Now I can use that to get her back safely, so please give me the phone.'

'I don't have it,' he lied.

'What? Where is it? I thought you had it? I told you to bring it.'

'It's safe, and, until I get my daughter back, it stays with me.'

'Listen, Amos, it's not what you think.' Beth's hands clasped together, pleading with him as she stepped closer.

'Don't come any closer. And how do you know my name?'

'Mary told me. She told me everything about you.'

Amos turned and walked towards the door.

'Where are you going? Beth said.

'You have no idea where Mary is, so you're no help to me. I'll find her myself,' he snapped, then marched out of the warehouse, leaving Beth alone. With no need for a covert exit, he walked straight for his car. The small wooden door clattered against the faded building as Beth chased after him, calling for him to stop.

'Look, Beth, or whatever your name is,' Amos snapped, as he turned to face the woman. 'I don't care which branch of the police you work for. If they think I've gone to the police, then Mary is dead.' He turned, continued his march towards his car, and slammed into the driver's seat. Beth followed, still shouting for him to stop.

OK Sapper, what's the next move? The phone. Check the phone.

The sounds of Beth's protests were drowned out by the diesel engine roaring to life. Turning right, he headed back the way he came and headed towards Glasgow Road.

It was a little after 1.30 pm now, and he was beginning to feel weak. *Eat when you can.* That was the training all those years ago, and he would need to keep himself fuelled. *I'll be of no use to Mary if I don't have the energy to save her.* Amos headed for a local café he had frequented when he oversaw a demolition project nearby a couple of years before. The food was good, and the car park was hidden from the main road, which was an added benefit.

Chapter 5

The bell in the café chimed as he pushed the door open. The place hadn't changed much since he was last here. The same five small booths sat under the same four large windows that faced onto the river Clyde, although the seats in the booths had been reupholstered with fresh red vinyl. Four smaller tables were dotted randomly in the remaining space. Each table had two chairs with matching red vinyl cushioned seats. A small L-shaped counter faced the door and was staffed by the same two plump ladies that had served him years ago. One smaller, approximately five-feet-five, and the other, two inches taller. The familiar smell of fried sausage, onions, and eggs wafted from the open kitchen door and service hatch that lay behind the counter. In the kitchen, another two ladies busied themselves cooking and preparing a wide range of fried foods. Only two tables were occupied. The lunchtime rush must be over.

'What can I get for you, honey?' asked the shorter of the two women from behind the counter. Her small, round face was flushed and sweaty but welcoming. Amos ordered the full breakfast with coffee. The order was repeated to the kitchen staff, and he took one of the booths by the window. He unzipped his breast pocket and took out Mary's phone. It prompted him to enter the passcode. *Shit*. After a moment, he glided his fingers over the screen and entered Mary's birthday. It was rejected. The phone informed him that he had two more chances before it would lock itself for five minutes. Sophia's birthday was his next guess. This was also rejected. This time, a message flashed, showing him that he had one more chance. Sandy's birthday was his last try, but it was rejected, and the phone locked itself. *Damn.*

'Here you go, honey.' said the smaller lady, placing the plate on the table in front of him. He put the phone back in his pocket and thought of his next move.

With his food finished, Amos wiped away the grease that dripped from his mouth and sipped the last of the coffee. The food was disappointing, but the coffee was good enough to order a second cup. Caffeine and calories were exactly what were needed. He looked out of the window at a lonely tugboat as it sloshed aimlessly past on the river. The lady arrived with the second cup of coffee and two small milk portions. He poured half of a single portion into his cup and watched it swirl in the dark liquid. Mary always wanted to drink the other half of his milk portions when she was a child. They were closer back then. She used to be such a daddy's girl. Often, whenever they were shopping with Sophia, he and Mary would get bored, so they would play silly games and make each other laugh. Then, when she was a little older, Mary would go running with him. They used to enjoy taking Krav Maga and boxing classes together too. Fitness and combat were what they bonded over. Thinking back, it was hard to pinpoint when they started to drift apart. When she stopped talking to him, and gravitated towards Sophia. It was probably around the time she started high school. That was when she started to spend more time in bed, glued to one device or another. Then the arguments would start when Amos tried to get Mary out of bed. She claimed stress and depression stopped her from going to school or doing the things she used to enjoy. She stopped running and boxing, and some days she wouldn't even leave the house. Depressed? What did she have to be depressed about? She had a good life — no hardships or real responsibilities. She had no idea what stress was. She never had to do a rest tour in Ireland, locating and defusing IEDs. She never had to do minefield and boobytrap clearance in Afghanistan. She never lost friends in battle, unable to talk to friends or family because they didn't have the right security clearance. That was depressing. That was stressful. She was just being lazy. Too lazy to work. Too lazy for school. She was even too lazy to think. She once forgot his birthday, even though it was the code for her phone.

Wait.

He frantically fished the phone back out of his pocket. He held his breath and entered 170170. The phone lit up. *Yes.* He navigated to the picture album first. No luck. It was empty. He tried the video library next. Empty too. The audio files and iTunes library offered the same results. No documents, no media, nothing. Confused, he navigated to the storage section in the phone's settings. Only two files showed to be storing any data. The phone book and the secure file vault. The vault required additional security to access, and somehow, he didn't think his birthday would be the answer this time. He made his way to the vault, nonetheless. It asked for the six-digit code. A birthday? Could it be that easy? This time, the phone offered the entire keyboard and not just numbers. This complicated things. A quick calculation told him that there are one million possible permutations of a six-digit number. That had now multiplied to an almost infinite number of letter and number combinations. He entered the same code as before. This time, the rejection message said he had two more chances before the information was locked forever. Too risky. *Damn.*

The phone book offered only a handful of names, including his and Sophia's. But calling any of the others would be dangerous. *If the phone really is that important, I can't risk letting the wrong people know who has it.* The only one who knew he had it was Beth, and she was obviously law enforcement of some kind and therefore another risk. He looked through the phonebook again, hoping a name he recognised would stand out. *What were the names of Mary's friends? Think, Amos, think.* No use. He didn't know any of her friends. He didn't know much about her at all, actually. Ashamed and embarrassed, he placed the phone face down on the table and picked up his coffee.

The phone sprang to life, vibrating violently on the table. He snatched it up, looking for a caller ID, but there was none. Not a phone call, it was a message. The message was on something called Snapchat. He'd heard of the app before, and, as far as he could remember, it was a service that deleted the message automatically after it'd been viewed. A perfect messaging service for people who have something to hide, which apparently Mary did. Knowing that the message would delete itself, he asked one of the serving ladies for a pen and paper. He switched the phone to his left hand and the pen to his right, ready to copy the message. His thumb glided over the yellow square icon, which had a white ghost shape inside, and opened the message. Reading the message, he smiled and put the pen down. The message was an address, one he didn't need to copy down because he knew it well.

Chapter 6

'What do you mean she doesn't have it? Where is it?' Mr B screamed, the muscles in his jaw tensed, and the sound of his teeth grinding against one another was only drowned out by the pounding of his own heart. His eyes widened, burning a hole into the two idiots standing in front of him. The bulging vein on the right side of his temple pulsed quicker, and he felt the blood rush to his face. 'Where is the phone?' he asked again in staccato, stabbing each word individually.

'She didn't have it on her, boss,' the larger of the two men said nervously.

'I sent you to get her *and* the phone. Do you know how important that phone is? Do you know why I need it back?'

'Yes, boss,' both men replied sheepishly.

'Then where is it?' Mr B yelled as he slammed his fist on the desk. The venetian blinds at his back split the bright daylight into slits, forcing the two men who stood opposite him to squint hard. They both shuffled awkwardly and said nothing. Mr B let an uncomfortable silence settle in the room before he slithered forward in his chair and spread his hands across the black desk. Two twelve-inch-thick gold columns served as legs, which held an eighteen-inch thick, six-foot wide tabletop. 'Do you know why I had this desk made?' he asked rhetorically. 'It's a perfect replica of the desk Tony Montana had in the movie Scarface. It's a symbol of power, of status, and of intent. It's a personification of my ambition, and the lengths I'm willing to go to, to achieve my goal. It's a reminder that in life, you've got to make the money first. Then, once you get the money, you get the power.' He stood up from the black leather chair and rested his arm on the gold ornate trim on top of the chair's tall back. The centre of the chair back, which was custom made to match the table, was monogrammed in gold lettering with Mr B's initials in the same style as the chair from the movie. 'I, like Tony Montana, have built my empire up from nothing. This current deal has been eighteen months in the making, and now I am three days away from making the biggest deal this city has ever seen. Three days from a multi-billion pound agreement that will make me the most powerful man in Scotland.' Mr B slipped out from behind the desk, stalked past the big goon, and stood between the two henchmen. 'Now, I gave both of you one simple task.' In one smooth movement, he glided to the smaller of the two. His six-foot-six, slender frame towered over the man by five inches. His long, sinewy fingers slipped into the lapel of the man's sports coat to adjust it, then flattened it back into place. 'And a man of my position and power cannot tolerate failure.' With that, Mr B grabbed the goon by the lapel he had just fixed and slammed his forehead into the man's nose. The sound of the nose breaking cracked loudly in the otherwise silent room, and blood exploded over the henchman's face. Mr B then grabbed the neck of his dazed victim, quickly pivoted, and slammed his face onto the edge of the custom-built table. His body slumped to the floor, and Mr B crunched the heel of his expensive black Oxford shoes against the victim's face again and again until the henchman stopped groaning.

Mr B composed himself as the body lay motionless at his feet. Gliding left, he now stood facing the gorilla. 'You're lucky we are family, or this would've ended very differently.' He said as he plucked a handkerchief from the breast pocket of his pin-striped suit and wiped the blood of the unconscious man from his bony chin. The body on the floor spluttered and choked on the blood that pooled in his mouth, then stopped. 'Fortunately, I put a tracker on the phone.' Mr B said, then slid back behind his desk and opened the laptop. After a few quick clicks, he scribbled down an address and handed it to the large man. 'Here,' he said, then gestured to the lifeless body on the floor. 'Get that thing out of here and bring me the phone. Oh, and George, if you screw it up again, I'll tell Aunt Sandra you overdosed on the steroids again. Only this time, they won't be able to restart your heart like they did last time. Do you understand?'

'Yes, boss.'

Chapter 7

Amos turned left, off the Edinburgh city bypass and onto the A7, and headed west towards the small suburb known as Little France. A series of badly timed traffic lights brought the traffic flow to a crawl and slowed his progress. Finally, the pristine white walls of the Royal Infirmary of Edinburgh peeked out from behind the trees to his right. He turned left when the traffic lights turned green and arrived at the address a little after 3 pm. The house was a small sandstone bungalow that was tucked into the corner of a quiet little dogleg street. The trees that ran the length of the street protected the houses from the golf course that lay behind them. The red gravel driveway of the bungalow ran from the pavement to the garage at the rear of the house. Two aisles of slabs split the gravel and offered a runway long enough for two cars, so Amos parked his Audi behind the Tesla already parked there. He unplugged Mary's phone from the Audi's charging port, zipped it into his breast pocket, and got out of the car. He made his way along the narrow path, which ran under the bungalow's large front window. Amos climbed the single red quarry step, pressed the doorbell, and stepped back to wait.

He pressed again.

A muffled voice called from behind the door. 'Alright, alright, I heard you the first time.' There was the metallic sound of a door chain sliding from its slot. Then came the heavy clunk of a Yale lock sliding from its strike plate. Then, finally, a key turned in the lock. The man who opened the door was the same age as Amos, although his greying hair and gold-rimmed glasses made him look five years older. He was heavier than Amos too, maybe carrying an extra ten pounds, but he was not what Amos would consider fat. The jumper, trousers, and penny loafers gave him a smart but relaxed look.

'Amos?'

'Hi, Gerry.'

'What are you doing here?'

'Not sure yet. Can I come in?'

'Of course, Buttercup.' Gerry O'Hara stepped aside, pulled the door open wide, and waved his friend into the hallway. 'I've just made a fresh pot of coffee. Everything OK? How's Sophia?' he asked and closed the door.

***

The smell of freshly brewed, expensive coffee filled the air. Gerry poured two cups and handed one to Amos. A small round wooden dining table with two chairs sat opposite the patio doors of the modest farmhouse-style kitchen. Gerry gestured for Amos to sit and pulled a chair for himself. A small brass Jesus hung from a crucifix above the kitchen door and watched the two men drink.

'Mate, I'm so sorry,' Gerry said. 'Sophia was an amazing woman.'

'Thanks, but I can't think about that right now, I've got other things to worry about.'

'What do you mean? Like what?' Gerry asked incredulously. Amos explained about the intruders, the kidnapping, Beth and the phone. He explained about the secure file vault and the message with the address that brought him to Gerry's door.

'That's why I'm here,' Amos said. 'Why did you send Mary your address?'

'Mary messaged me yesterday. She said she needed my help, but I was in Manchester with a client. I just got back this morning.'

'Did she say what she needed your help with?'

'No, just that it was urgent and asked me not to say anything to you about it.'

'To me? Why?'

'Don't know, but she sounded worried, and I wasn't going to say no to my Goddaughter.'

'OK, it must have something to do with whatever is on this phone.' Amos unzipped his pocket and placed the phone on the table between them. 'Can you have a look at it for me?'

'Of course, but mate, you need to go to the police. This is serious.'

'I can't. They'll hurt her, or worse. I need to know what is on this phone, find out where Mary is, and get her back. Gerry, I need your help. Please.'

Gerry picked the phone up from the table and stared at the blank screen. 'OK, let's get to work.'

The small home office was dominated by a large pine desk with three 24-inch screens sat on top, all angled to focus on the swivel chair in front of them. The whirr of the cooling fan from the black tower unit on the right-hand side of the desk was the only sound. The room had one small window to the left of the desk and was covered by a blackout roller blind, which plunged the room into almost complete darkness.

'Jesus, Gerry,' Amos said. 'You sure it's dark enough? You need to get some daylight in here.'

'Listen up, Buttercup, I don't come to your office and tell you how to draw pictures.'

'Structural designs Gerry, not pictures.'

'Same thing,' Gerry said, flicked a switch on the wall, and four uplights gave a soft, low-level glow to the room. 'Now, step aside and let the big boys work.' Gerry walked behind the desk, tapped the keyboard, and all three screens sprang to life simultaneously. He plugged the phone into the PC, sat in the swivel chair, and cracked his knuckles in an overly dramatic gesture. 'OK, let's see what we have here.' His fingers clicked furiously on the keyboard. Amos watched him work, but the information on the screens might as well have been in Chinese. It was a mix of letters, symbols, and numbers that meant nothing to him but was obviously making sense to Gerry.

'I just need to know what is in that vault and what could be so important,' Amos said.

Gerry said nothing.

'Can you even get into the file vault if it's password protected?' Amos asked, pacing nervously.

'Of course I can; it's me you're talking to, not some second-rate wannabe hacker. Seriously, Amos, you should've come into Army Intelligence like I told you to do when we were signing up.'

'Computers weren't my thing, mate. Still aren't. Besides, I can't spend all day in front of a computer screen. I needed to be where the action was. That's why I joined the Engineers. People think the infantry guys are the fighters, but the Royal Engineers are the first ones in and the last ones out of every fight. That's why our motto was Ubique.'

'I know, "Everywhere". Not a great motto, if I'm honest mate. Has no ring to it. No punch. No pizazz,' Gerry jibed, as his fingers continued to dance across the keyboard.

'Oh and "Manui Dat Cognitio Vires" just rolls off the

tongue, does it?'

'Yes, it does. And it's true, Knowledge *does* give Strength to the Arm.'

'If you say so. Computers won't save you on the ground, though. You can't replace a soldier's instincts,' Amos said, now pacing the full length of the small room. The sound of the keyboard clicking filled the room again.

'Huh, that's strange.' The clicking on the keyboard stopped.

'What?' Amos asked.

'A brute force attack can generate ten thousand six-digit combinations per second. It should be able to crack this passcode in less than sixty seconds. But this code looks like it's constantly changing. This isn't your average file vault here; this is some serious software. It must be hiding something big.' Gerry said, looking at Amos over the top of his glasses.

'So, you can't break it?'

'Hey, I didn't say that. I spent fifteen years in Army Intelligence and now run one of Scotland's top elite cyber security firms. It'll take more than a clever phone app to beat me. It's just going to take me a little—' Before Gerry could finish his sentence, the left-hand screen flashed an alert, accented with a loud beep.

'What was that?' Amos asked nervously.

'We may have a bit of a problem.'

'What?'

'There's a tracker on this phone.'

'A tracker? Does that mean they know where we are?'

'Yip, and its location has been pinged.

Chapter 8

The black Land Rover rolled quietly to a stop in front of a small sandstone bungalow that was tucked into the corner of a quiet little dogleg street in Little France. The silver Audi in the driveway told George that he was in the right place. He reached over, pulled the latch to open the glove compartment, and lifted the silencer from inside. Glancing left and then right, he then pulled the Berretta M9 from his shoulder holster and screwed the silencer to its barrel. The Berretta's slide pulled back smoothly and slickly and clicked softly when it reached the stop, exposing the 9-mm parabellum in the chamber. There was no need to check the clip; he had loaded a fresh magazine before he left. George looked left and right again; the street was empty. There was no sign of anyone walking their dogs or the twitching curtains of nosy neighbours, curious about a strange car in the street. With no onlookers, there was no need to hide the Berretta in his jacket. He locked eyes with himself in the rear-view mirror.

'OK, George, no mistakes.' He said it resolutely, then pushed the heavy door of his car open and eased out. He held the gun tight to his right thigh and walked smoothly towards the bungalow, pivoting his head left and right as he went. A silver Audi and a red Tesla were sitting on the driveway's paved aisles, forcing him to walk on the gravel, removing any chance of a silent approach. Despite the slow, careful pace, the red gravel crunched under each footstep. A frontal assault would be too exposed, he thought, and would offer no tactical advantage, so he continued down the gravel driveway towards the rear of the house. He pressed his back against the wall of the house and edged his head around the corner.

All quiet.

A raised wooden decking offered three steps to reach a set of patio doors and was much quieter than the gravel in the driveway. He cautiously climbed the steps. Still hugging tight to the wall, George stole a quick glance through the patio doors and discovered a modest, rectangular farmhouse-style kitchen with a table and two empty chairs opposite. The patio door slid along its rails smoothly and quietly. The long nose of the silencer, held at head height, crossed the threshold first and swept left to right. The room was empty, and the thick smell of freshly brewed coffee hung in the air. Slowly and silently, he slipped inside the kitchen, keeping the Berretta raised. Out of the corner of his eye, George caught a glimpse of something metallic above the kitchen door; the small brass Jesus looking down on the armed intruder. George shook his head in disgust and gently pulled down the handle of the kitchen door and eased it open. The door opened onto a narrow hall that spanned the length of the house. He stepped slowly into the hall, pointing the gun left. The front door, ten feet from where he stood, faced him head-on at the end of the hall. Another door was to the right, halfway along the hall. *The living room, probably*, he thought. He swivelled the gun one hundred and eighty degrees down the length of the hall, which stretched another twenty or thirty feet. One closed door faced him at the end of the hall, with another on the right, halfway between the kitchen and the door at the end of the hallway. A third door on the left was further along. A loud toilet flush came from the door on the left. He smiled and tip-toed forward, stopping with the Berretta at head height outside the door and waiting. Light spilled from the bathroom, and a man he didn't recognise stepped out and stopped when he saw the gun pointed at his forehead.

'Hey there, Buttercup,' the stranger smiled.

'Where is he?' George asked in a soft growl.

'Jesus, Amos wasn't lying! You are a big bit of a boy, aren't you? Your balls must be the size of peanuts with all those steroids.'

George swiftly stepped forward and pressed the muzzle of the silencer into the stranger's forehead. 'Don't get cute with me, sir; I'm not here to hurt you. Now, where is Mr Fisher?'

'Sir? I wasn't expecting manners from an armed thug. I almost feel bad for you now. I'm sorry, but this is going to hurt a little.' The man's eyes glanced at something over George's shoulder, but before George could turn, everything went dark.

Chapter 9

The pain in her cheek had faded, but the ringing in her ear persisted. Mary flexed her jaw and turned her head left and right, checking her reflection in the mirror. The swelling wasn't as bad as she feared, and make-up would cover the fresh bruise. Small beads of sweat stung the cut on the corner of her mouth. *That will need more than a layer of foundation and a smear of lipstick to hide,* she thought. It had been three hours since George and the new guy broke into her dad's house, killed her dog, knocked her father out, and kidnapped her. Three hours of kicking and screaming. Three hours of slamming her fists against a locked door. Three hours of nobody listening. Now her arms were slumped at her side, too heavy to move the strand of hair that had dropped across her face and now irritated her nose. The harsh glow of the LED strip light built into the vanity mirror accentuated each imperfection her face had to offer. It showed the bruise and the cut, the streaks of mascara that stretched from her eyes to her chin, the hairstyle that she went to great lengths to perfect, which was now a scattered mess, and the dark bags hanging from her eyes; all with frightening clarity.

The black and gold, straight-edge design of the custom-built table in Mr B's office was a motif that Mary had continued into the bedroom. Gold voile curtains hung loosely from the black, super-king-sized, four-poster bed. Matching gold curtains covered the patio doors that led to the balcony. The black damask-style bedsheets were stitched with an extravagant gold inlay, and the pattern continued onto the bed pillows and the cushions of the vintage chaise lounge. The large, palatial bedroom was by no means the smallest prison ever built, but it felt just as claustrophobic to her now. Mary turned away from the mirror and stared at the sandwich and orange juice sitting on the black table beside the bedroom door. She had no appetite when the tray was placed there an hour ago by one of his lackeys, but she felt weak now, almost shaking with hunger. Mary stood up and dragged herself to the sandwich. The tray felt heavy. She took it back to the dressing table and placed it on the edge farthest from the mirror. She sat back down on the cushioned stool, picked up the sandwich, and turned to face the door while she ate.

The sandwich was adequate. Not good, but adequate. *At least the orange juice was fresh*, she thought. *A coffee would have been better, though. Calories and caffeine — that's what I really need.* The food had barely settled in her stomach when it began to churn, and nausea began to slowly creep up from her stomach. She stood and made her way to the ensuite bathroom, but the cool air rising from the tiled floor quelled the nausea instantly, or maybe it was the short walk. The large grey marble bathroom offered a bath and shower. Mary opted for the shower. She stripped her clothes off and turned the shower's pressure and temperature up high. Steam instantly filled the room and turned the clear glass shower cubicle opaque. A thundering cascade of hot water from the shower head, which hung from the ceiling, crashed down on top of her. She closed her eyes and raised her face toward the downpour. The sweat was cleared from her cut lip, the mascara was washed from her face, and the tense muscles in her shoulders relaxed.

Coconut and lavender scented steam flooded into the

bedroom as she opened that bathroom door. *It's amazing the regenerative power a long, hot shower can have*, Mary thought as she towelled the excess water from her hair and made her way to the wardrobe. The walk-in wardrobe was split into two sections. His to the left, and hers to the right. Mary carefully assembled an outfit of black combat trousers, a black long-sleeved V-neck top, and tan boots and got dressed. Checking herself over in the full-length mirror, she thought, *Give a girl the right shoes, and she can conquer the world.* It was a great quote, even if she couldn't remember who said it. *Was it Coco Chanel? Or Vera Wang? Doesn't matter.*

The dull clank of the bedroom door being unlocked jolted her from her train of thought. Slowly and carefully, she stepped out of the wardrobe. It was him. His six-foot-six, lean, angular figure loomed over the dressing table, his back to her. The pin stripe of his suit accentuated his slender frame and made him look almost gaunt, yet he still dominated the room. Watching. Waiting. Taking a step closer, she sensed a familiar tension in him. He seemed calm, but experience told her that he was coiled and ready to strike. Slowly, she slid her right foot back, offset her shoulders, and softened her knees. Ready to strike back.

'Feel better?' he asked, without turning. His voice was soft but menacing.

'What do you care?'

'I care very much. That's why I sent George to bring you home.'

'You kidnapped me, Boydie. That's not how normal people show affection.'

He turned to face her; the harsh lighting from the table lamp cast deep shadows on his face, which sunk his eyes deep in his skull. 'I love you, Mary. I need you here with me. I don't blame you for the things you did before. Losing your mother must be scary for you, and you took that fear and frustration out on me. Once you have calmed down, you'll remember that you belong here. You'll thank me for bringing you home. I just want to go back to the way things were. Please.'

'No, Boydie. I meant what I said. I'm done.'

'Is this because I hit you?' he asked, as he took a step forward. Instinctively, Mary's hands sprang up into a fighting position, fists clenched, ready to strike. Boydie stopped. Slowly, he stepped back, raised his hands to his shoulders with palms out in a surrendering gesture, and bent his knees in a half crouch. 'Wow, calm down, baby.' he said. 'You know I would never hurt you. I've just been under a lot of stress with this deal coming up.'

'Really? And what is your excuse for the second bruise and my burst lip?'

'Look, I'm not here to fight. I've come here with an olive branch. I know you've been worried about your dad. I just wanted to let you know that he's OK. In fact, I've sent George to go get him.'

'Leave him alone, Boydie. If you bring him here, he *will* kill you.'

'I think we can handle one old man,'

'He was a soldier and once a soldier, always a soldier.'

'He was an engineer. He built bridges,' Boydie scoffed.

'No, he was a Royal Engineer.'

'OK, so he built bridges for the Queen.'

'You don't get it,' Mary said, as she lowered her hands to her side and relaxed her stance. 'Royal Engineers are some of the toughest soldiers, physically and mentally, the army has to offer. First ones into the fight, and last ones out. They are a law unto themselves. And you just pissed one off.'

Boydie struck forward and grabbed Mary by the throat, his tight grip constricting her airway. She dug her nails into his hands and pulled at his fingers, but she couldn't pry them away. She struggled, gasping, clawing, and fighting for a breath that wasn't coming. Blood drained from her face as her knees buckled and blackness began to creep in, and she could feel her eyes begin to roll into her head. Suddenly, Boydie released his grip, and Mary fell to the floor, landing hard on all fours. She fought to regulate the air that flooded back into her lungs. She fought to control the coughing as her vision cleared. Mary craned her head upwards at the figure that now dominated her as well as the room.

'I tried to be nice, Mary,' he said. 'I even tried saying please, but you're too stubborn.' He stepped over her and paced back and forth along the foot of the bed. Tears blurred her vision now, and she strained to watch him, twisting her body to keep him in view. 'You are the only person I've ever met who refuses to be scared of me,' he continued, 'and I don't know if that turns me on or infuriates me. Probably both. But that's why I can't let you go, Mary. Only love can make a man this happy and this angry at the same time. I am doing things. Big things. I'm making all the right connections. I'm making the right moves. This is my time. My time. And with the right woman by my side, there's no stopping me. I could go right to the top.'

Mary coughed and caught her breath.

'Seriously, another Scarface quote? You really need to watch more movies. Scarface wasn't even that good.'

A quick kick to Mary's ribs forced all the air back out of her lungs and she fell sideways. She curled her knees to her chest, protecting herself from another kick and coughed uncontrollably. Pain radiated through her entire body as she waited for his next attack with her eyes shut tight.

The next blow never came.

The bedroom door slammed. Slowly, Mary opened her eyes. She was alone again.

Chapter 10

The harsh ammonia of the smelling salts jolted the gorilla awake. He shook his head and groaned. *Probably dazed and confused,* Amos thought. *A concussion, too, possibly.*

'Hey there, Buttercup.' Gerry cheered as he tapped the keyboard of the laptop in front of him. 'You have a good nap?' He sat at a small rectangular metal table beside two rows of seven-foot server racks. Wires ran vertically and horizontally from unit to unit while lights flashed at random intervals, displaying a complicated flurry of activity. The whirr of the room's air conditioners and server fans filled the otherwise quiet room.

The big man who had invaded Amos's home earlier that day tried to stand, but the rope around his legs held him tight to the metal chair beneath him. The rope around his chest and arms bound him to the chair's high back, while his hands were tied to the chair's back legs. He tried to speak, but the rag around his mouth made it impossible for him to form words. The giant man's face flushed red, and he raged against the ropes, screaming what Amos was certain would be a collection of the most colourful profanity ever uttered in anger.

'Hey, calm down there, Buttercup.' Gerry said. 'You'll hurt yourself, and we wouldn't want that.'

'There's no point struggling,' Amos said coolly, 'The ropes holding you in place are ten-millimetre, high-modulus polyethylene rope, which has a breaking strain of eight thousand kilograms.'

'Cut a long story short, Sweet Cheeks, unless those steroid muscles can bench press two elephants and a BMW, you're going nowhere,' Gerry quipped, then resumed typing.

'So why don't we just calm down a little and talk this out?' Amos continued. 'Now, you have something I want, and I have something you want. I'm sure two intelligent men like us can come to some sort of agreement where everyone walks away happy. I'm going to take the rag out of your mouth now, OK?' He stepped forward and slowly pulled the rag out of the restrained man's mouth. The gorilla drew a deep breath in and flexed his jaw. *Probably sore from the rag.*

'Where am I?' the big man growled.

'Safe, for now,' Amos replied. 'Where is my daughter?'

'She's safe for now. Untie me from this chair, and I'll make sure she stays that way.'

'We have no reason to hurt you, but we also don't have any reason not to. Do you understand?' Amos said, repeating the same threat the gorilla gave him just hours earlier.

The big man scoffed, 'Cute. Look, untie me, give me the phone, and I'll be on my way. No need for anyone else to get hurt.'

'This phone?' Amos held up the phone, which was connected to the laptop with a long wire, then tossed it back onto the table beside Gerry, who was still typing furiously with complete focus. The restrained man followed the phone with his eyes and smiled.

'OK, Mr Fisher, you want to talk? Let's talk. How do you think this is going to end?'

'Mary safe at home and your boss in prison would be nice.'

'Mary is home, Mr Fisher. And Mr B will never see the inside of a cell, that much I guarantee you.'

'Why do you call him Mr B?' Gerry asked without looking up from his laptop. 'Does he think it makes him sound mysterious? Is he trying to frighten people by not having a name? It doesn't work; he just comes across weird.'

'Intelligence is the key to war; without it, you cannot win. And Mr B is a very clever man.'

'Is that right, Sun Tzu?' Gerry replied. 'Well, he sounds like a paranoid schizophrenic if you ask me.'

'I don't care who or what he is,' Amos shouted. 'I just want my daughter back. Now where is she?' His fist slammed down onto the table, sending the phone jumping before settling face down on the table.

The large man watched the phone settle, then locked eyes with Amos. 'You think you frighten me, old man? My employer is one of the most powerful men in Scotland. He has endless resources and a vicious temper. I have watched him stamp a man to death. He has no fear, no remorse, and no tolerance for failure. He has a bold plan for the future, and he has the ruthless ambition to see it to fruition. You cannot frighten me, Mr Fisher. There is no greater illusion than fear.'

'I bet that sounded really cool in your head. Oh, and there's no point stalling for time there, D-ball.' Gerry said, referring to the anabolic steroid Dianabol. 'I found the tracker on the phone and rerouted the signal through twenty-six different locations. Your balls will grow back to their normal size before anyone traces your location.'

The gorilla roared, lunged, and raged against the ropes. The ropes held.

Amos stepped forward, pushed the rag back into the big man's mouth, and muffled the screams. Leaving the man to tantrum, Amos turned to Gerry and leaned close.

'Thank you,' Gerry said. 'If I had to listen to another one of those Chinese proverbs, I was going to hit him myself.'

'Did you get anywhere with the vault yet?' Amos whispered.

'No use, mate. It seems to be missing something, like this phone only has half of the key. The other half must be on a different device. The vault will only open when you have both halves together. It's quite a clever design, to be honest.'

'Great. Where is the other half?'

'You'd have to ask philosopher roid-rage over there.'

The phone began to vibrate on the table.

The philosopher stopped his tantrum and froze. The metallic rattle of the phone vibrating against the table filled the room, then stopped. Amos looked at the phone, then at Gerry. Gerry looked at the phone, then at Amos. The phone vibrated again. They both looked at the man tied to the chair. He looked back at them. Amos turned to Gerry.

'Go on then,' Gerry said. 'They can't trace the call.' The phone began to vibrate for the third time, and Amos picked it up, unplugged it, and held it to his ear.

'That better be you, George,' growled the same voice that Amos heard that morning in his kitchen.

'Your man is safe. For now. Where is my daughter?'

'God dammit! Aunt Sandra will be devastated.'

'Where is Mary?' Amos asked again.

'Where she should be. She's asking for her phone, though. Give it to George, and he'll make sure she gets it,' Mr B said.

'No.'

'Give the phone to George, or I'll kill her. Don't test

me, old man.'

'No, you won't. She's your only bargaining chip. And if you harm even one hair on her head, then the only time you'll see this phone is at your trial. Do we have an understanding?'

'You have pissed off the wrong man, Amos. You have no idea what I am capable of.'

'Yeah, yeah, endless resources, stomped a guy to death, and all that. I got the spiel from your buddy already. Now let me give you mine. I am a man with over a decade of specialised training and nothing to lose. I have been shot at, stabbed, and even died once. I have single-handedly razed buildings to the ground and toppled cities. I am the most capable and dangerous man you will ever meet. And you have taken the only thing left in this world that I care about. I am coming to get my daughter, and if I have to kill everyone you care about to do it, then so be it.' Amos ended the call and shoved the phone back into his pocket.

Gerry turned to George and said, 'Now that's how you make a threat.'

Gerry closed the door behind him, leaving the muscled thug that Mr B identified as George to tantrum alone in the server room. Amos could hear his own heartbeat thunder in his ears as he paced back and forth in the narrow, dimly lit hallway. The sound of his teeth grinding reverberated through his jaw and filled the silence between beats. His fingernails dug deep into his palms, almost drawing blood. He then turned to face Gerry and said, 'What now?'

'Now we hunt the bastard down.' Gerry smiled.

'We?'

'I'm not going to let you go alone. You'll need help.'

Amos shook his head. 'You're not a fighting soldier; you're intelligence. I need you working on the phone. I need intel, like what my next move is. And I need you to keep an eye on our guest in there.'

'I don't like this. I'd rather be there to watch your back, but I suppose you're right.' Muffled screams echoed from behind the closed door. 'It's a good job we moved him here,' Gerry said. 'There's nobody around for miles to hear him.'

'What about the people who work for you? Won't they hear him?'

'I only have one employee and he's in Dubai at a conference until next week.'

'Did you get any information from the phone? What's my next move?'

'Here's that list of recent addresses in the phone's maps you asked for. I don't know how useful it'll be, but it's a start. Maybe we can shake something loose.' Gerry handed him a small sheet of paper. 'The first address is to something called Onion.'

'Onion?' Amos asked.

'Aye, I don't know if it's a farmers market or something.'

'Thanks Gerry. I really appreciate this. Oh, can I keep a hold of your baseball bat for now?'

'Sure. I'm surprised you didn't break it when you knocked that maniac out, though. Here, take his gun too. Just in case.' Gerry held George's Beretta by the barrel and offered Amos the grip. Amos stared at it, then shook his head.

'You might need it if he gets loose,' Amos said.

'He's not going anywhere; he's tied up pretty tight. I don't like guns anyway, and like you said, I'm not a fighting soldier.' Amos reached for the pistol. The textured grip felt cold but familiar, like the handshake of an old friend. He spun to face away from Gerry and quickly went through the routine that was trained into his bones a lifetime ago.

Remove and check the magazine. Pull the slide until it locks, and inspect the chamber. Release the slide, point the pistol, and pull the trigger to perform a control shot, then replace the magazine. The whole process took no longer than three seconds. He had become slow in his old age and was out of practice. The gun fit snugly in his jacket pocket. Amos pulled the phone from the other pocket and checked the maps. His destination was thirty-two miles from where he stood. Thirty-two miles from the converted barn Gerry bought from a farmer friend years before. It was an ideal location for keeping homicidal henchmen of psychopathic crime bosses, although that was not its intended purpose when Gerry bought it. The barn, affectionately named "The Shed", long ago housed a large number of cows. It has since been refurbished and repurposed into a large, comfortable office space, miles from any prying eyes.

The Audi's engine coughed to life, and Amos slipped Mary's phone, the gun, and a pack of zip ties into the glove box and closed it, then tossed the baseball bat onto the back seat. He typed the GPS coordinates into the car's satnav and set off slowly south along the dirt road. *I'm coming, Mary.*

Chapter 11

Nine hours after saying his final goodbye to his wife and leaving the hospice, Amos was back in his car, heading east out of Edinburgh. The sun was getting low in the sky, and the temperature was slowly dropping from its midday high of ten degrees. The satnav told him to get back onto the M8, and although he only had thirty-two miles to cover, he knew that heavy traffic meant it would take him over an hour. The delay would give him time to think, and that was time he really needed.

Problem solving, planning, and organisation were listed as some of his best attributes by his instructors at Garelochhead during basic training decades ago. It was these innate skills and an uncontrollable need to push himself to his limits, that guided him into the Royal Engineers. It was these same skills that helped him become the fourth youngest staff sergeant in the Corps' history. It was a rank he held with pride until he retired years later. The same set of skills, and a few others he picked up along the way, helped him build a successful structural engineering and demolitions business after his retirement from Her Majesty's Service.

That was all before the incident. Before the attack. An unprovoked attack by an unknown attacker in the car park of an industrial estate landed Amos in the intensive care unit. Along with two broken ribs, a fractured eye socket, and a severe concussion, the perpetrator left him with permanent brain damage. RHD, the doctor called it, right hemisphere damage, and went on to explain that it would affect his attention, reasoning, and problem solving. The brain damage also accounted for the short-term memory loss. He had lost all memory of the day of the attack and could not tell the police who had attacked him or why he was even in the empty car park of an abandoned factory.

He recovered better than the doctors had expected, though, and his intellect remained intact, but the process had slowed somewhat. Information took longer to take root, but given enough time, he could still solve almost any problem. Facts had to be planted slowly and with care. Too much, too fast, and too soon would only suffocate his mind and drown any ideas before they had the chance to blossom. They needed time and space to grow. An hour of silence, alone in his car, would give him just that.

Amos focused on his breathing and slowed his heart rate, which he now realised had been pounding loudly in his ears since the two men broke into his house that morning. He assembled all the facts he had and displayed them on a wall in his mind, like a map. The map displayed Mary at its centre, and branches from her picture spread in all directions. One branch led to a question mark with "Mr B" underneath. A second branch led to a picture of Beth with the word "police?" underneath. The third pointed to the phone with the word "info?" Two branches were attached to Mr B. The first was a picture of the muscled thug called George, who was currently tied up in Gerry's server room. The newest branch led to another question mark with the word "Onion" underneath. Outside, the traffic had ground his progress to ten miles an hour, and he used this time to let the image of the map solidify itself in his mind. *Let it take hold, Sapper; don't suffocate it*, he thought.

The car's satnav announced his arrival a little earlier

than he first anticipated. The mind map was now thoroughly in place, and he knew from experience that his subconscious would work on the problem while he was busy with other tasks. Tasks like finding an onion — whatever that was — in Coatbridge.

The Cliftonville area of Coatbridge had recently been named as one of the most impoverished areas in Scotland. Looking at the three dull tower blocks in front of him, Amos could see why. They emanated a depressive energy that seemed to grey the sky around them and sapped the lives of the people walking past. They loomed oppressively over the landscape and drained the colour from the surrounding trees. Amos checked the list, slid the baseball bat down the back of his jacket like a sword, and headed for the first block. Oversized grey letters at the base of the building identified it as High Coats Tower. He approached the red security door, which was sunken in one of the tower's two recesses at the front of the building. A silver panel to the left offered a ten-digit keypad with numbers zero to nine and a call button. He typed the number Gerry had written down and pressed call. A harsh metallic buzz echoed loudly off the walls of the recess.

No answer.

He buzzed the number again. Five seconds passed. Ten seconds. Then a loud click crackled over the panel's speaker.

'Hello? What do you want?' came an impatient voice.

'Mr B sent me,' Amos lied.

'Mr B sent you? Why? I'm going there next week.'

'Well, he sent me today. Do you want me to go back empty handed because you told me to come back next week?'

'No, God no. It's fine. Jesus, man.' A harsh metallic buzz sounded, and Amos pulled on the handle of the security door.

The elevator doors slid open once he reached the fourteenth floor. A dismal blue fluorescent light bathed the bleak grey stone hallway and left it devoid of hope. Amos turned right and was faced with three doors in an L-shaped formation. Two faced him straight on, and one to his left, facing the length of another hallway. Before he could look at their numbers, the centre door was pulled quickly open. The blue glare from the florescent light penetrated the gloom beyond the door enough to reveal a shabby bearded man drowned in a dirty brown bathrobe.

'You're not George,' the shabby man said.

'You're right,' Amos replied, then lunged at the man, slamming into his chest. The force of the collision sent the straggly stranger tumbling backwards into the short wall of the L-shaped hallway behind him. Amos spun and slammed the door shut, plunging them both into darkness. His eyes struggled to adjust, but he made out the shape of the scrawny man who was back on his feet, dazed and confused.

'What the hell, man?' the grubby man said. Amos pounced again, grabbed the ill-fitting bathrobe, and tossed the stranger to the left, slamming him into the long wall of the hallway. The man gasped, panicked, and tried to escape down the length of the hallway but stumbled the whole way. Amos followed close behind. Three feet away from the door at the far end of the hallway, the shabby man fell on all fours, breathing heavily. Amos raised his leg and, with the heel of his foot, kicked the bearded stranger through the door he was so desperate to reach. A high-pitched scream rang out from inside the room, where the frightened man now lay face down. Amos caught the door as it swung back and closed it softly behind him. He turned and faced the shaggy stranger, who had spun and was now on his back, arms defensively outstretched. Amos turned to the half-naked, still-screaming girl on a sofa and raised his finger to his lips to shush her. The screams dulled to a whimper that were rhythmically interrupted by gasps. The room was small and dull, and the air was thick with a distinctively pungent stench. Dark blue bedsheets nailed to the wall served as a curtain over the room's only window, which Amos guessed hadn't been opened in a while, judging by the smell. The stranger had squirmed his way onto the sofa opposite the door, beside the now quiet girl. The grimy grey sofa, peppered with burn marks, faced directly onto a sixty-five-inch flat screen TV, which was hung on the wall behind where Amos stood. Thick, malodorous smoke hung in the air and stung his eyes as he stepped towards the couch where the two strangers cowered.

'Who are you, man? What do you want?' the shabby man pleaded.

'Answers,' Amos replied as he pulled the bat from his jacket. 'Onion?'

'What?'

'Wrong answer.' He turned and swung the bat as hard as could. Shards of the sixty-five-inch television exploded over the filthy carpet.

'Wow, wow, wow. Stop, man, OK? I'll answer whatever you want.'

'What is onion?' Amos demanded as he pointed the bat at the shabby man.

'Me. I'm Onion. It's my name, OK? Now please stop

smashing my things, man.'

'Your name?'

'Aye, man. I'm Onion.'

'OK, Onion, where is Mary?'

'Who?'

'Wrong answer again.' He wound the bat back and aimed for Onion's legs.

'I'm telling the truth, man; I don't know any Mary. I wish I did.'

'Then why is your number in her phone?' he demanded, still poised to swing.

'I don't know, man. I sell weed for Mr B, that's all. I don't know you or this Mary bitch.'

Amos relaxed his shoulders and lowered the bat. 'Damn,' he growled through gritted teeth.

'Listen, man, you don't know who you're dealing with here. You better get lost before...'

'Dealing?' Amos interrupted then paused a moment. 'You said you were going there next week. Going where?'

'To the warehouse, man. To deliver the cash and get supplies.'

Amos grinned. 'Get dressed, Onion. We're going out.'

Chapter 12

The sun had fully set now, and Amos's black clothes offered him better cover in the darkness than his frightened and unwilling companion's dirty brown housecoat. Amos rubbed, then blew into his cupped hands.

'We shouldn't be here, man. Mr B is going to kill us both,' Onion whimpered.

'Don't care. Now shut up, I'm trying to think.'

'Will you at least cut this off?' Onion held up his hands, gesturing to the zip tie that was cutting into his wrists.

'I'll let you go once I'm done here,' Amos replied coldly, then turned to survey the converted warehouse on the other side of the road. A dimly lit sign above the double door read *24-hour Cash & Carry*. The unassuming building lay nestled amongst others like it in the Kinning Park industrial estate, just off the M74. They both sat and watched the building from the corner of an almost empty car park that lay opposite. Three transit vans had come and gone in the hour they had been watching, and if Onion's estimations were correct, each van was delivering over ten thousand pounds in cash. The vans would then be loaded with weed, cocaine, heroin, and anything else the seedier side of society chose to turn to when hiding from their pain and misery, and head back to their allotted patch to peddle their temporary happiness.

'Talk me through it again,' Amos said, without turning his attention from the cash and carry.

'For the last time, the cash and carry is a front, man. I

mean, the front shop is like a legit shop and stuff, but the real money comes from the stores in the back. I come here once a week to drop off the cash and get more stuff. Anything you want or need, man, I can get it from right here.'

'And you can make ten thousand in a week?'

'No, we've been through this already, I average around three to five a week. But my patch isn't exactly the most lucrative area in Scotland, if you know what I mean. But guys come from all over the place, and they can make ten grand a week easy, OK? Now, can you cut this off? My hands are going numb.'

'Not yet. Wait here,' Amos said, stepped out of the car, locked Onion inside, and stuffed his hands into his jacket pocket. Amos gripped the pistol in his pocket. It felt cold against his hand as he made his way across the street to the double doors.

Inside the cash and carry, the roar of indistinct chatter reverberated off the high ceiling and rained back down on top of Amos, drowning out his thoughts in a monsoon of noise. The clattering wheels of large trolleys, piled high with fruit, bottles, and other goods, thundered around him. Defective fluorescent strip lights flashed erratically overhead and crackled audibly above the noise. Huge metal racks which shelved pallets of varying goods lined the east and west walls. Randomly placed islands dotted the remainder of the floor space and displayed everything from birthday cakes to industrial cleaning fluids. Wave after wave of impatient shop owners and bargain hunters pushed past, barging each other aside, grabbing for this and that. A small armada of cashiers rushed customers through the checkouts near the front of the store in attempts to ease the growing swell. Amos ducked his head down and weathered through the chaos towards the storerooms at the rear of the building.

A huge white wall spanned the width of the warehouse and separated the chaotic front store from the storage room at the back. A single grey door lay tucked in a dark corner, ten feet from the eastern wall. Amos posted himself at the end of the closest aisle, ducking behind a stack of kitchen rolls, and watched the door. He watched as a tall, heavy-set man wearing a T-shirt bearing the cash and carry's logo swiped a key card in front of a small, dark rectangular box above the door handle, pushed open the door, and disappeared inside. The door slammed shut behind him. *There goes any chance of a stealthy approach*, he thought. The chaos and chatter ebbed and flowed around him while he waited and watched.

Ten minutes had passed before a young blonde girl wearing the same T-shirt as the heavy-set man approached the door. Amos bounced from his position and marched towards her. As she began to push the door open, he lunged forward and grabbed the back of her arm. Before she had time to turn, he whipped the gun from his pocket and jabbed it into her back.

'Don't make a sound. I'm not going to hurt you,' he said quietly, and ushered her through the door.

The girl was greeted with a smile by a small, bald man standing guard on the other side of the door. That smile quickly faded when Amos followed behind. The small man's hand grabbed quickly at the inside of his jacket, but came back out empty to grab the stumbling girl who had been pushed into him. Amos charged forward with the pistol raised high and brought the butt of the gun crashing down onto the small man's eye again and again.

The guard's body went limp and fell to the floor as the girl screamed and ran for the open shutter door at the north end of the storeroom.

More organisation and thought had gone into the layout of this part of the converted warehouse than its legitimate counterpart on the other side of the wall. Clearly labelled pallets boasting a wide selection of narcotics were stored vertically on racks secured to the south, east, and west walls. A few pallets of overstock were organised neatly on the vast empty floor space in front of the racking. A makeshift office adjacent to the shutter door stretched along the remainder of the northern wall. Two men busied themselves loading the back of a transit van that had parked inside the shutter door with bags and bricks of varying sizes and colours. Through the office's window, Amos could see two men filing handfuls of cash into the top of a machine that spit them back out the front. The girl's screaming had interrupted everyone from their tasks. The two men inside the office jumped to action, and the office window exploded outward, sending shards of glass flying as the bullet whizzed past Amos and lodged into the wall behind him. Instinctively, he dived behind a nearby pallet of white bricks stored on the floor in front of the racking. A rapid succession of small explosions continued from inside the office as tufts of white powder were punched from the tightly wrapped bricks beside his head.

The firing stopped.

Broken glass crunched under heavy boots as the men advanced on his position. Slowly, the crunching grew louder, but the pace slowed. Then the crunching turned to shuffling. Guns poised and fingers tight on the triggers, the two men sidled to the corner where Amos hid. The point man paused a beat, then lunged forward, pivoting to take aim, and found nothing. Amos took advantage of the momentary confusion, bounced up from the rear side of the pallet, and launched a white brick at the head of the second gunman. The force of the collision exploded the brick against his face and sent him to the floor, while the first gunman choked on a cloud of fine powder. Keeping low, Amos rushed forward, rammed his shoulder into the gunman's gut, and lifted him off his feet. What little air was left in the gunman's lungs was forced out completely when Amos slammed him to the floor. Three blows from the butt of Amos's stolen pistol were all that was needed to leave him unconscious. The second gunman groaned and stirred, but a single kick left him in the same condition as his two friends. Three Tangos down, all clear.

***

Information came quickly over the crackling headset as his pen scribbled furiously on the notepad. He raised his hand to press the earpiece closer and listened intently. The crackling stopped, and he ripped the page from the pad and dashed from his seat. The narrow hallway and tight corners made his hurried pace difficult to maintain, but he made the journey in under a minute, nonetheless. He flattened the wrinkles the rush had put in his shirt, took a breath, and gave three rapid knocks on the door. He paused for a beat and rapped the door again.

'Yes, yes, come in,' came a stern voice.

'DCI Clarke? Sir?' said the young man, as he pushed open the heavy pine door. Inside, Detective Chief Inspector James Clarke sat behind a cheap fake pine desk, frowning at a laptop and typing angrily.

'Yes? What is it, Johnson?' Clarke said, without raising his head from his laptop, his fingers still clicking away on the keyboard.

'Sir, a call just came into Glasgow City Police. Reports of shots fired at the cash and carry at Kinning Park.'

'What?' Clarke snapped as the clicking stopped. 'I gave no orders to raid.'

'Sir, it wasn't us,' the young man replied nervously.

'Then who? Nobody is stupid enough to start a war with him right now.'

'Sir, I believe it was the father.'

'The father? Where is he? Bring him in now.'

'Sir, we can't find him. The tracker on the phone shows him in twenty-six different locations simultaneously.'

'Get McGuire in here, now.'

Chapter 13

The morning of Mary's fifteenth birthday began the same way it had done fourteen times before. Amos woke up early and prepared his daughter's favourite breakfast. This year, she preferred pancakes and bacon covered in maple syrup. Then he set out her gifts neatly in the lounge. The sweet and savoury scent filled the kitchen and stirred Sandy from his dog bed near the kitchen heater. More often than not, Amos would toss the dog scraps as he glided back and forth from the stove, and today was no different. It was part of the daily ritual that Sophia hated. She had protested many times before that this was teaching the dog to stare at people while they ate, but Amos ignored her. The two males had an arrangement. Amos fed the dog scraps, and the dog loved him unconditionally. It was a simple contract, and one they both honoured and enjoyed. Sensing the end of the routine, Sandy retreated to a spot by the patio doors to bask in the warm sunlight and watch the birds come and go in the garden. The smooth vocals of James Taylor that sang from the smart speaker on the worktop about an imaginary visit to Carolina, coupled with the bright summer sun, gave the morning a relaxed and enjoyably lackadaisical quality.

James Taylor had moved on to singing a story of a young cowboy who lived on a range when a familiar, heavy sound thudded from the room above the kitchen. Slow and lazy footsteps travelled into the hallway and trudged downstairs. The sound stirred Sandy from his comfort and set his tail slapping against the tile floor in muted excitement. Amos slid a plate of food onto the centre island and pulled out a tall stool as Mary shuffled into the kitchen.

'Good morning, Peanut,' he said cheerfully, 'Happy birthday.' Sandy padded towards her, panting and nudging at her leg. Mary groaned and ignored the dog, then she lifted the plate from the island and left Amos alone in the kitchen with Sandy. Amos frowned, then raised one eyebrow and locked eyes with Sandy. 'What's wrong with her?' he asked, as though the dog possessed some insight into his daughter's mind that he was not privy to. Without waiting for an answer, he marched out of the kitchen and into the lounge, where Mary now lay, huddled under a shawl on the sofa, shovelling a piece of pancake into her mouth.

'What's wrong with you this morning?' he demanded.

'What?' She scowled. 'Nothing.'

'Then what's with the attitude? You completely ignored me when I was just being nice. It was completely uncalled for!'

'What are you talking about? I didn't do anything,' Mary protested.

'Exactly. I made you breakfast and said happy birthday and you don't even have the decency to say thanks.'

'Oh my God. Thanks. You happy? Can I eat my breakfast in peace now?' Mary picked up the remote control and turned her attention to the television. He felt anger boil in the pit of his stomach.

'Why are you wrapped in a shawl anyway?' he said.

'I'm cold,' she snapped in reply.

'How? It's the middle of summer, you can't be cold.'

'Well, I am. You can't tell me how I'm feeling. You might not be cold but I am.'

Blood rushed to his face and his jaw clenched.

'Turn that T.V. down. It's far too loud.'

'I can't hear it,' Mary complained.

'I said turn it down!' he barked and stormed back to the kitchen. The TV volume remained unchanged. He scowled at the birds in the back garden, pecking his garden for worms. Sandy, sensing the mood, had now retreated to his bed and tucked his head low.

'What's going on?' Sophia asked softly, as she wiped sleep from her eyes. Amos spun, and his hard eyes softened as he watched her shuffle sluggishly into the kitchen. Her long, bare legs stretched out from under an oversized blue and white striped shirt. Her dishevelled hair hung to her shoulders, framing her soft features and accenting her natural beauty.

'It's her,' he scoffed. 'She's in a mood, again.'

'Why?'

'Who knows?'

'Did you ask her?'

'Of course, but all I got was attitude. She has no respect for anyone or anything.'

'Amos, we've been through this, she's a fifteen-year-old girl, not one of your soldiers. You can't treat her like one. You need to listen to her and be patient.'

'So, it's all my fault? She can treat everyone like crap, and we've all got to deal with it? That's not how the world works, Soph.'

'I didn't say it was your fault, Amos. I'm saying you need to try and understand her a little better.' Sophia wrapped her arms around his waist and looked up into his eyes, tiptoed, and softly kissed his nose. It was a trick she used to calm him down. A manipulation he was all too aware of but was incapable of resisting. The blood drained from his face and returned it to a more natural colour. His fists unclenched, and his jaw loosened. 'I'll go talk to her,' Sophia said, and glided on tiptoes out of the kitchen.

Chapter 14

Rachel McGuire stood beside the heavy pine office door and patted the creases from her suit jacket. She glanced at her watch again, then palmed her head, flattening any stray hairs she may have missed the first two times. The quiet, muffled chatter from the office behind her grew gradually louder until they became angry shouts, which reverberated down the narrow hall. Five seconds after the shouting stopped, the office door opened, and a short, nervous man clutching a laptop stumbled out. He glanced at her long enough to adjust his glasses on his nose, then rushed awkwardly down the hallway.

'McGuire. Get in here, now,' barked the angry voice from inside the office. McGuire pushed the door open, stepped inside, and closed the door softly behind her. Detective Chief Inspector James Clarke stood staring out the large office window, silhouetted in the glow of the floodlights of Ibrox football stadium across the street. McGuire stood at attention and waited. The clock on the wall ticked loudly in the quiet of the room. 'Apparently, we can't track the phone,' Clarke said finally. 'For some reason, it shows in multiple locations simultaneously, and my computer boffins have no idea how.' He paused again and turned to face her. The clock ticked loudly again. 'Three months, we've had Mr B's operation under surveillance. Countless man hours and resources you've thrown at this thing, and we have nothing. We can't bust him on the drugs operations because, despite everything that we've accumulated during our surveillance, we found nothing when we raided. And, even if we did find something, his retail management agency only owns the building and rents it out. So, we have no concrete connection between him and the drugs. We have no witnesses, no dealers, and no buyers. In fact, we have no evidence of any kind whatsoever. He's been one step ahead of you the whole time. The only thing we do have is a phone full of evidence collected from your informant, and it's currently showing up in twenty-six different places at once.' Slowly, Clarke took one step forward and lifted the cover of a manilla file that lay on the desk between them. 'And now we have reports of this "Amos Fisher" breaking into the cash and carry and starting a fire fight,' Clarke's fist slammed hard on the desktop, 'threatening our entire operation!'

'Sir, Mary's father has the phone. I'm confident I can retrieve it and bring the situation under control.'

'Except you have no idea where he is, do you?'

'We have officers at his home, and we are looking at known associates. We will have him soon.'

'How do you know he even has the phone?'

'Sir, I made contact earlier today, both on the phone and face to face. He confirmed that he is now in possession of the phone and that my informant has been abducted. Just give me seventy-two hours, and I will retrieve the phone and, more importantly, the girl,' she said.

'I don't give a damn about the girl,' Clarke roared. 'You've got forty-eight hours to get that phone on my desk, or you'll be demoted back to sergeant, and you'll spend your entire career making tea for the real men who can actually get the job done.'

'Real men, sir?' McGuire quizzed.

'Watch your tone with me, young lady, and be careful what you are insinuating. The last female officer to submit a chauvinism complaint against me is currently stacking shelves at Tesco. Now, I want to know the instant you make contact with this Amos Fisher. I want to know every move that is made from now on. Anyone so much as farts without my say-so, they will be out of here faster than a packet of biscuits at a Weight Watchers meeting. Am I understood? Dismissed.'

'Yes, sir. Thank you, sir.' McGuire spun on her heels and marched out of the office. The heavy door slammed shut behind her as she strode down the hallway and turned the corner. Alone and out of sight of Clarke's office, she pressed herself tight against the wall and shook her trembling hands. A few deep breaths quelled the nausea churning in the pit of her stomach. *Get it together, Rachel*, she thought, *you've got work to do.*

Chapter 15

The M8 going back to Edinburgh was almost deserted. The heavy rush-hour traffic that stalled Amos hours before had dwindled to a few HGVs and the occasional boy racer. He had driven twelve miles before a dull ache began to set into his forearms. He loosened his grip and shook his hands one at a time. It was then that he looked at the speedometer and noticed he was doing over ninety miles an hour. He eased his foot from the accelerator and slowed to a steady seventy. The last thing he needed was to be stopped by the police with a gun stashed in the glove compartment and the stolen laptop on the passenger seat. His mind, however, was still racing as one thought crashed into another. Ideas collided violently with emotions and smashed any clarity that either one would provide, were they to exist on their own. Answers hung just out of reach, obscured by a fog of uncertainty and fear. Faded images flashed one after another without any detail or discernible pattern. Adrenaline dumps were hard enough when he was younger and more practised. It had been some time since his last real fight, and that was when it was only his life that was on the line. This fight was much more important. *Come on, Amos, just slow down. Just slow everything down and think.* Slowly, he drew a deep breath in through his nose and held it for a long time. Then he opened his mouth slightly and let it out again. Control your breathing, and you control your heart. Control your heart, and you control your mind. It was an effective technique learned from his old drill sergeant, which he used countless times when he was still on active duty. It took five controlled breaths before his hands stopped shaking and ten before he gained full control of his legs. The images in his mind, however, refused to slow down. They flashed randomly and made no sense, filling every space in his mind and suffocating all reason and logic.

His arms grew heavy and sluggish. He forced his eyes open as they began to sting. It was a fight now to keep his head straight and concentrate on the road ahead. The car window rolled down at the touch of a button, and brisk night air flooded into the car. The radio blasted some awful dance music on a station he would normally avoid as he strained to focus on the road ahead. *Almost there, Amos. Just ten more minutes.*

The Audi rolled to a stop outside Gerry's converted barn a little after ten o'clock. Security lights, triggered by his approach, popped to life. Amos groaned and raised his hand to shield his eyes from the blinding glare. His feet dragged along the gravel path to the barn door. He stopped at the entrance and glared at the grey steel door. The whole barn had been painted grey with thick black timber beams framing its edges. The new roof had been painted black to match the beams, and large solar panels were installed. The steel door had black straps across the top and bottom, connected by another diagonal beam, completing the Z pattern. The whole structure looked oddly modern against its farmland backdrop. Of all the times Amos had visited his old friend's barn, this was the first time he had truly noticed how odd it looked.

The mind can take you to strange places sometimes, Sophia had said to him one day when she caught him deep in thought. He was watching Mary play in the garden with the new Golden Retriever puppy they'd bought days before. When she asked what he was thinking about, he told her of his time in Afghanistan when he watched a young girl playing with one of the stray dogs that wandered the streets. The girl, no more than five, ran in circles, chasing the stray, and laughed. He told her how he remembered being lost in the innocence of the moment. How the girls laugh sounded sweet and angelic, and how much he laughed watching them play. He also told Sophia how the laughter stopped when the gunfire started. How he instinctively rushed for the child, scooping her up, and dived for cover. He told her of the screams of the frightened child and how he would have given anything in that moment to make her feel safe. He told her that once the shooting stopped, the child fled, crying, and he never saw her again. A tear welled in his eyes, but he choked it back before it fell. He told Sophia that he would never let Mary feel that kind of fear. Ever. Sophia smiled, hugged him tight, then stretched up and kissed his nose.

'Are you coming in, Buttercup or you just gonna stand there looking pretty?' crackled a voice over the intercom. Amos held the stolen laptop to the camera above the door.

'I brought you a present. Let me in.' The door buzzed loudly, and he pushed his way inside.

Gerry took the laptop to his office across the hall from where George was still strapped to a chair. The spacious office matched the barn's exterior with its grey and black colour scheme. The grey walls were broken by thick black picture frames housing various qualification certificates, awards, and pictures of his army past. Gerry placed the laptop on the large grey wood effect corner desk and sat on the executive, high-back, black leather office chair.

'How has our guest been behaving?' Amos asked.

'He's been fine, actually. Civil almost, and quite the conversationalist. And, if I'm being totally honest, quite a looker too.'

'Gerry! Seriously?'

'What? All I'm saying is, if I had met him in a club under different circumstances, I would have climbed that man like a tree.'

'Honestly, mate, I have no idea how you made it through fifteen years of service without anyone finding out you were gay.'

'I'm just that good. Where did you get this laptop, anyway?'

'Long story. Let's just say, I've got Mr B's attention now. What's on it, anyway?

'No idea. I'll need a bit of time to go through it all.' Gerry scanned Amos's face. 'You look like crap — you should sleep.'

'I will. You got anything to eat?'

'Yeah, I ordered pizza for Confucius and me. There's plenty left over in the kitchen.'

'Oh, before I go, I brought you this in case you needed it.' He handed Gerry the handgun he took from one of the guards at the cash and carry then headed for the door.

The small kitchen was at the far end of the barn. Two pizza boxes sat on the worktop between the kettle and microwave. Amos opened the cupboards, which hung on the wall above. The plates sat on the higher shelf with a small portable camping stove and one pot underneath. He picked one of the smaller plates from the shelf, took two slices from the box, and sat them on the plate. Then he opened the small refrigerator underneath the counter and took a can of Irn Bru. Amos carried the feast to the small

72

round table opposite, pulled out one of the two folding chairs, thumped himself down and ate. The images in his mind had slowed now. They still flashed with no obvious pattern and offered no insight, but their frequency had diminished somewhat. Answers still floated just out of reach, like a ghost taunting the notion of truth without delivering anything useful. A long, heavy sigh escaped his lips. His shoulders sagged, and he chewed slowly.

Only twenty minutes had passed since he first sat at the table with the pizza, but it had felt like an hour. The weight of his eyelids was now unbearable. The weight of the whole day was unbearable, if he was being honest. *Don't think about it. You still have a job to do. There's time to grieve once Mary is safe.* He washed his plate and returned it to the cupboard where he found it, then shuffled back to the office where Gerry sat, still typing furiously.

'Find anything?' Amos asked, as he lowered himself into one of the two small black tub chairs, which sat opposite Gerry's desk.

'It looks like a logbook recording their transactions. Large sums of money and products. It's all coded, though. It'll take me a bit of time to decipher it.'

'Did you get anything else from the phone's data?'

'Only that more than one person has tried tracking it. We know Mr B tried because he sent our oversized friend next door to get it. But there's also been another attempt to track it. I'm not sure who yet, but I'll know soon enough.'

'Can they track us here?'

'You forget who you're talking to? They'll spend a fortnight chasing ghosts around the country before I let them get anywhere close to having an idea of what country we might be in.'

'Good,' Amos sighed. His head fell into his hands, as he rubbed his eyes.

'Mate, you look like crap. There's a sofa in the office next door, go get yourself some sleep. I'll wake you if there's anything new.'

'Yeah, thanks. It's been a long day.'

'And tomorrow is gonna be even longer. Go and get some rest.'

Amos slapped his hands down on his knees and pushed himself up off the chair. He pulled open the frosted glass door and shuffled into the hallway. The door clicked softly behind him. He stood alone in the empty hall and heaved a heavy sigh. A picture of Sophia flashed in his mind and a lump formed in his throat. *No*, he thought, and swallowed hard. *Not yet. Not until the child is safe. Then you can miss her.*

Amos dragged himself slowly to the office next door and gently pushed the door open. The office, which was smaller than the one Gerry occupied, was more homely decorated. Pictures of a young family hung on the walls and a rug on the floor gave it a much more welcoming feel. The sofa at the far end of the office was low and deep. It was ideal for napping and came complete with a thick shawl that hung over the back. he plumped one of the cushions and pulled the shawl over him. Another five controlled breaths slowed his mind enough for him to focus on the present moment. He pushed all thoughts out and concentrated on the sound of the air passing through his nose. In and out. In and out. In and out. In and...

Amos drifted off to sleep.

The office door exploded inward. 'Amos, wake up. You'll never guess what I found,' Gerry called excitedly.

'Jesus, Gerry,' Amos said as he bounced from the sofa and rubbed the sleep from his eyes. 'What time is it?'

'Five-ish, I think. Doesn't matter. Hurry up and see what I have found.'

'What?'

'Come on,' Gerry said, then rushed out of the room.

Chapter 16

The bedroom door exploded inward and clattered against the wall with such force that the door handle left an indent in the plasterboard wall. Boydie charged into the room, barking an indecipherable string of angry curses. His hands waved violently as he spat threats at the invisible victim in front of him. Luckily, the bedroom furniture took the brunt of his rage as the outburst continued for a few more minutes before he eventually clamped his teeth around the foreknuckles of his fingers. Mary sat in the farthest corner of the bed with her knees tucked to her chest. She had pulled the covers to her face when he crashed through the door and watched the whole vicious episode in silence. Experience told her not to interrupt him when his temper had gripped him so violently. It was better to wait until the fire had burned itself out. But the blaze did not burn itself out this time. It merely settled into an inferno. She watched him slither back and forth at the foot of the bed.

Then he stopped.

His eyes narrowed and trained on Mary. She watched him slide slowly around the bed. His fists coiled around the edge of the cushioned stool at the dressing table. He dragged it behind him, took up position on the opposite side of the bed, and sat in silence. He stared at her with a long, well-practised, penetrating gaze that was designed to unnerve and distress. A predatorial stare that, in the past, had reduced the most hardened of men to squirming, nervous wrecks. Mary, however, was not a man. She stretched her legs out and lowered the covers. 'Let me guess,' she said, 'you've just found out that Pacino didn't get an Oscar for Scarface, and now you're pissed?'

'Where is he?'

'Pacino? No idea, probably sniffing coke out of a hooker's bellybutton somewhere.'

'Enough!' Boydie screamed, slamming the palm of his hand against the post of the bed.

Mary said nothing.

'Your dad. Where is your dad?' he hissed.

'How should I know?' Mary said, trying to sound nonchalant.

A tense, palpable stillness settled in the room. The same type of stillness that could be found on the floor of a rainforest in some remote part of the world. A stillness shared between a defensive mouse and a hungry viper. The mouse, not daring to move for fear of startling the snake into action. And the snake waiting for the perfect moment to catch its prey off guard before striking.

'I have just spent three hours with the police because your dad broke into one of my warehouses. Obviously, they can't connect the drugs to me.'

'You're welcome,' she snipped.

'Then I spent another two hours on the phone with the Pakhan,' he continued, ignoring her interruption. 'It wasn't easy, but I calmed things down. I had to give up some collateral and make some assurances, but I did it. Now just tell me where he is, Mary.'

'I warned you, Boydie. I told you, he's tougher than you think. He will tear your whole operation apart piece by piece to get to me. You can't intimidate or frighten him. Your best bet is to let me go and forget all about me.'

'All I wanted was the goddamned phone,' he spat venomously. 'I had no interest in hurting him or you. But now, not only has he cost me a lot of money, but he has also made me look weak and threatened this deal. I can't have that, Mary. I have worked too damn hard on this to let some pensioner destroy it. I have built this whole empire from scratch. I started with nothing, and now I own this damn town. I am going to find him, Mary, and I am going to kill him.'

Chapter 17

Gerry rushed back into his office and sat behind the grey wood-effect desk. Amos shuffled in, yawned and stretched, pulled out the same small black chair as before, and slumped himself down. He wiped the sleep from his eyes and then waited for his blurry vision to clear. Staring across the grey desk, he saw dark rings had formed under Gerry's bloodshot and sunken eyes. Cans of energy drinks and empty nicotine gum wrappers littered the desk and overflowed the small wastepaper basket on the floor. 'Jesus, Gerry,' Amos said. 'When was the last time you slept?'

'Don't know, it doesn't matter. That's what caffeine is for. Listen, Amos, there's a lot of stuff on this laptop. I've been at it all night, and I've barely even scratched the surface. It took me three hours just to get past the firewall. Where did you get it from?'

Amos recounted the whole story about the shabby man called Onion and their little shopping trip to the cash and carry. He told Gerry about the warehouse hidden at the back of the cash and carry, with pallets of various drugs stacked high on tall racking. He told him about the three Tangos he left unconscious before acquiring the laptop and leaving Onion cuffed to a lamppost.

'Well, that cash and carry you "acquired" this thing from isn't the only one this maniac has,' Gerry said. 'He has one in Glasgow, one here in Edinburgh, and one in Dundee. Each of these "hubs," for lack of a better term, services around thirty dealers spread out across the country, and he has them all networked together through a secure site on the dark web. The security on the site is pretty sophisticated, too. I could only get access to parts of it so far. There is an in-depth statistical analysis of the drug habits of the entire country here. He knows exactly which drugs to push and where to push them. This arsehole has dragged drug dealing into the twenty-first century. He's smart, Amos. I've never seen anything like it. This thing is a lot bigger than we thought. It might be time to call in the cavalry.'

'I can't get the police involved, Gerry, he'll hurt Mary.'

'I'm not talking about the police, mate. I've found communications between these hubs warning when the police plan to raid. Christ, he's even got files with the names and addresses of the undercover agents staking these places out. I'm not sure how he's doing it, but he's been two steps ahead of the police the whole time. Philosopher roid-rage next door wasn't joking, mate — the police will never catch this guy. They're useless. I'm talking about bringing in the big boys, MI5; they'd cream their Y-fronts over something this big.'

'If his operation is that big, he probably has someone on the payroll. I mean, it's not like MI5 to let something that big go unnoticed, is it? And, anyway, I don't know anyone I can trust.'

'What about your old pal? What's his name? The spook you met during your tour in Afghanistan back in 2001?'

'Farmer? I haven't spoken to Brian in years. He was working with Special Branch last I knew,' Amos said.

'You still have his number?' Gerry asked.

'I have an email address. I don't know if he still uses it, but it's worth a shot, I suppose.' Amos took a pen and a pad of post-it notes from the desk tidy on Gerry's desk and scribbled the details from memory, then handed it to Gerry.

'I'll track him down. Now, Amos, there's something else.' Gerry paused and took a deep breath. 'I found a list of sixteen names. I haven't had a chance to look at all sixteen, but the three names I have checked out so far have been reported missing in the past few days. I haven't found any connections between them yet, but mate...' He paused again. 'Mary's name is on the list.'

'What? Mary? Why?' Amos cried, as he lunged forward in the chair.

'I don't know, mate.' Gerry said, holding his hand up in a futile attempt to calm his friend down. 'It looks like her name was added to the list two days ago.'

'He will know,' Amos snarled, jabbing his finger towards the server room, where their unwilling guest was still strapped to a chair. He then pushed himself up from the chair and started towards the door. Gerry bounced from his high-backed chair and blocked the door before Amos reached the handle.

'Wait,' Gerry said. 'Don't do anything stupid here. You don't want to do something you'll regret.'

'I'm done being nice, Gerry. They have kidnapped my daughter and got her locked-up, God knows where; I don't even know if she's alive. And now her name is on a list with fifteen other names who, we can only assume, have all been reported missing. It's time I start getting answers, or people are going to get hurt.' Amos reached into his pocket, fished out the folding knife, and flicked the blade open. 'Now, move!' he ordered. Gerry held his hands up and stepped aside. Amos pulled the office door open and disappeared. Gerry steadied himself for the screams that were due at any minute. He knew his old friend would barge in heavy-handed and demand cooperation, and he knew that George would refuse. He knew from experience that his friend would start punching, but the escalation to cutting would be very quick. This was the darker side of war. It forced good men to do bad things for what seemed like the right reasons, and no man walked away with his soul intact.

Gerry held his breath and waited.

But there was no shouting.

There was no screaming.

There were no sounds at all.

Only silence.

The office door opened slowly, and Amos staggered back in. His face was two shades whiter than when he had left moments before. The frayed end of a climbing rope hung loosely in his hand at his side. 'What's wrong?' Gerry asked.

'He's gone,' Amos replied.

The sound of screeching tyres and the wail of a car engine protesting at high revs shook both men from their disbelief. Amos raced down the narrow hallway towards the barn door, his legs powered by panic. In the two-point-eight second dash from Gerry's office door to the barn's entrance, his mind played out three different scenarios. The first of these was that George had stolen the Audi and was on his way back to Mr B with the Shed's location. He would return sooner rather than later with a small army and lay siege until the converted barn was nothing more than a smouldering pile of ash.

The second scenario to play out in his mind was that George had revved the Audi and was waiting for his captors to appear before releasing the handbrake and launching the car straight through the barn door, killing them both in one swoop.

The third, and least desirable scenario, was that George had found the gun, which was still in the glove compartment, and had revved the car's engine as a decoy to lure him and Gerry outside, where they would be gunned down and Mary would be lost forever. Both scenarios one and two would at least give him options for countermeasures. The gorilla would rely heavily on luck for either of these to be successful. The third meant game over for him, Gerry, and Mary. The math came to him instantly, he calculated an almost sixty-seven percent chance of death when he opened the door. He had survived worse odds before, but that was with a team of highly trained soldiers behind him. Now, he was blindly running at a door, and his only backup was an IT guy on the wrong side of middle age with little to no battle experience. This realisation pumped adrenaline into his legs faster and pushed them forward, independent of thought or reason. Amos did not fight his legs, though. His gut had made the decision to kick open the door, and he had learned long ago not to second-guess his instincts. He had seen firsthand how dangerous that kind of indecision can be. At its worst, it creates confusion that jeopardises not only the mission, but also risks lives. At its best, it crumbles the confidence of battle-seasoned soldiers and jeopardises not only the mission, but also risks lives.

He lowered his shoulder and charged into the emergency exit door, catching the release bar with his hip. The door swung wildly as he barged through just in time to see the brake lights of his car speed along the dirt track. His heavy panting hung motionless in the cold morning air.

'Damn it!' he shouted. Gerry reached the door three seconds later. 'He's gone,' Amos said. Upon hearing those words, Gerry instantly slumped forward, bracing his hands on his knees in a half-collapse, wheezing and coughing. After a moment, the coughing eased.

Gerry, half composed himself, then pointed to the distant taillights and shouted, 'Shite bag!'

Chapter 18

Gerry thudded back into the high-backed chair behind his desk, pulled a fresh packet of nicotine gum from his desk drawer, and popped two into his mouth. Amos slumped forward in the small black chair opposite, rested his elbows on his knees, and cradled his head in his hands.

Scenario one. Thank God.

'I'm so sorry, Gerry,' Amos finally said. 'I shouldn't have come here. I shouldn't have got you caught up in this.'

'I'd be pissed if you hadn't, Buttercup.'

'He'll be back, and he'll bring backup. They'll send a team out here to burn this place to the ground. I've destroyed your business and potentially killed us both. We've got to get out of here.'

'Don't worry about my business,' Gerry said. 'We just need to get Mary back safe. How much time do you think we have?'

'Don't know. Forty-minute drive at the most, depending on how much of a risk he wants to take by speeding. A couple of hours to get a crew, equipment, and a plan assembled, and an hour's drive back here with a van full of guns and guys. Three hours at the very most, I'd say, and that's being generous.'

'Good. I've got some stuff I need to finish first. We'll be out of here in about two hours max.'

'Gerry, we need to get as far away from the Shed as possible. We need to go now.'

'Listen up, Buttercup, I'm going nowhere. These scumbags have my goddaughter, and there is nothing on this earth that will stop me from getting her back. I have loved that girl like she was my own since you and Soph showed me the scan pictures. I've been there for every birthday and every Christmas. I taught her how to code. She's a better programmer than half the guys I interview. Her first word was "Gerry" for Chrissake. I was the one she came running to when you guys had an argument. And I was the one she called when this thing started. She came to me for help. She knew she was in trouble, and she came to me. Now I don't care who these people are or what they want, but they better bring a goddamned army because I'm going nowhere until I find her.'

'Actually, Gerry, her first word was "Mum",' Amos said.

'I'm having a moment here, Buttercup, don't ruin it.'

'OK, Gerry,' Amos said, holding his hands up in mock defeat. 'Two hours, but we need to be gone before they get here. OK?'

'OK. I just want to have another pass at the file vault on the phone.'

'Oh shit!'

'What?' Gerry asked.

'The phone. It's in the car.'

'What? Seriously?'

'I put it in the glove compartment and forgot to take it out. There goes my bargaining chip,' Amos said, slapping his thigh.

'Look, we've still got the laptop. Let's focus on what we have and not beat ourselves up about what we don't have. Let me work on this, and we'll take it from there. There's a shower at the end of the hall, next to the kitchen, if you want to freshen up,' Gerry said, then cracked open another energy drink and began typing.

The two-hour mark was approaching fast. Amos had

taken advantage of the time, as Gerry suggested. He found bread and a toaster in the kitchen, made a quick breakfast, and washed it down with one of Gerry's energy drinks. *Caffeine and calories. Eat while you can.* A long shower helped clear his head, stay focused on what lay ahead, and not muddy his thoughts on things he couldn't control or change. He needed to stay sharp. Sitting now in the kitchen, he had time to breathe and organise his thoughts. Time, however, is a double-edged sword. The quiet inactivity gave his mind the chance to wander, and thoughts of Sophia intruded into his train of thought once again. Pictures of her radiant smile and deep green eyes, so full of colour and life, were scattered amongst the images of her pale, gaunt features lying in the hospice bed. A knot formed in his throat, and his vision blurred. He gripped his trembling knee tight and swallowed hard. *Not yet, Amos, you can't afford to fall apart now.* He bounced from the chair, shaking his hands and his head. Movement helped. Movement distracted. Keep moving. He paced back and forth in the empty kitchen, shaking, bouncing, and moving.

'Amos?' Gerry's muffled voice called from the office. Amos stopped bouncing and started towards the office.

'You finished?' Amos asked, as he opened the office door.

'No, not yet,' Gerry replied, distracted by the computer screen in front of him.

'What is it?'

'Come have a look at this.'

Amos walked around the desk and stared at the footage of the security camera covering the front door. The face on the screen was discoloured by the night vision, but he recognised it instantly.

'Is that live?' he asked.

'Yes. Isn't that your car?' Gerry replied.

'Yes,' Amos said, incredulously.

'Do you know who that is?'

Without reply, he left Gerry alone at the desk and headed for the front entrance. He pushed open the release bar, and the door opened outward. The figure stepped back into the flood lights that thumped to life.

'Beth?' Amos said.

'Hello, Mr Fisher. Did you lose something?'

Chapter 19

Gerry sat in his high-backed leather chair behind his desk. Amos sat in one of the tub chairs opposite and gestured to McGuire to sit in the other. She ignored his request and opted to tower over the two men, who stared at her in silence. She allowed herself a small, cocky smile. Then, squaring her shoulders, she stood as tall as she could. 'OK, gentlemen. I understand you will have a lot of questions, and I will answer as many of them as I can. But first, I need you to answer some of mine. OK?' She paused a beat, then continued without letting either of the men answer. 'Mr Fisher, I need to know how you found out about the cash and carry and why you were there last night.' With one smooth movement, she slipped her black trench coat off her shoulders and dropped it over the back of the empty tub chair. The slim grey pinstripe trouser power suit she had chosen that morning was for precisely this eventuality. The fitted blazer accentuated her slim waist, and the high-heeled shoes elongated her athletic legs. The saleswoman had advised that this suit combined authority with style. Forging her professionalism and femininity into a perfect weapon against unsuspecting men. Now, with her hands on her hips, she pressed Amos for an answer.

'I needed toilet roll,' he said.

'Don't get cute with me, Mr Fisher. I know you coerced a low-level street dealer, known as Onion, into divulging the location to you. I need to know why you were there and what you found.'

'If you already know so much, what do you need me for?'

'I need to know how much damage control I need to do to get your daughter back safely.'

'Get her back? You have no idea where she is, do you? Why should I trust you? You won't even tell me who you are,' Amos said. McGuire paced the length of the office, feeling the eyes of the two men burn into the back of her head. Small beads of sweat had begun to form on her brow. She quickly mopped them away before turning to face them again.

'OK, Mr Fisher, Mr O'Hara. I am Detective Inspector Rachel McGuire, and I am with the special investigations unit with Strathclyde Police. That is all I am at liberty to tell you right now, but please believe me; my highest priority is Mary's safety.'

'All you want is her phone,' Amos spat.

'If that were true, then I wouldn't be here.' McGuire pulled the phone from her trouser pocket. 'We found it in the glove compartment of your car. After your little shopping trip to get toilet paper, we put out an All-Ports-Warning for your car. It was picked up sixteen miles from here, being driven by a known associate of Mr B. I have him in custody at a safe house not far from here. He's refusing to speak, obviously, so I checked the recent locations on the car's satnav, which led me here.'

'Give me that,' Amos said as he bounced up from the chair to grab the phone. McGuire snatched it away, stashed it back in her pocket, and folded her arms. From her training, she knew that this was the wrong body language to use right now. She wanted to stay open and project authority and trust, but she needed to hide her trembling hands. She cleared the lump from her throat and forced eye contact with the angry man who stood opposite.

'Mr Fisher, this phone is crucial evidence in an ongoing investigation.'

'Why?' Gerry said. 'What is on there that is so important? I've tried to crack the file vault on it myself, but the security is solid. And if I can't crack it, then your guys have no chance. I wouldn't trust those clowns to hack a calculator, never mind something as sophisticated as that.'

'To be honest, Mr O'Hara, I don't know what's on the phone,' she admitted, a little more sheepishly than she would have liked.

'What?' Amos barked. 'You don't know? Are you serious?'

'Look, I have been after Mr B for a long time. I have been trying to get wiretaps, surveillance, and undercover operatives to bust him, but I couldn't get the evidence to support the authorisation. Then, around four months ago, Mary reached out to me, and using the information she had gathered, I was granted resources to put a surveillance team together. We staked out the warehouse at the cash and carry, and when we had gathered enough intel, we raided it but found nothing. It's like he knew we were coming. I know there are drugs moving through that warehouse, but I can't prove anything. That's when Mary told me she could get concrete evidence. Then last week, she called to tell me she had the exact thing I needed downloaded on her phone. I was to rendezvous with her to do the exchange, but when I called to confirm yesterday morning, she told me she wasn't going to go through with it.'

'Wait,' Amos said. 'That was you she was talking to? I heard her talking when he was in my house, but I thought she was talking to that psychopath.'

'Yes, that was me. I was calling to confirm the meeting, but she was upset about something and hung up.'

'She was upset because her mother had just...' Amos broke off. She watched him swallow hard as he raised his hand to cover his eyes.

'Mr Fisher, I am so sorry for your loss. I had no idea.'

'Of course you didn't!' he snapped, looking up at her. 'You were too focused on your primary objective. Well, now you have it. What more do you want?'

Before McGuire had a chance to answer, a vaguely familiar Cardi B song blasted from the phone in her pocket. She quickly pulled it out and stared at the screen. Slowly, she turned the phone to show the two men. The name on the caller ID only showed the letter B. She answered, turned the loudspeaker on, and waited.

'Amos,' said the voice on the phone. 'Are you trying to get your daughter killed? What exactly were you trying to achieve with your little stunt? Other than pissing me off, I mean.'

'I got your attention, didn't I?' Amos said.

'Oh, you've got my attention, old man. Now let's see if I have yours. Say hello to Daddy.' Sounds of muffled screams blasted over the phone's speaker, which then gave way to angry shouts.

'Mary!' Amos yelled.

'Dad, I'm OK.' Mary shouted. 'Don't give him the— ' A loud slap silenced her momentarily, and her shouts were muffled again.

'Well, do I have you attention now?'

'You bastard! If you hurt her, I'll—'

Mr B interrupted, 'Bring me the phone and the laptop, or she dies. I'll text you the details.' The phone went dead.

Amos dropped back into the chair with his head in his hands. McGuire stared hard at him for a long moment, one eyebrow raised.

'What laptop?' she asked. Gerry explained about the laptop and the encryption key on the phone. McGuire glanced over to where Amos sat. In that moment, with his shoulders hunched over and his head hung low, he looked lost. Up until now, he projected an air of defiant confidence — a self-assured anger that suggested weakness was an emotion he was not capable of feeling. He was the personification of the toxic masculinity that the woke generation likes to rant about on social media and at university rallies — the latest hook that pseudo-intellectuals like to hang the world's problems on.

After a few minutes of stunned silence, Amos shook his head and said, 'Something is wrong.'

'You think?' Gerry replied sarcastically, then he turned to McGuire. 'OK, so what's our next move?'

'*We* don't have a next move,' she said. 'I will get a unit mobilised. We'll set up a sting at the rendezvous once Mr B has confirmed the time and location. We will secure the area, arrest Mr B, and get Mary back safely.'

'Something isn't right, but I don't know what. I can't think,' Amos murmured.

'None of this is right, Mr Fisher,' McGuire said, then turned back to Gerry 'I can't risk two civilians getting in the way and jeopardising the whole operation.'

'Lady, we have got more info on this maniac in one day than you lot have managed in three months,' Gerry said.

'No, something was wrong with the phone call I mean. Something he said. Something's missing,' Amos said.

'Missing?' McGuire quizzed. 'Like what?' She watched as Amos closed his eyes and mumbled. Confused, she looked at Gerry. Gerry looked back and shrugged. 'I need to get the phone and the laptop back to my team, so they can be analysed properly.'

'The phone and the laptop,' Amos said. 'That's what he said. He wants *me* to bring the *phone* and the *laptop*.'

'So?' McGuire said.

'Why didn't he instruct us to give them to his man, George, like last time? Why didn't he ask about the hostage?'

Chapter 20

Rachel McGuire stepped out of the office with her phone in hand. Gerry turned to Amos and said, 'I like her, she did well. She took command of the conversation early and maintained authority without being bossy. She asked questions, listened to your answers, and offered just enough of the truth to gain our trust. Other than the folding of her arms to hide her shaking hands, it was textbook advanced interrogation techniques perfectly executed.'

'Yes, she worked hard at hiding her insecurities. A solid eight out of ten, I'd say.'

'You OK, mate?' Gerry asked softly. 'That was a tough phone call.'

'It's proof of life, which is the best I can hope for right now, I suppose.'

A familiar, niggling feeling was beginning to form in the back of Amos's mind. Like a distant and muffled voice shouting a warning. The words themselves were indistinguishable, but the tone was undeniable. He had heard those same muffled cries many times before during some of the more questionable mission briefings in Iraq, Ireland, and a dozen other countries around the world. Missions that lacked solid intel, or when something he couldn't quite pinpoint, just seemed off. It was a gut instinct with no clear cause or point of origin. And on those missions, nine times out of ten, something went seriously wrong, and someone ended up hurt or dead.

'I have a bad feeling about this, buddy,' Gerry said.

'Me too. Something doesn't feel right.'

'About Rachel? I mean, can we trust her?'

'Not even a little. Someone is clearly feeding this arsehole police intel. I don't know if it is her, but until we're sure, we can't trust anyone.'

'So, what do we do now? I mean, you know it's a trap, right? If you take the phone to wherever this lunatic wants, he is going to kill you.'

'I know, but I don't know what else to do.'

The draught excluder on the office door brushed loudly against the carpet. McGuire marched back in, stuffing her phone into her pocket. 'OK, Mr B has sent the rendezvous location,' she said. 'It's an abandoned church not far from here. We have three hours, so that gives me time to get a surveillance team in place and get you wired up.'

'No,' Amos said. 'I won't risk it. Your team could be spotted. It could get Mary killed.'

'Mr Fisher, I wasn't asking. This is a police investigation, and we are your best shot at getting your daughter back safely.'

'She's right, mate,' Gerry said. 'We're out of our depth here. We need help.' Amos stared at McGuire, who pulled her shoulders back and tried to make herself look big again. *Seven out of ten*, he thought as he closed his eyes. The muffled voice in his head began screaming something inaudible again. A warning of some kind, but of what, he wasn't sure. He pictured the mind map again. The question mark with the word "Onion" underneath had now been crossed out, and the name "Rachel McGuire" had been assigned to the picture that was labelled "Beth". Three locations Mr B was using as warehouses and the laptop had been added. Something isn't making sense. Why risk taking Mary? What was on the phone? Why didn't he ask about George? Three hours? The shadow of an answer loomed in the corner of his mind.

'Three hours?' he finally said.

'What?' McGuire asked.

'You said three hours. The meeting time is three hours from now. Why? And why a local church?' The shadow crept closer.

'Looks like your team has arrived,' Gerry said, as he turned one of his CCTV screens around. It showed a black Land Rover rolling to a stop at the front door and four men dressed in black stepping out.

'That was quick,' McGuire said.

'Why that church? How did he know where we were?' Amos said. The gloom was slowly fading, and details were beginning to form on the shadow's figure.

'I'll go and brief the team, then we'll get you wired up, Mr Fisher. OK?' McGuire said this and headed towards the front door. Her high-heeled shoes clicked on the hall floor loudly and quickly at first, but quietened and slowed as she neared the barn's entrance. Then Amos bolted from his seat and flung the office door open.

'Rachel, don't open the door!' he shouted, as he sprinted towards her. He launched himself forward and tackled her. They hit the ground just as the door handle exploded inward. They both scrambled up from the ground as two more shots shattered the door's hinges, and the door began to flop inward. Amos kicked it as hard as he could, sending the door crashing into the man holding a shotgun on the other side. He pushed McGuire down the hall and followed her back towards the office. The front door dropped heavily on the floor behind them as they stumbled along the hallway. Gerry emerged from the office and pointed the stolen handgun straight at them.

'Get down!' he shouted. Amos and McGuire dived for the floor as gunfire exploded overhead. 'Move!' Gerry yelled. Keeping low, Amos and McGuire scrambled down the hall while Gerry fired a few covering shots, then followed. They ran past the office and ducked into the kitchen.

'Friends of yours?' Gerry shouted at McGuire as he took cover in the doorway, firing more shots towards the Tangos advancing down the hallway. McGuire shook her head, gasping.

'Is there another way out?' Amos asked.

Gerry sidled to the kitchen door, ducking shots from their attackers. 'Yes, an emergency exit at the back,' he said, cracking off two more shots in a violent question and answer. Amos dived for the cupboards, flinging the doors open. 'What are you looking for?' Gerry said.

'I saw a camping stove earlier. You got any propane?'

'Bottom cupboard, next to the fridge.' Gerry fired two more shots, then ducked back inside as a hail of bullets thudded into the wall next to his head. Amos grabbed two small propane canisters and a can of spray polish and strapped them together with duct tape he found in a drawer.

'Give me the gun,' he said to Gerry, and they switched positions. Without looking, Amos tossed the cans down the hall towards the attackers. The hail paused. Whether the Tangos were reloading or confused at the projectile that was tossed in their direction, he wasn't sure, and he didn't care. He took advantage and spun into the hall with one hand wrapped around the pistol's grip and the other cupped underneath. *Can't afford to miss.* One shot was all he would get, and if he was half as good a shot as he was back in the day, then one shot was all he needed. His heart thumped slowly in his ears as he watched the cans tumble in slow motion on the hard floor. The fluorescent light in the hall flickered and glinted against the handgun of Tango number one as he began switching his focus from the projectile on the floor to Amos. The switch, in real time, probably took a split second but seemed like almost a minute to Amos. Enough time to perfectly align the pistol's rear and front sight dead-on his target. Enough time for him to push all the air out of his lungs. Enough time for him to time the shot between heartbeats. All unnecessary for a target at such a short range, but when the stakes were literally life and death, he didn't want to take any chances. He squeezed the trigger quickly but gently. The gun rocked his hands back hard. The crack of the gun was amplified by the narrow hallway walls. The average bullet can cover a distance of roughly 370 metres per second. The improvised explosive he tossed was no more than five metres away. The bullet took approximately 0.014 seconds to hit the target, yet to Amos, it seemed to take a lot longer. He watched the muzzle flash explode from the end of the gun. He watched as the bullet travelled agonisingly slowly through the air towards the cans. He watched as Tango number one raised his gun, aiming to fire at Amos, who was a sitting duck in a narrow hallway. He watched as the nine-millimetre parabellum pierced the propane can, scraping against it and creating that all-important spark that would ignite the contents. He watched as the hall filled with a toxic mixture of fire, propane, and furniture polish. Tango one had squeezed off a return shot, but not before the cans exploded, sending his aim wide of his target. His shot buried itself deep into the wall beside Amos's head. The sound of gunfire was replaced with coughing and choking. Gerry and McGuire did not wait for the all-clear before scrambling from the kitchen and rushing for the emergency exit at the rear of the building.

Luckily, the four Tangos did not have the training or foresight to cover the rear exit. Amos followed Gerry around the side of the Shed and headed for the car park at the front. Gerry stooped at the corner and held his fist high. Amos instinctively dropped to one knee and ushered McGuire down behind him. He watched Gerry and waited with the pistol pointed low but ready. The signal was given, and the three bolted from their cover and headed straight for the Audi. Gerry jumped into the passenger seat, while McGuire clambered into the back. Amos circled around the car, then stopped to watch as the four attackers fell out of the Shed's front door, choking and vomiting. He allowed himself a small smile, then raised his pistol. There was no need to rush this time. The Tangos were in no condition to fire back. He lined up the first target and squeezed the trigger. Four quick shots rang out over the empty fields, and the four tyres of the Land Rover gushed and collapsed. The four men, still coughing and vomiting, dropped to the floor and covered their heads.

'So, what now?' Gerry asked, as the Audi sped away from the barn for the second time that morning.

Chapter 21

The hum of the tyres on the road filled the silence of the Audi. Amos squinted and flicked the sun visor down, but the low morning sun shimmered on the slick tarmac and obscured his vision just the same. He took random turns, heading nowhere in particular, just staying on the move. He glanced in the rear-view mirror at McGuire. Her brow was buried deep into her nose, and her eyes shifted left and right but focused on nothing. He had seen the look before, sometimes in the mirror. Doubt was sometimes a useful tool, but it became a dangerous weapon when wielded against yourself.

'I need to call this in,' she said, breaking the silence. She fumbled her phone out of her pocket. Amos watched as she shook her free hand and pumped a fist over and over.

'Control your breathing,' Amos said. 'Deep breath in and slow out.' His words seemed to shake her out of a daze.

'Huh?'

'Control your breathing, and you control your heart. Control your heart, and you control your mind.'

After a few deep breaths, McGuire made the call and requested officers attend the barn to arrest the gunmen. She confirmed the address and gave instructions to keep her posted, then returned the phone to her pocket.

Silence fell back into the car.

'Why three hours?' Amos said. 'Why wait so long? And why that church? How did he know where we were? Where is the safehouse that you're holding what's his name in?'

'George,' Gerry offered. 'His name is George.'

'I'm not taking you to a police safehouse, Mr Fisher. There are regulations in place, and for good reason,' McGuire said.

'Do me a favour; call and check on your suspect,' he said. McGuire pulled her phone from her pocket again and dialled.

'What now?' Gerry asked again.

'First, we need to get rid of this car,' Amos said. McGuire's voice was low and rushed in the back seat. 'The police and the enemy are on the lookout for it now,' he continued.

'I know a guy who might be able to help; he owns a scrapyard.'

'Can we trust him?'

'I helped him out last year when someone hacked his computer and tried to blackmail him. They threatened to send compromising pictures to his wife. I saved his sham of a marriage and upgraded his security.'

'Tell me you weren't *in* the compromising pictures, Gerry.'

'A gentleman doesn't kiss and tell, Buttercup, you know that.'

'What?!' McGuire yelled into the phone. 'On whose authority?' Amos glanced in the mirror. Her brow was buried deeper, but this time not with self-doubt. 'What do you mean, no reason to hold him? He's a known associate of a suspected drug dealer, driving a stolen car. When was he released?' She paused and listened to the reply. 'I want his location now,' she demanded, then slammed the phone back into her pocket. 'Damn it.'

'That's how he knew where we were,' Amos said. 'That was the reason for the three hours. He wanted us to stay in the Shed. And why he didn't ask us to release George.'

'Take the next left,' Gerry interrupted.

***

Gerry's directions led them along a picturesque country road that ran parallel to the curving River North Esk. Great oak trees, which hugged both sides of the road, stretched their branches overhead and created a tunnel overhead. The warmer spring mornings had spurred the trees into sprouting leaves early. Sunlight fell through the treetop canopy and cast soft shadows on the road ahead. Long, slow bends in the winding road rocked the car lazily left, then right. The soft melodies of birds rousing in their nests accompanied the babbling river and created a natural symphony that, on any other occasion, would have been relaxing. No sign or billboard advertised the turn for the scrapyard or even acknowledged its existence. A break in the tree line, however, revealed a small side road, one that Amos would have missed had Gerry not warned him in advance. He slowed the car and swung left. The hum of the tyres changed to a more jagged rhythm as they left the smooth tarmac for the rougher track.

The scrapyard itself lay three hundred yards ahead, at the end of the single-track road, nestled in a nook between high bushes and dense woodland. The narrow road, flanked by trees and unkempt undergrowth, led to a tall steel corrugated gate that stretched between two stone pillars. On the other side of the pillars, a tall, barbed wire fence circled the yard. It looked odd and out of place amongst the natural surroundings. *A strange place for a scrapyard*, Amos thought to himself. A single camera high on the right pillar pointed onto a small intercom on the opposite side. Gerry got out and pressed the button on the intercom. The loud, harsh metallic rattle of the buzzer sounded just as out of place as the gate had looked. An unnatural voice mumbled over the speaker, and Gerry waved at the camera opposite. Then, the heavy, slow whirr kicked the gate into life, pulling it behind one of the stone pillars. Gerry sat back in the car, closed the door, and said, 'He's a bit security conscious after his issues last year.'

'So I see,' Amos replied, then rolled the car slowly through the gate. The car ambled thirty yards before stopping outside a large white cabin marked *Reception*. The trio stepped out of the car and waited. The green wooden door of the cabin swung inward, and a large, greasy man bounded from inside.

'Gerry,' boomed a deep, eastern European accent. 'Welcome, my friend. If I had known you were coming, I would have cleaned up a little. Come, come, I will put the kettle on.' It was hard to pinpoint the accent exactly. It seemed to be a strange mix of broad East-Coast Scottish with a Slavic origin. Two accents rammed together in a head-on collision. Usually, in any other circumstance, a smash like this would result in wreckage that would see its victims brought to a facility just like this one, but the greasy giant had welded the two together seamlessly, and it fit him perfectly. The three followed him inside.

The inside of the cabin was surprisingly clean. A small, two-seater sofa sat against the far wall, left of the door, and at the other end was a neat and modest desk. On top of the desk, a small pink ceramic vase filled with fake flowers sat next to a computer screen and a desk tidy. The cabin's ceiling cleared the big man's head by only a few inches. Rough, oil-stained skin around the huge man's eyes and mouth was stretched in a welcoming grin that revealed immaculately white teeth. The teeth, like the gate and the buzzer, looked out of place among their surroundings. His hard, protruding powerbelly peaked from the bottom of an ill-fitting, sleeveless T-shirt. His broad shoulders and huge bulking arms were spattered with more engine oil, and a thick smell of diesel seemed to ooze from his pores. 'Amos, Rachel, this is Damir Volkov. Damir, these are my friends Amos Fisher and Rachel McGuire,' Gerry said. Volkov's huge hand engulfed Amos's and shook it with the energy and enthusiasm of an old friend, meeting up after years apart.

'Good to meet you, my friend,' Volkov said, then turned to face Gerry. 'So, Bratishka, what can I do for you?' The word Bratishka not only told Amos that the giant was Russian, but that he regarded Gerry with enormous respect and love.

'We need a car, Buttercup,' Gerry replied. 'Nothing fancy, just something to get us from A to B. Can you help us out?' Volkov's sturdy stomach bounced as he bellowed a hearty laugh.

'Of course, little brother. I have a few lying around the back. Help yourself. First, you must stay for breakfast, though, yes? My wife is making kasha and zapekanka.'

'That's very kind of you, but—' Amos began, but was cut off by the loud Russian.

'Come, come, my friend, I insist. I will make coffee, and you can rest from whatever it is you are running from,' Amos's eyes widened, and he rocked back, instinctively looking for the door — looking for an exit.

'Calm yourself, my friend. I know a man in trouble when I see one. You are safe here.' Volkov looped a huge arm around Gerry's shoulder and pulled him close. 'Any friend of Bratishka is a friend of mine. Come, come, sit.' Volkov released Gerry and gestured towards the small sofa. 'Sit, relax. I will bring coffee.' He turned to McGuire and pointed to the office chair behind the desk. 'Please, please, krasivaya dama.' McGuire accepted his offer and sat down. Volkov smiled once more, ducked back through the door, and disappeared.

Silence.

The adrenaline was wearing off, and the trio was beginning to feel the effects. McGuire slumped in the office chair, and Gerry stared blankly at the wall. Amos couldn't tell if he was lost in thought or fighting exhaustion. Neither would have surprised him.

'Can we trust him, Gerry?' Amos asked, shaking Gerry from his gaze.

'Don't worry, Buttercup, we're safe here.'

'If you're sure, *Bratishka*,' Amos said, nudging Gerry with his elbow.

'What did he call me? McGuire asked.

'Krasivaya dama,' Amos said. 'It means beautiful lady.'

McGuire's cheeks flushed red. 'So, what do we do now?' she asked, changing the subject.

'First, we eat,' Gerry said. 'Anya makes a lovely zapekanka.'

Chapter 22

The coffee was strong, and the Zapekanka was sweet. Gerry was right; it was lovely. Volkov was a warm and welcoming host. He asked no questions about their predicament, which Amos appreciated, and offered levity with amusing anecdotes from the old days. It was a small and welcome distraction from the morning's stresses. *This guy knows what he's doing*, Amos thought. McGuire finished her meal and excused herself. 'I need to make a few phone calls,' she added, leaving the cabin. The empty cups clinked against one another as Volkov placed them back on a rectangular tray.

'More coffee?' he asked nobody in particular, 'Aye, more coffee,' he continued without waiting for an answer. Then he picked up the tray and ducked back out of the door. Amos smiled a quick thank you, but the smile faded as soon as the door swung closed and clicked loudly into place. He sat forward, resting his elbows on his knees and his head in his hands. A long, deep sigh escaped from his lips, and rushed into the silent void that now filled the room. The sigh reverberated, then died quickly. A hand gently squeezed his shoulder, stirring him from his despair.

'We'll get her back, mate,' Gerry said. 'Everything is going to be fine.'

'It's all my fault, Gerry.'

'How? How is it your fault that Mary was kidnapped by a psychopath? Or that Sophia...' Struggling to find the right words, Gerry opted for silence to finish the sentence for him. 'It's not your fault, mate, you can't blame yourself.'

'It is my fault,' Amos said as he pulled his head from his hands and stared at his friend. 'Not about Sophia, I mean, but Mary. She left because of me. I love Mary with every fibre of my being, I really do. Always have and always will, but she became someone I couldn't understand, someone I just—' He swallowed hard and slumped his head back into his hands. 'Someone I didn't like. Her own father didn't like her. That's why she left.'

'No, Buttercup, she left because she wanted to make her own way in life. She knows you love her; you've always been a loving father. You're just overthinking this. I bet she didn't even know you felt that way.'

'Of course, she knew,' Amos snapped as he bounced up from the small sofa and began to pace the small office floor. 'How could she not know? How could a child not sense that her own father doesn't like her? She would've felt it every day. Saw it in my eyes when I looked at her. Hell, even the way I spoke to her, she would've felt my anger, my disappointment, and my impatience. Children sense these things, Gerry; trust me on that one. I know what I'm talking about.

'Sophia tried warning me about it, but I knew better. I was a soldier. I trained hundreds of men. I knew how to break them down and build them back up. I created warriors, and I was good at it. Soph warned me, but I wouldn't listen. I didn't know how to. And by the time I learned, it was too late. The damage was done. And my little girl was gone. She hated me, and I don't blame her. I wasn't her father; I was her commanding officer. But damn, Gerry, that little girl is the toughest soldier I've ever seen, and I've seen the best. She's fearless and stubborn, just like her mother.'

'Sorry, Buttercup, you're pointing that finger in the

wrong direction there. She gets that stubborn streak from you. I once watched you tell a two-star Yankee general to run his arse up a cheese grater because you had a funny feeling about his briefing.'

'That guy was an idiot.'

'Aye, and he almost got you court martialled. The only thing that saved your career was the fact that you were right. By sheer luck, you were right.'

'It wasn't luck, it was a gut feeling. I've served too long to ignore my instincts.'

'The intel looked good. The lead looked solid. And, despite all evidence to the contrary, you said the location was wrong and you were too stubborn to back down.'

'And I was right.'

'Mary gets that from you, Buttercup.'

Amos said nothing and kept his stride, walking back and forth.

Gerry stood up and blocked his friend's path.

'Amos, you are a great father. Yes, you may have been a bit too strict sometimes, but that was because you cared. Mary knows that. She knows you're a stubborn, pig-headed prick, but she never once doubted your love.' A small chuckle escaped Amos's lips before he caught himself. 'Now,' Gerry continued, grasping Amos's shoulder, 'let's get our shit together, hunt this bastard down, and get my goddaughter back.'

A nod between the two sealed the pact. Amos swallowed the lump in his throat and grunted.

The door swung open again, and Volkov returned, balancing four cups on a tray. 'OK, my friends, now we see about the car, aye?' Amos smiled at the car crash accent again.

'Aye,' he replied.

The coffee helped fight the brisk morning air as they trudged through the scrapyard. Wreckages were piled high, and engine parts were scattered around. There seemed to be a degree of organisation to the chaos, though. Tyres were piled next to alloys, suspension arms next to springs, and engines next to gearboxes. That was the extent of Amos's automotive knowledge. *Give me two sticks of dynamite, and I can bring down a skyscraper, but don't ask me to change a spark plug*, he thought. Volkov paced in front, while the two men followed.

'Are you sure about this, my friend?' Volkov bellowed. 'The Audi is a nice car, and I have nothing of that value here.'

'Yes, Damir,' Amos replied, 'I won't be using it again. I'm not looking to match the value. I just need something reliable that will last a few days.'

'Not a problem, my friend. I am guessing you don't want any paper trail with the Audi?'

'I'd prefer if there wasn't, if that's OK?'

'Don't worry, my friend. It will be as though it fell off the face of the earth.'

'Thank you, Damir,' Amos said, as mud pulled at his boots.

'Here we are,' Volkov said. 'This is the most reliable thing I have. I bought it last week from a couple of kids who owed money to their dealer.' He stood waving a great big hand towards a sky-blue Ford Focus RS with black alloys and a spoiler to match.

'Do you have anything a bit less conspicuous?' Gerry asked.

'Nyet.' The giant smiled.

'It'll do. Do you have the location of any of the names on the list?' Amos asked Gerry. 'I need to know what that list is, and why Mary's name is on it.'

'I found the last known address for one name.' Gerry fished his phone from his pocket and began swiping at the screen. 'Alex McDonald, he lives in Govan, or used to, at least. I'll text you the address and the names of the other people on the list.'

'That's my next move then.'

'I'll keep working on the laptop,' Gerry said.

'The laptop? That's back at the Shed. How can you work on it?'

'First thing I did was back the hard drive to my server. I can access it anywhere. Damir, could I use your computer?'

'Of course, Bratishka. I will tell Anya that you are staying for lunch,' Volkov said, then marched towards a second, larger cabin at the north end of the yard.

High-pitched yelps rang out from behind the two men. They both spun to see McGuire squelching barefoot towards them with mud stretching up both legs of the trousers of her power suit. 'What happened to you?' Gerry asked.

'I lost my shoes,' McGuire said, looking dishevelled and harassed. 'What the hell is that?' she said, pointing to the Ford.

'That's our new car,' Gerry chirped.

'Jesus. Doesn't he have anything a bit less obnoxious?'

'Nope,' both men answered in unison.

'I need to get back to Glasgow. My superior is hunting for my head. And I need to find out how my suspect got released. I obviously have a mole in my department. Someone is clearly leaking information to Mr B, and I need to find out who it is.' Amos shot a side glance at his friend, who was returning the look. The two men, obviously sharing one thought, then looked back at McGuire.

'OK then,' Amos said, 'I'll go to Govan to find out why Mary's name is on this list. McGuire, you go back to your department and try to uncover your leak. And Gerry, you stay here and work on the laptop information. Agreed?' The others nodded, then exchanged phone numbers. 'OK, McGuire, get in the car. I'll drop you off on the way,' Amos said. McGuire staggered towards the Ford, pulling her feet from the thick mud.

'Can we trust her?' Gerry whispered as she clambered into the car.

'We don't have much of a choice right now,' Amos whispered back.

Volkov marched back with the keys and tossed them to Amos. 'Come, Bratishka, Anya has made more coffee,' he cheered.

Amos trudged into the driver's seat. 'Where to?' he asked.

'First things first,' McGuire said. 'I need a shower and a change of clothes.' She gave him an address and he started the engine.

Chapter 23

The evening of Mary's fifteenth birthday had shed most of its tension from breakfast. Sophia had smoothed their tempers and brought the argument from a boil back to a gentle simmer. The nose kiss soothed Amos as usual, and a forty-three-minute chat with Mary had calmed her temper too. *Men are so much easier*, Sophia thought, as she left Mary alone in the lounge that morning. This thought now repeated itself in her mind as she and her husband sat in silence in the kitchen. It was a little after 5 pm, but the old soldier always liked to be early. *To be on time is to be late*, he would say.

Amos looked at his watch for the fourth time, huffed loudly, and began to bounce his leg. Sophia knew that he would jump from his seat at any minute and begin to pace the floor, then the grumping would start and soon lead to moaning. If left unchecked, he would work himself into a rage by the time Mary finally appeared. Sophia stood and instructed Alexa to play Van Morrison. She then glided across the tile floor, scooped up Amos's hands, and pulled him off his stool. She wrapped his arms around her waist, then clasped her fingers behind his neck. Alexa complied with the request and played *Have I Told You Lately*, and Sophia sang along, staring deeply into her husband's eyes. It was another cheap manipulation, and one she knew Amos could see through but was just as powerless against it as the nose kiss. His shoulders relaxed under her arms, and his eyes softened. *Still got it*, she thought, as they drifted back and forth on the kitchen floor.

Neither of them heard the song end or another one

start. They had not noticed the second song end and the third song begin. And they were both oblivious to Mary, who had thumped down the stairs and was now standing in the doorway, staring at them. 'What are you doing?' she said, with the typical impatient and irritated teenage tone. Sophia saw Amos's nostrils flare and his eyes close. She felt his chest swell, then heard the slow, quiet huff from his nostrils. He was pushing his anger down and this effort deserved a reward. She clenched the chest of his shirt in her fist, pulled him close, reached up, and met his lips with hers. The kiss felt like it lasted as long as the dance. The moody teen voiced her disgust again: 'Ugh, can we just go?'

'We waited on you long enough, you can wait on us,' Amos said softly.

'Come on,' Mary said. 'We need to pick up William, remember?'

'Come on, let's go,' Sophia whispered, then sealed the moment with another kiss.

***

Sophia sat in the passenger seat of the Audi while Amos drove, and Mary dictated directions from the back seat. The fifteen-minute drive took them deep into Drumchapel.

Every city around the world has a dark side. A side they don't advertise in the glossy tourist magazines. Districts that they hide from fat wealthy Americans hoping to submerse themselves in the local culture whilst trying to connect with their ancestral home.

Drumchapel was such a place.

The large post-war housing scheme, known as The

Drum, was built by Glasgow City Council during the 1950s and then forgotten. Row after row of cheap tenement buildings, which housed some of the city's most deprived families, were left to decay and crumble for decades. Alcohol abuse, drug addiction, and gang violence became the preferred pastimes of the area's bored and neglected youth. Amos made a left and then a right at Mary's instruction. 'Where did you meet this boy?' he asked.

Sophia hoped Mary did not hear the subtle disapproval already in her father's voice, *but Mary is a clever girl; she's bound to have noticed it.*

'Through a friend,' Mary replied. 'We all hang out at the skate park at Southdeen. Stop over there; I told him we would get him there.' Amos steered left and rolled to a stop outside a small, abandoned corner shop with the name *Jaffas* above the door. The steel shutter and the plywood boards covering the windows had all been heavily graffitied by bored local kids who would soon graduate to drugs and violence. Mary unclipped her seatbelt and slid out of the car. Amos's head swivelled side to side, and his hand tapped an erratic rhythm on the steering wheel. The leg would be next; he always started tapping his fingers, then the leg would bounce. This detour threw him off schedule even more, and he was fighting the frustration. These were his mechanisms. His routine. Soon, he would make the transition from irritated to frustrated before finally resting on anger. Sophia reached across and gently squeezed his knee. The erratic tapping stopped, and his leg remained still. His head snapped towards her, his eyebrows furrowed, and his lips tightened.

She smiled softly and whispered, 'I love you.'

Instantly, Amos's brow relaxed, and his lips stretched to a smile. His hand dropped from the wheel and rested on hers. The routine was broken.

The back door pulled open, and Mary slid back into the seat, shuffling behind the driver seat. A tall, heavy-set teenage boy slumped into the seat behind Sophia. 'Mum, Dad,' Mary said, 'This is William. William, this is my Mum and Dad.'

'Call me Sophia,' Sophia said.

'Call me Mr Fisher.' Amos said.

'Don't listen to him,' Sophia interrupted. 'His name is Amos.'

'Nice to meet you,' the boy replied politely. Amos shot his wife a sideways, disapproving glare. She winked and blew a kiss.

'Right then,' Amos said, as he pulled the car from its parking spot. 'We should still make the reservation time.'

Romano's Italian restaurant in the heart of Bearsden was only a short drive from the Fisher household and had been a family favourite for quite some time. Over their many visits, they had become friendly with the owners, brothers Alfredo and Stefano Romano. This friendship led to Amos helping the brothers with various building projects. His expertise and advice had saved the brothers money and delays on the restaurant's renovations a few years earlier. This had earned Amos and his family larger than standard portions on their visits and free coffee for life.

Tonight, Alfredo's welcome was exaggerated, as he knew this was Mary's birthday ritual dinner. He greeted each of them with a hug and a European two-cheek-kiss greeting. 'Buongiorno,' he smiled. 'Welcome, my friends. Ah, there she is, tanti auguri di buon compleanno, Mary.' Although born in Scotland, Alfredo picked up his Italian accent from his parents, and he could switch between the two effortlessly. Mary smiled and thanked him for the birthday well wish. 'Oh my, who do we have here?' Alfredo said, looking at the tall, plump boy. 'My, you are a tall one, aren't you?' William offered his hand, but Alfredo ignored it, stretched up, and pulled the awkward teen down for the traditional greeting given to Amos and the girls. Amos watched this and stifled a smile at the boy's discomfort. 'We don't greet family with a handshake here.' Alfredo said, 'And if you are with Mr Fisher, then you are family.' He turned his attention back to Amos. 'Come, Mr Fisher, I have the best table in the house for you over here.' A corner booth at the back of the restaurant had been reserved for the occasion. This was the premium spot, which was close enough to the air conditioning unit to offer a gentle cool breeze on a hot summer night, but not too close as to make the patrons uncomfortably cold. Amos followed behind as the host weaved his way through the tables towards the booth at the back.

'Alfredo, how many times I have I told you? Call me Amos.'

'Yes, Mr Fisher. As you wish. Can I get you anything to drink?' They all slid into the booth. Amos and Sophia were on one side, and Mary and William sat opposite. Mary sat closest to the wall, and William perched himself at the open end. All four ordered soft drinks, and Alfredo handed them menus, before bowing away. Now that they had all taken their seats, Amos watched William as he gazed at the menu and talked with Mary. He watched the boy's eyes as they shifted back and forth. The way the boy sat stone still in his seat. No uncomfortable shuffling, no nervous hand movements, or uneasy glances around the room. A distant voice wailed at the back of Amos's mind. Something wasn't right. Something indescribable. An instinctual warning, but of what? Sure, the boy was big, towering over him by at least five inches, but he was still a child. What threat could he possibly pose that would set off his alarm like this?

'So,' William said, 'Amos is an unusual name, Mr Fisher. Is your family Greek or something?'

'It's a family name. My dad was named Amos, and his dad before him, and so on. It's from the Bible.'

'I see. And Mrs. Fisher, Sophia is such an exotic name too.'

'Actually, Sophia is my middle name. My real name is Agnes, but I hate it, so I go by my middle name.'

'So, William, what school do you go to?' Amos asked.

'Drumchapel High,' William answered matter-of-factly, then poured himself a glass of water from the jug at the centre of the table.

'What year are you in?' Sophia asked.

'Fifth year.'

'Fifth year?' Amos said. 'You mean you'll be starting fifth year after the summer?'

'No, I'm in fifth year now. I'll be going into sixth year after the summer.'

'That means you must be, what, seventeen?' Amos heard the indignation in his own voice and did nothing to hide it.

'Aye, I'll be eighteen in three months.' William held his glare. It was Amos's experience that people generally felt uncomfortable with a prolonged silent stare. They would do almost anything to fill the void and release the anxiety it creates. The boy sitting diagonally across from him now, though, did not flinch. He simply held Amos's gaze. The corners of his mouth twisted upwards, creating dimples in his chubby cheeks. His lips parted, exposing his top and bottom teeth. His eyes, which stayed fixed on Amos, were wide and smooth.

The distant voice in Amos's head began shouting again.

The boy's eyes narrowed, and his head tilted almost imperceptibly. 'This is a lovely—' he began, before his hand, which swept a wide arch over the table, gesturing to the room, knocked over the glass of water he had poured moments earlier. The water spilled over the table and onto Mary's lap. She jumped back and yelled. Alfredo leaped into action, bringing a cloth and napkins before the sound of Mary's cry had time to reverberate around the room. With the speed and precision of a Formula One pit crew, he mopped up the mess and replaced the empty glass, apologising for the inconvenience.

The warning cries in Amos's head grew louder.

Two courses had come and gone, with accompanying small talk. They had mindlessly talked about the weather, school, exams, skateboarding, and a cacophony of other meaningless subjects that Amos had no interest in. He could not shake the uneasy feeling about the young man now holding his daughter's hand. The hairs on the back of his neck refused to settle back into their resting position. What was it about this boy, this child, that made him feel so on edge?

'So, William,' Amos said, 'What are your plans after school? Are you going to college or straight to university?'

'No,' the boy replied.

'Sorry? What do you mean, no?' Amos frowned.

'I'm not going to college or university. Higher education is a waste of my time.'

'Really? Why?' The voice in his head was wailing now.

'Twenty years ago, a university degree was worth ten times what it is today. The number of students achieving a first-class honours degree has gone from twenty-three percent in the nineties to over seventy percent today. The government tells you it's because of the quality of the education system in Scotland, but really, they use it as a statistic to make themselves look good and justify their pay rise each year. These days, every Tom, Dick, and Harry has a degree. They're literally not worth the paper they're printed on. The whole education system is a lie told to the masses to make themselves feel better, when in actuality all it does is make the rich richer and keep the poor in their place. University is not for smart people, Mr Fisher.'

'You have something against wealthy people?' Amos asked.

'No, Mr Fisher, I have something against poor people,' William replied coldly.

Alfredo appeared at the table with his well-practised, warm smile. The corner of his eyes pinched, and his eyes swooped left and right long enough to make each guest feel special. 'Are you ready to order dessert?' he asked. They all nodded and ordered, and Alfredo vanished as quickly as he appeared.

'Erm, where is the toilet?' William asked.

'I'll show you,' Mary said, and the two teens shuffled from the booth and headed for the back of the restaurant. A sting shot up Amos's arm, jarring him from his stare.

His head spun towards the source, only to see Sophia glaring at him, her eyebrows pulled together, and her nose pinched high. *She is so cute when she's angry.*

'What are you doing?' she chided in a shouted whisper.

'What?' he said, rubbing the sting from his arm.

'You know what.'

'I don't like him, Soph.'

'Really? You hide it well.' Sarcasm dripped from her perfect lips.

'There's something not right about him.'

'Like what?' she demanded.

'For a start, he's almost eighteen; Mary just turned fifteen today. That means they met when she was only fourteen. She's a child, and he's almost an adult. Secondly, I think he tipped that glass over on purpose. Then he didn't even apologise for it. That would've been involuntary for most people. Then there's that smile — it was a fake, forced smile. He's hiding something, Soph, I'm telling you; I can feel it.'

'Why would he tip the glass on purpose? Eh? He's a nervous child, meeting his girlfriend's parents for the first time. Of course, he's going to be a little off, you need to give him a break.'

'I'm telling you, Soph, I've met guys like him before. The dead eyes, the uncomfortable grin — he's dangerous, and I don't want Mary around him.'

'Well, that's not up to you, Amos. That's Mary's choice. We have to let her make her own decisions. You're just being overprotective because she's your little Peanut.'

'Maybe, but my gut is telling me something is wrong, and I've—'

'You've served too long to ignore your gut,' Sophia interrupted. 'I know. But you're not in the army anymore, and he's not a soldier. Now, try to relax, and let's just enjoy the rest of the meal, OK? For me?' Her eyes had softened, and her touch now soothed the arm she had slapped moments before.

'OK, I promise.'

Sophia only had to kick Amos twice under the table to keep him from straying from his promise, before they finished their meal and filed back into the car. She prattled on with the young couple in the back seat while he drove silently with one eye on the road and the other watching the tall, chubby boy taking up most of the space in the rear-view mirror.

'Where do you live, William?' Sophia asked. 'We can drop you off at home.'

'Oh, just drop me at the corner shop where you picked me up, please.'

'Don't be silly, we can take you home. It's no problem,' she said.

'Honestly, it's fine. I live two minutes from the corner, and it's easier for you to get turned around there.'

'Are you sure?' Mary asked softly.

'Aye, the corner is perfect, thanks,' the boy insisted. Amos swung the car left and rolled to a stop at the abandoned corner shop in Drumchapel. The boy said his thank you, then slid out of the car, and Mary shuffled out after him for a private goodbye. The leather of the steering wheel crackled under Amos's twisting grip. The sound matched that of his teeth grinding in his mouth. It sounded so loud in his head that he worried Sophia would hear it and hit him again. The door pulled open again, and Mary climbed back into the back seat. Amos loosened his grip and widened his jaw to relieve the tension.

***

Amos had spent the whole drive home rehearsing his speech in his head. Now that they were all standing in the kitchen, he decided this was the moment to deliver it. 'Mary, I don't want you seeing that boy again.' Mary closed the refrigerator door and glared at her father.

'Excuse me?' she said. Her tone was a mixture of anger and confusion. 'Why?'

'He's too old for you.'

'He's seventeen and I'm fifteen, how is that too old? There's five years between you and mum.'

'There's something not right with that boy, Mary. I can't explain it. but I see something dangerous in him. He's trouble, Peanut, believe me.'

'Amos, that's enough,' Sophia snapped.

'Well, it's not your decision, Dad; it's mine, and you can't make me stop seeing him. I love him.'

'You're fifteen; you don't know what love is. And I can stop you. He'll be eighteen in three months. That will make him an adult and you a minor,' he said.

'What are you going to do? Phone the police?' Mary yelled.

'If I have to.'

'Amos!' Sophia barked.

'What is wrong with you?' Mary screamed as tears raced down her cheeks. 'Why can't you just let me be happy? I'm not one of your soldiers. You can't order me around. You know what? Phone the police. See if I care.' With that, Mary stormed out of the kitchen, slamming the door behind her. The dull thuds of her stomping upstairs thundered in the kitchen, followed by the slamming of her bedroom door.

'What did you do that for?' Sophia demanded.

'He's dangerous, Soph. She'll thank me one day.'

'No, she won't, Amos. You just don't listen, do you? She's a kid. She has to make her own mistakes, and you need to let her. She's not like you and me. She doesn't think the same way we do. But it's not her fault that you can't understand her. You need to listen to her and try to understand her more. You can't issue orders and demand obedience. That's how your father raised you, and you hated him for it.'

'My father was an angry alcoholic who used his fists to get respect. I have never raised my hand to Mary. Never,' he growled.

'It's not about the abuse, Amos; it's about you listening to her and connecting. It's about patience and understanding. It's about putting your bloody ego aside and being the father she needs, not the drill sergeant you think she needs. Now, I'm going to hug my daughter. You can sleep on the couch.'

Chapter 24

Amos and McGuire spent most of the forty-minute drive in complete silence. This was partly due to the scope of the daunting tasks that lay ahead of them both, but mostly because the noise from the definingly loud engine that thundered inside the car that made conversation almost impossible. The loud and obnoxious popping that spat from the car's double exhaust each time it accelerated drew disapproving glares from the malcontent suburbanites making their way to their boring jobs in their boring cars. The Ford's aftermarket bucket seats were made more uncomfortable by the lowered and stiffened suspension. The only benefit the car offered was the illegally tinted windows, which protected its occupants from the stares of unhappy commuters.

He followed the Ford's built-in satnav to the address that McGuire had given him. At the centre of Parkhead, on the east end of Glasgow, the car instructed him to turn right. The robotic feminine voice announced that their destination was at the end of a small row of modern flats on the left of the street. A line of parked cars outside the flats had left only a narrow passage down an already narrow road, forcing the car to creep slowly towards the pinpoint displayed on the satnav's screen. This did not quieten the car, though. The roar of the engine echoed off the flats, and Amos was once again glad of the tinted windows. He slowed the car to a stop at the end of the row of flats, pulling into the only parking space left on the street. He waited for Rachel to finish connecting his phone to the car's Bluetooth system before he killed the engine. He hadn't asked her to do it, but he didn't complain either.

A long moment of welcomed silence was broken when the bell of the school opposite the flats rang loudly and ushered a hoard of excited children outside to enjoy a short break from their morning lessons. 'Amos, I am really sorry about your wife. I had no idea, and I promise, we will get Mary back safely.'

'I don't need your sympathy. I need my daughter back,' he said. His eyes stayed fixed on the road ahead. He felt her eyes on him. He felt her anxiety and longing for his forgiveness. His rational side told him that none of this was the fault of a self-conscious and frightened twenty-something-year-old trying to make a living in a largely male dominated environment. After all, despite McGuire's inexperience, she hadn't done anything wrong. All the moves she made seemed to have been the best options available. Things just got a little out of control. The girl deserves a break. *She deserves your forgiveness.*

Amos, however, was not feeling very rational.

After what seemed like an hour but was in fact closer to a minute, McGuire reached for the door handle, stopped, and turned back towards him. 'Mary had said something to me when she first reached out. She said she had made a lot of bad choices in the past, but she is trying to make the right ones now. For her family. She was trying to make you proud, Amos.'

The chaotic screams of children playing in the school filled the silence.

'Check in with Gerry every hour,' he finally said, turning to look at her for the first time since leaving the scrapyard. 'And be careful.' It was the best he could offer her at that moment. McGuire nodded and slipped out of the car, slamming the door behind her. Angry pops and bangs from the Ford's double exhaust changed the playful shouts from the school into frightened screams. Amos ignored the speed signs advising that twenty is plenty and charged forward.

Chapter 25

Glasgow's Govan district lay on the city's south side, on the opposite side of the river from Parkhead. The once bustling shipyards, which dotted the district for over one hundred years, gave many of Govan's residents not only an income but a sense of purpose and self-respect. Poverty and tradition forced many young boys to leave school early and find jobs working in the shipyards. There, hard times and harder jobs forged these boys into toughened men. Over the generations, hordes of welders, engineers, mechanics, and metal workers would jump from their beds each morning and march themselves to the docks to build legendary ships that were the envy of the oceans. Pride flowed easily in the streets when the clocking-off whistle blew, and the docks gave their workers to the pubs.

In the late 1980s, when all but a few of those yards had closed, and bored men who would have spent their days toiling and building vessels like the Queen Mary 2 found other, less productive ways to fill their days. Men, angry that their livelihood and sense of pride had been stripped from them by an empty suit and an empty promise, raised angry boys, who themselves then raised angry boys. And so they continued the vicious new tradition until the reason for their anger had long been forgotten, and all that was left was the rage. Crime, drugs, and alcohol abuse were now the trade of most men.

The address Gerry had given him led to a small housing development in the heart of Govan. The boisterous sky-blue Ford blended into the area perfectly. It seemed like every second house had a garish two-door hatchback with a ridiculously oversized spoiler and aftermarket body kit sitting out front. A few of these ostentatious ornaments had their bonnets propped open, and a collection of greasy large men operated on the engines while drinking from long-neck green bottles and blasting terrible, thumping music. Children, who should have been at school, milled around the street corners, shouting obscenities at dog walkers and postal workers and throwing empty cans at the buses that passed by periodically.

The satnav announced that Amos had arrived at his destination. The end terraced building was split into two houses. The door on the face of the building led to the house on the bottom, while a small set of stairs at the side led to another house above. The small garden at the front of the building was owned and kept by the occupants of the lower house. A ring of rosebushes reflected the floral pattern of the curtains hung in the window that overlooked it. A stone bird bath and matching feeder sat at the centre of the neatly trimmed and vibrant lawn. The regimented height of the bushes and the neatly trimmed edges of the grass suggested to Amos that its gardener had spent some time in the armed forces, and the discipline he or she had learned there had now become a lifelong habit, but he couldn't be sure.

The garden at the side of the house was separated from its counterpart at the front of the building by a stone path and did not receive the same level of care and attention. The owner of this garden had clearly never spent any time in the service or had any self-discipline whatsoever; that much was clear. Uncut grass stretched knee high and wrapped around an old, rusted washing machine, which lay abandoned at the garden's edge. Patches of creeping thistles jagged out from between the cracks in the paving stones, snatching at his trousers. A waist-high wall served as a handrail for the six steps that lead to the door of the upper house. The red paint on the cracked and broken coping stones, which topped the wall, had chipped and faded over many years of neglect. A familiar, thick stench emanated from the door and reminded him of his encounter with the shabby-looking drug dealer the day before.

A gut feeling, confirmed by a quick check of the door numbers, revealed that this was the house he was looking for. He pressed the small white button beside the door and waited. And waited. He pressed again and leaned closer, putting his ear to the frosted glass at the centre of the door. A faint bell rang on the other side. He waited. He pressed the button again and hammered on the door. Getting impatient, he raised his fist to pound the door again when he heard a faint thumping of feet descending the stairs on the other side of the door.

'Alright, alright. I'm coming, man,' a voice mumbled. The door swung inward, and a shabby bearded man stared wide eyed and slack-jawed at him. 'Onion?' Amos said.

***

Onion sat on a tattered and dirty armchair. That, and a grubby couch, were the only furniture in the room. He was staring hard at the ceiling and pinching his nose at the bridge. His eyes had glazed over, and tears were edging their way down his cheeks. The bruising under his eyes was beginning to form, and his rhythmic swallowing suggested that the blood was now flowing down the drug dealer's throat instead of out of his nose.

'Let's try that again,' Amos said, rubbing the sting from his knuckles, 'and this time don't lie. I'm looking for Alex McDonald. Where can I find him?'

'I told you, man, I don't know an Alex McDonald. I've never heard of him.'

'This was his last known address.'

'I don't know any Alex McDonald!' Onion shouted, over-pronouncing each word.

'Bullshit. What are you doing here anyway?'

'This is my girlfriend's house, man. She lives here with her flatmate. We came here to get away from you after you kicked my door in.'

'Shouldn't you be in a jail cell?'

'For what, man? I was the victim of a crime. I was kidnapped by a crazed psychopath and left to freeze to death, cuffed to a lamppost. Anyway, even if I wasn't an innocent victim of a brutal attack, I work for Mr B, man. He wouldn't allow me to go to prison. You have no clue who you are dealing with, man. He's going to kill you slowly.' The blood had stopped now, but the man's nose was beginning to swell. The delicate and sharp sounds of his consonants dulled as they hit a wall of dried blood in his nose. T's became D's and soft G's became hard and clumsy.

'Aye, so I've heard,' Amos said, sarcastically.

The slamming of the front door jolted Amos into action. He lunged forward, circling behind the frightened man on the armchair, and clamped his hand around his bearded mouth. Before Onion could react, Amos whipped the black Smith and Wesson tactical blade from his pocket, snicked the blade from the handle, and pressed it tight against his victim's throat. Onion now sat petrified between his captor and the person now stomping their way up the stairs.

'One sound out of you and a broken nose will be the least of your problems,' he whispered into Onion's ear.

They waited.

The door to the living room swung carelessly open, and a pretty, dark-haired girl screamed at the stranger with a blade pressed to her boyfriend's throat. For a moment, Amos didn't recognise her, but the scream was distinctive. There was no doubt that this was the half-naked girl he shushed the day before in Onion's flat. He made the same gesture today, and the result was the same. The girl quietened to a whimper. Amos flicked the blade in the direction of the grubby couch, which sat perpendicular to the grubby armchair. The girl, now wearing considerably more clothes than their first encounter, sidled her way nervously to the couch and sat. He unclamped his hand from the man's mouth and circled around, keeping both his hostages in view. He kept the tactical blade pointed at the idiot, still holding his nose, although he had no real intention of hurting either of them. Keeping the blade in view was enough of a threat to ensure their cooperation. They were just kids, after all. Stupid kids who made really bad life choices and could benefit from the kind of structure and discipline that he had found in the armed forces. But kids are lazy these days. They don't want to do any hard work. *Well, life is hard work; get used to it.*

'What do you want?' the dark-haired girl asked, shaking him from his inner monologue.

'I'm looking for a man. This was his last known address. One of you must know him,' Amos said.

'I told you, man, I don't know any Alex McDonald,'

Onion said. Amos pulled his hand back to hit the drug dealer again.

'Wait,' the girl said, saving her boyfriend from the impending blow. 'You're looking for Sandy?'

'What did you say?' Amos asked.

'My flatmate, Sandy. Sandy is her nickname. Her real name is Alexandria McDonald.'

'Alex is a girl?' he asked.

'Yeah,' the girl replied. Confusion now replaced the fear in her voice. 'Is that a problem?'

'Where is she?' he demanded.

'We don't know, man,' Onion whined. Amos swung his free hand and caught the bearded man high on his cheek with the palm of his hand. *No point risking a broken hand on this idiot.* The dark-haired girl stifled a scream and stiffened to attention.

'I wasn't talking to you,' he growled and turned his full attention to the girl. 'Where is Alex McDonald?' he asked again.

'I don't know,' the girl snivelled, 'I haven't seen her in over a week. She does that, though. She disappears for a few days at a time, then pops up.'

'Where does she go?'

'I, I don't know.' She sniffed hard and wiped at her cheek. 'She fell in with some bad people. I tried to warn her, but she was making a bit of money. She wouldn't tell me where she went or where she got the money.'

'What people?' he pressed. 'I need a name.' He was towering over the girl now, and he could see her shake. Her slim frame and high cheekbones reminded him of Mary. There could not have been more than two or three years between this poor girl and his daughter. A churning swelled in the pit of his stomach, and he fought the urge to sit by the girl's side and reassure her the way he did with Mary when she had bad dreams about scary beasts as a child. A child. The thought struck him like the slap he gave Onion. This child was terrified, and he was the cause.

He was the beast.

He swallowed hard and pressed her again. 'A name!'

'I don't know a name, I promise,' the girl cried, hiding her face behind her hands. 'Ask Onion; he introduced her to them.' These words quelled the nausea in his belly. The drug dealer did not deserve his sympathy. The grubby idiot did not have any delicate features that would evoke sympathy. There was nothing about this parasite to pity. He was a vulture, feeding on the corpses of the vulnerable and profiting from their misery.

Amos felt himself grin as he turned slowly to face the man sitting in the armchair. He was still rubbing the cheekbone where he had been slapped moments before. Onion glanced up, clearly oblivious to what the girl had just said and therefore oblivious to what was coming next. Confusion swept across the idiot's face as Amos took a slow step forward, folding the blade of the knife back into the handle and returning it to his pocket. He squared himself to the shabby man and took another slow step. The drug dealer shuffled farther back into the armchair, his eyes shifting left and right. Amos tilted his head forward, his eyebrows furrowed, and his jaw clenched hard. His grin had now stretched into an uneven smile that pulled higher at one side. He took one last, slow step.

'What?' Onion asked nervously.

Chapter 26

A hot shower cleansed more than the mud from around McGuire's feet. It seemed to clear her mind too. The warm cascade washed away some of her anger, which ran rampant in her mind in the overly loud Ford. 'Going full Hulk mode doesn't help anyone.' She said out loud with forced confidence. 'That is what a man would do, and you've come too far to be that stupid.' She turned her face to the warm downpour and rinsed away the last of the shampoo from her hair. McGuire then squared her shoulders, took a deep breath, and let the steam fill her lungs before turning the temperature control hard left. She then began to count. 'One. Two. Three.' An icy blast pounded down on her head, stealing her breath away. Still counting, McGuire fought to regain control of her breathing. 'Ten. Eleven. Twelve.' Her heart began to pound in her chest as adrenaline flooded her body. 'Nineteen. Twenty. Twenty-one.' Her skin tightened, and her senses sharpened in a fight-or-flight response. 'Thirty-eight. Thirty-nine. Forty,' she cried, and snatched at the controls, shutting the water off. 'A new personal best.'

Despite having lived in the flat for three years, the bedroom's bare walls still had the original magnolia paint, and the grey carpet remained unchanged since she moved in. The black curtains served no other purpose than to minimise the amount of sunlight pouring into the room on her days off. The small bedroom could not accommodate a king-size bed, so instead, McGuire settled for a double. She now stood, inspecting herself in front of the full-length mirror at the foot of her bed. The damp towel, which was coiled around her head, fell to the floor, and her unnatural blonde hair flopped to her shoulders. Leaning in close to the mirror, she clawed at the wet hair. Brown roots were sprouting like weeds. They would have to be dealt with soon, but right now, she had a job to do.

A thousand voices in her mind had been shouting a thousand questions. Each one drowning out the last, like a room full of second-rate journalists hurling questions at a corrupt politician over the latest sex scandal. The cold blast had cleared her head and brought a degree of clarity and focus, quietening all but three of the voices. Three voices with three important questions. A plan had begun to formulate in her mind. But before going into battle, she had to choose her armour. McGuire loosened the towel wrapped around her body and let it fall to the floor. The power suit she chose for her interrogation at the Shed was not going to cut it now. *No*, she thought. *These men are far too arrogant for that approach. They're too chauvinistic to be intimidated by a woman. I need something a little more subtle. Something professional yet delicate. Suggestive but respectable. I don't want them to think with their heads.* Opening her wardrobe, she filed through the selection of suits hanging on the rail.

Two pairs of trousers and a high-waisted maxi skirt were considered but tossed onto the bed and rejected. McGuire pivoted in front of the mirror, admiring the snug fit of the pencil skirt that now pulled in her waist and accentuated her curves. *No underwear*, she thought. *Better not distract them when they're perving.* Next was the shirt. A fitted white shirt blouse with the top buttons left strategically undone, teasing a promise of the ample bosom beneath, was simple but effective. Tucking the shirt into the skirt, she turned her attention back to the wardrobe. A black single-breasted blazer would complete the look. The blazer's one button pulled in at the waist and highlighted her trim hourglass figure. The lapels bunched and strained against the fullness of her breasts, accenting her subtle but powerful cleavage perfectly. A pair of black point-toe stiletto ankle strap pumps elongated her athletic and tanned legs. McGuire then tied her hair into a high bun to accentuate her long and slender neck and slipped on a pair of black rimmed glasses that made no difference to her vision.

The armour was complete. Time to go to war.

***

Helen Street police station was heralded as the flagship station of a modern-day police force. Its five floors, countless offices, and state-of-the-art technologies served as a base of operations for the very best that Police Scotland had to offer. Since its opening in the 70s, Scotland's most dangerous and prolific criminals have been detained and questioned within its walls. The high security cells, two levels below ground, had held terrorists, gang bosses, and serial killers alike. It was at this station that the notorious serial killer, Bob White, was interrogated and later charged with the kidnapping, rape, and murder of three nine-year-old girls.

McGuire flashed her ID card to the guard posted in the small white cabin at the eastern car park entrance. The officer on duty glanced at the card, then at her, nodded, and pressed a button, raising the red and white-striped barrier.

McGuire parked her car, climbed the concrete steps to

the entrance, and pushed the revolving door. Inside, fumes from the bleach mixture on the freshly mopped floor attacked her eyes. The large open foyer was a hive of activity. Busy people bustled between rooms while the low rumble of a hundred voices filled the large hallways. The booming yet soft voice of the receptionist answering phone calls echoed around the foyer's entrance. McGuire stood for a moment to adjust herself to the sensory onslaught before stepping towards the metal detectors. A uniformed officer in a stab-proof vest stood to attention behind a desk. 'Good afternoon, ma'am.' He said this and subtly ran his eyes up and down her body. McGuire cleared her throat, jolting his attention back to the job at hand. The officer shyly offered her a basket.

'Please place your phone, keys, and any metal objects in the basket,' he said. This irritated McGuire. *I know the drill. You know I know the drill. It's the same process every single day, yet you feel the need to explain it to me every single time.* She tossed the items in the basket as requested and stepped towards the detection gate.

'Thank you, ma'am,' the officer continued robotically. 'Please step through the gate here for me.' McGuire gritted her teeth and stepped through the gate without incident. 'Thank you, ma'am. Please collect your belongings and swipe your ID card on the scanner.' McGuire snatched her phone and keys from the basket, stepped towards the turnstiles, and swiped her ID badge as the officer instructed. A small LCD screen on the turnstile flashed *"Detective Inspector Rachel McGuire,"* and a green light confirmed the turnstile was now unlocked. She pushed herself through with her hips, and DI McGuire marched down the long hall. Her stiletto heels clicked loudly on the tiled floor, announcing her presence. The clicks seemed amplified by the hall's concrete walls and would have made her feel self-conscious, but the sound was drowned into obscurity by the cacophony.

Halfway along the wide hallway, McGuire stopped at a set of elevator doors and pushed the call button. The number on the digital display above the doors began working down from four.

'McGuire,' a voice called from behind. She clenched her teeth and braced herself, then forced a smile and turned.

'Superintendent Graham, Good afternoon, sir,' she chirped.

'Good afternoon,' DSU Graham replied. The words dripped from his mouth as he eyed her from head to toe, making no attempt to hide his ogling like the uniformed officer at the entrance. 'You looking for a promotion, McGuire?' he continued, in a practised tone that could be described as a light-hearted joking in a sexual harassment hearing.

'I thought you were at the conference in Aberdeen,' she said, ignoring the comment.

'It has been postponed until next week,' Graham said. His eyes lingered a second on her legs before turning his attention upwards. A small ding announced the elevator's arrival, and the doors slid silently open. Graham smiled and ushered her inside, ahead of him. Traditionally, it was a gentlemanly gesture, but McGuire suspected ulterior motives. She felt his eyes on her as she stepped inside. She turned around just in time to see Graham snap his head upward. He smiled a broad, toothy grin, tucked his hat under his arm, and smoothed his silver hair back before striding into the elevator. With his free hand,

Graham stretched across her, turning so they were now face-to-face, and pressed number five on the control panel. 'Fifth floor?' he asked.

'Yes, sir, thank you.' She squirmed, taking a half-step backwards. The doors slid silently closed. They rode upwards in silence until the digital display changed from G to one.

'So, McGuire, Chief Inspector Clarke tells me you're making headway in the drugs case? I thought you hit a dead end with that after the raid was a bust?'

'Yes, sir. New information has come to light, and I believe I will have something solid very soon.'

'From what I can tell, this Mr Boyd character seems nothing more than a successful entrepreneur. Something we are sorely in need of in Scotland at the moment. Don't you think?' The thick, rounded, overpronounced words of his posh East-Coast Edinburgh accent grated on McGuire's nerves. He bore an unmistakably upper-class, daddy-paid-for-everything, St Andrew's University type of arrogance and swagger. And he knew it.

'Yes, sir, I do, but Mr B, I mean Mr Boyd is not—' she began, before she was cut off.

'If you have no evidence against this Mr Boyd, then I'm afraid I'll have to shut this investigation down. Effective immediately. I'm not wasting any more resources on this just to be embarrassed again. I expect a full report on my desk by the end of the day. Understand?'

'But, sir.'

'No, McGuire, no buts. You have had this man's business under surveillance for three months now, with nothing to show for it. I now have the Chief Superintendent breathing down my neck, looking for results.'

The digital display had passed two and was approaching three. McGuire gulped hard, adjusted her decorative glasses, and turned to face him. The man was pure sleaze. His mere presence made her skin crawl. But at this angle, she had to admit that he wasn't an ugly man. Most men in their late fifties had accepted age with an undignified grace. Superintendent Fraser Graham was not most men. He had taken great pride in his appearance. His perfectly trimmed silver beard highlighted his well-tanned face, and a sparkling white smile complimented his deep, husky blue eyes. His trim and slender physique was not something she found attractive, but she could see why so many women had.

'Sir,' she spoke, softening her voice, 'I would love to go over some notes from the investigation with you.' She let a knee bend a little, exposing an extra inch of her thigh. Then, her right hand softly grabbed for her left elbow, bunching her breasts together while pushing them closer to the opening of her blouse. 'Maybe you could give me some pointers and show me where I went wrong.'

Graham smiled, and his eyes widened, drinking in the view she was offering.

'I'm sure I can make room in my schedule for a one-on-one tutoring session. I could maybe extend your deadline a little.' Another small ding announced their arrival on the fifth floor, and the doors slid open to a small procession awaiting the elevator's arrival. Graham quickly composed himself and returned his hat to his head. 'Make an appointment with my secretary at your earliest convenience, DI McGuire.' Graham said this and marched out of the elevator cabin.

'Yes, sir,' McGuire replied and gulped down the lump of disgust that was lodged in her throat.

Chapter 27

DI Rachel McGuire took a long, deep breath, held it, and then slowly let it go. Her heart slowed after three more breaths. Summoning the same forced confidence she had used in the shower, she knocked on the heavy pine door. The stern voice from the other side granted her access.

'Good afternoon, sir,' McGuire said, focusing intently on her own voice, trying to sound confident without being arrogant. DCI James Clarke was stationed at the same spot he was the last time she entered his office, gazing over to Ibrox football stadium from his large window with his back to her.

'Have a seat, McGuire,' Clarke instructed. She complied. 'Superintendent Graham has ordered me to shut this investigation down, effective immediately.'

'Yes, sir, he spoke to me in the lift.'

'He wants my report of this investigation, along with any evidence collected, and a review of your performance on his desk by the morning,' Clarke interrupted.

'My performance, sir?' McGuire felt the blood drain from her face.

Clarke spoke as he turned. 'He is questioning your competence, Rachel.'

McGuire said nothing.

'He sees you as nothing more than a man-hating feminist, imposing your "woke" agenda on an honest businessman,' he continued.

She felt her throat tighten and her mouth dry up.

'Graham is an idiot,' Clarke spat.

The words slapped her out of her daze. She glared at him with the same look a deer might give a set of oncoming headlights.

'Sir?' she finally managed.

'You heard me,' Clarke said, as he sat, rolling his chair into the desk. 'The man hasn't spent a single day on the street. Hasn't spent a single sleepless night working a case or put in the hours catching real filth like you and me. Nepotism got that prick where he is now. I never liked him. He's a cowardly little shit who wouldn't know a good officer if she slapped him with a sexual harassment suit.'

McGuire didn't know what to say. So, she said nothing.

'You're a damn fine investigator, McGuire. And I'd rather have my balls chewed off by a pack of rabid squirrels than let a slimy prick like Fraser Graham ruin your career.'

'Eh, thank you, sir.'

Clarke either didn't hear her or didn't care that she spoke. 'He's part of the funny handshake brigade too. Did you know that?'

'Funny handshake brigade, sir?'

'Freemasons, McGuire. How do you think he got to the rank of Superintendent? It wasn't through hard graft, that's for sure. He knows the right people.'

'I had no idea, sir.'

'Yes. He and the Chief Constable are lodge brothers for Chrissake.' Clarke paused and seemed to compose himself. 'But that's not why I called you in here,' he said.

'It wasn't, sir?'

'No. I called you in here, because we have a mole in the department.'

The blood that had flushed from McGuire's face moments ago flooded back. Her cheeks burned, and the room temperature seemed to jump up ten degrees.

'A mole?' she said.

'Don't play dumb with me,' Clarke barked. 'Only three people would have the authority to let your suspect go, and I assume it wasn't you.'

'No, sir.'

'Then that only leaves two people, and I'm guessing, since you tried playing dumb, you suspect me.'

'No, sir. Not at,'

'Of course you do,' Clarke interrupted. 'You'd be an idiot not to, and you're no idiot, McGuire. Here.' Clarke tossed a manilla file across the table. 'The release papers for your suspect. Check the signature at the bottom.'

McGuire opened the file gingerly. 'Superintendent Graham?' she gasped.

'Exactly.'

'But why?'

'Money? Power? Who knows? We can ask the slimy prick when we arrest him. One release paper isn't enough, though. We need concrete evidence. Where are we with the phone?'

'We believe the phone is one half of an encryption key to Mr Boyd's network on the dark web. This network links all his illegal businesses, including the three warehouses full of drugs,' she explained.

'So, if we get the phone, not only do we bring down this scumbag, we would be able to get definitive proof that Graham is on Mr Boyd's payroll? Two shits with one flush! I like it.' Clarke laughed and slapped the desk hard. 'So, where is the phone?'

'Amos Fisher still has it,' she said. 'I made contact, have arranged a meeting for tonight, and will have the phone by tomorrow morning.'

'Good work, McGuire. We need that phone. It's the key to bringing these assholes down.'

'Yes, sir. But what about Superintendent Graham? He wants this wrapped up by the end of the day?'

'Don't worry about Graham, I'll handle him. I want that phone in my office first thing tomorrow morning. Understand?'

'Yes, sir,' McGuire replied and left the office.

Once out of sight of Clarke's office, McGuire slumped backwards against the wall and huffed. Her hands cupped over her eyes, physically holding back the tears she felt welling behind them. A great weight, which she didn't know was there, had been lifted from her shoulders, and a swell of relief brought a flood of tears with it. But she held them back. *Do not get emotional, Rachel! Don't let them see you cry! Don't you dare! You are better than that. You are stronger than that.* After what seemed like forever, McGuire stood tall. She straightened her bunched-up blazer, flattened a few stray hairs back into place, and marched down the long hall.

She stopped outside a door with a name plaque that read *DI Rachel McGuire.* To say this was an office would have been not only generous, but a complete exaggeration. The small, windowless space had a desk pushed against the farthest wall with a laptop and a single filing cabinet. McGuire closed the door and dropped into the room's only seat behind her desk.

Silence.

She pulled open her laptop and logged in. Then she fished her phone from her blazer and called Gerry.

'What's up, Buttercup?' Gerry chirped.

'Gerry, it's Rachel. I think I've found something. I think I found out who the—' Her voice trailed off.

'Rachel? Everything OK?' Gerry asked urgently.

'What? Uh, yes, yes, I'm fine. Sorry, Gerry, I'm going to have to call you back.' With that, she hung up the phone and stared at her computer screen.

'Oh my God,' she gasped.

Chapter 28

I owe that poor girl a new housecoat, Amos thought as he stared at the blood-stained satin belt now biting into Onion's wrists. Onion groaned as he squinted up with his one working eye. The swelling had shut the left eye completely. He slumped back from his high kneeling position and rested on his heels. Dropping his head forward, he spit another tooth into his cupped hands, which were beginning to turn a bluish green colour. His nose, which now pointed in a different direction than it had when he woke up that morning, stained the front of his T-shirt with fresh blood. 'Please, man,' the drug dealer begged, 'No more. I'll tell you anything; just please stop.'

'Anything?' Amos said.

'Aye, man, anything.'

'Where is Alexandria McDonald?'

'I can't tell you where she is, because I don't know where she is. I've told you that already.'

'Not good enough!' he yelled, pulling his arm back for another punch.

'No! Please!' Onion begged, holding his bound hands high to protect his face.

'Tell me something.'

'I already told you.' Onion coughed. A spray of blood splattered the empty couch. 'I told you; they have a flat on Allison Street, over on the southside.' A watery mixture of blood and tears dripped from the corner of his mouth and pooled on the floor. 'That's where they keep all their girls. That's all I know, man, I swear. I don't know what more you want.'

Amos relaxed his arm and unclenched his fist. The leather belt unspooled itself from his knuckles, and blood rushed back into his fingers. *I already told you.* The words echoed in his ears, sending clumps of thick fog swirling through his mind. 'What do you mean, you told me already?' he said.

'What?' Onion said, peering up over his hands. 'I've told you like five times about the flat, but you just kept hitting me, man.' Amos looked around the room, searching for any clues to where he was and how long he had been there.

'The girl,' he demanded when his search reached the empty couch. 'Where's the girl?'

'What? What do you mean, where's the girl? You told her to leave. You called her Mary, a couple of times and said you didn't want her to see this.'

The swirling in his mind gave way to a howling gust, and the fog vanished in a rush. Reality crashed through in an overwhelming flood of clarity. His knees gave way, and he collapsed on the blood-splattered couch. *Get it together, Sapper; you've got a job to do. Get your head in the game. Focus; Mary needs you.* He flopped his head forward, catching his head in his cupped hands. Slowly, he slid his palms down his face, as though to wipe away the last few strands of confusion and bring himself fully to the present.

Two full minutes had passed before he realised that the drug dealer was talking.

'What?' Amos asked.

'Please let me go, man. I won't tell police, I promise. Just please let me go and I swear, you'll never see me again.' The shabby man held his hands high, pleading for his wrists to be untied.

'Give me the address again,' he said.

'Allison Street, above the barbershop. Please, man.' Onion thrust his blue hands forward again, palms pressed in prayer. Amos pulled the folding knife from his pocket and cut the satin belt that bound the man's wrists together. Onion instantly collapsed to the floor, curled into a ball, and wept loudly.

Amos strode back to the car and thumped down inside. The engine screamed inside the car once more as the tyres of the Focus screeched against the rough, uneven road. Loud pops and bangs echoed back from the houses on either side of the street, cueing a half-drunk would-be mechanic to stop mid-swig from his long-necked bottle and nod in appreciation. This respect was not shared by the truant children perched on the green street cabinet at the T-junction halfway along the street. They, instead, yelled and hurled stones at the sky-blue target as it barrelled past. All missed their mark.

Chapter 29

The streets of Glasgow passed by unnoticed as Amos drove. The sky-blue Ford turned left and right without a conscious decision being made by its driver. Muscle memory had now taken over, and he drove on autopilot. He guided the car into the empty car park outside a small row of shops on an empty street. The roar of the modified engine died, and heavy panting replaced it as the loudest noise in the car. Amos felt his nostrils flare with each heavy exhale. The trembling in his hands travelled through his wrists and into his tight arms. Prying his hands from the steering wheel, he wiped away the cold sweat dripping from his forehead before it reached his eyes. His heart pounded in his chest, sending blood rushing into his ears. Faster and faster, louder and louder. He frantically searched the car for something to drink. Something, anything. He found nothing. One of the shops along the strip would have a wide choice of drinks available, but his legs were shaking too violently to leave the safety of the car. He blinked hard, trying to restore his distorted and concaved vision. It was as though he was watching the world rush past through a fisheye lens. His heart pounded in his ears again, louder and faster.

His heavy head flopped back into the bucket seat and closed his eyes. 'Control your breathing,' he whispered. A deep breath filled his chest, and his lungs protested against the cold air that now stretched them. His heart began to slow with the long, exaggerated exhale. Eight more deep, concentrated breaths brought his heart rate back to normal. The tremble in his hands was now reduced to a slight tremor, and the blood quietened in his ears.

If he had not already closed his eyes, he would have felt his eyelids get very heavy. If he had checked if his vision had been restored, he would have noticed a shadow creeping on the edge of his peripheral vision. If he had not slowed his breathing, he would have noticed it growing slow and shallow.

And then darkness.

The sharp electronic ringing of the phone in his pocket jolted him awake. He fumbled the phone from his pocket and blinked to clear the blur from his eyes. The name on the caller ID read Gerry, although to him, the letters on the phone's screen may have well been hieroglyphs. A string of strange, indecipherable shapes with no purpose or meaning, either individually or strung together like they were on the phone. He stared at the phone until it went blank, and the ringing stopped. his blank expression was reflected back at him on the black screen as silence settled in the car again.

The sharp electronic ring blasted from the phone again, and the screen flashed Gerry's name once more. The world rushed into focus, and Amos was back in the present. 'Hello?' he said.

'Amos,' Gerry said, his voice a mixture of concern and relief. 'You OK? I've phoned you five times.'

'Five times?' he asked, now looking at the clock on the car's digital dashboard display.

'Yes, five times. I was about to phone Rachel and abort the whole mission.'

'No, I'm fine. I just left my phone in the car,' Amos said.

'Don't lie to me, Buttercup. I know you too well. It happened again, didn't it?'

'I'm fine!' he snapped.

'Amos, maybe we should let the police handle this. You're getting—'

'I said I'm fine!' he interrupted. 'I left the phone in the car while I interrogated Onion, that's all.'

'Onion? The low life drug dealer that took you to the cash and carry?'

'Aye, he was at the address you gave me. Turns out Alex McDonald is a girl and she's fallen in with some lowlifes on the southside. I'm heading there now to track her down.'

'The southside?'

'Aye, Allison Street, above a barber.'

'Allison Street? Why is that name familiar?' Gerry paused for a long moment. 'I'll do a little digging into that; something is ringing a bell with that street.'

'Has Rachel checked in yet?' Amos asked.

'Aye, she called about twenty minutes ago. She thinks she's found something. Didn't say what it was, but it sounds big.'

'Could be dangerous. Let me know as soon as she checks in.'

'Roger that,' Gerry replied smartly.

'Any update on the laptop yet?'

'Not yet, although there's something strange about its security protocols.'

'Gerry, let's imagine for a moment that I'm not a computer geek and explain it to me like I'm an idiot.'

'Hardly a massive stretch of the imagination now, is it, Buttercup?'

Amos could hear Gerry smirk at his own quip.

'Very funny. What's strange?' Amos said.

'I don't know yet. There's just something almost

familiar with the coding. I need to do a bit more work on it. Hopefully, it won't take long.'

'OK, keep me informed.'

'Roger that.' With that, Amos ended the call and returned the phone to his pocket.

OK, Sapper, what was that? he thought. *A panic attack? Really? You don't have time for that. You've got a job to do. Mary is in trouble. Now get your shit together and go save your daughter. You can fall apart later. Now, get a move on, soldier.* He slapped his palms against the steering wheel in defiance.

Defiance of weakness. He slapped again.

Defiance of fear. He slapped again.

Defiance of failure. He slapped again.

'I'm coming, Peanut,' he growled.

Chapter 30

Amos took a position at the window table of a small café on Allison Street. A thick smell of grease wafted from the serving hatch at the back of the café, choking the gaunt and haggard woman who stood behind the waist-high marble-effect counter. The low music from the small radio that sat behind the cash register did very little to drown out the clattering and sizzling from the kitchen. He swallowed down the last bite of his cheese toastie, pushed the empty plate aside, and washed it down with the last mouthful of his third coffee. The woman shuffled from behind the counter with a jug of hot coffee and offered him a fourth cup, eager to keep her only customer in his seat and spend more money.

'Please,' he replied and slid his cup across the table. He watched as she poured the thick black liquid into his cup, flicked her grey hair from her face to offer a crooked smile, and shuffled back to her post behind the counter. He sipped the bitter drink, then picked up a newspaper that had been left on the table by its previous occupant and pretended to read it again. He peered over the top to stare at the barbershop directly across the street.

During his three-hour surveillance, Amos had noticed that at regular intervals, a customer would enter the shop and speak to the large round man behind the reception desk. They would awkwardly shake hands before the round man would lead the customer through a door at the back of the shop. A few minutes would pass, and the large man would return to his post. Thirty minutes after the customer's arrival, he would emerge again from the door at the back and leave the barbers without having a haircut. He had dismissed it on the first occasion. He noted it as a coincidence when it was repeated by another customer forty minutes later. And recognised it as a pattern on its third instance forty minutes after that. *The entrance to the flat must be at the back of the shop,* thought Amos. 'Excuse me,' he called to the tired grey-haired woman, 'Is that barbershop any good?'

'Don't know, son,' the woman replied, her voice gravelled by decades of smoking. 'It's never very busy, and half the men who go in there don't get their hair cut. I think there's something funny going on there, if you ask me. It's run by some Russians, I think.'

'They're Lithuanian,' a deep voice corrected from the behind the serving hatch.

'Whatever,' the woman snapped back. 'It's run by a bunch of foreigners. They can't be trusted. Should be shipped back to wherever they came from,' she snarled.

'Time for a little trim I think,' Amos said to himself, as he ran his fingers through his hair.

***

The heavy-set man did not look up from his phone when the bell above the door announced Amos's arrival. He did not look up when Amos walked past the four empty barber chairs and stopped in front of the desk where he sat. The man's chubby fingers continued to scroll lazily across the phone screen when Amos cleared his throat. Finally, Amos broke the uncomfortable silence.

'Excuse me, I'm looking to get my hair cut. I don't have an appointment or anything. Do you have space?' The man nodded towards the bench that stretched from the entrance to the desk and looked onto the barber chairs opposite. He then lifted his heavy frame from the seat and pushed open the door at the back.

'Ramus!' he shouted, 'Kažkoks asilas nori apsikirpti.' His voice was deep and lazy. A mumbled voice shouted something indecipherable in reply, and the round man returned to his seat. The language was unknown to Amos, although he did pick out one familiar word.

Amos had earned the nickname *Asilas* while on secondment to the United Nations in 2001. He spent six weeks teaching mine detection and IED disposal to what would become Lithuania's first Explosive Ordinance Disposal Team. The moniker was given to him by the squad leader on the second day of training and was muttered in hushed tones during long drills. The day before his assignment came to an end, he asked his translator what the name meant. The translator smirked and told him it meant Jackass.

After a few minutes, a tall, trim man swung the door wide. Still chewing what Amos guessed was his lunch and wiping some sauce from his chin, he shrugged angrily at the fat man behind the reception desk. The receptionist glanced up from his phone and jabbed a chubby finger towards where Amos sat.

'Hello, my friend,' the angry man said, still chewing. 'What can I do for you?'

'I'm just looking for a quick haircut,' Amos replied. Through the door where the angry man stood, Amos saw daylight at the far end of a small sitting area and a man at an open fire exit, smoking. The thick stench of marijuana wafted onto the shop floor. The slim, angry man swallowed what was left of his lunch and gestured towards an empty chair. Amos took the seat, and the all-too-familiar dance between barber and customer began.

First came the paper collar, then the apron. Then came the question of preference and the awkward reply were followed by ten minutes of uncomfortable small talk while the heavy bass of an obscure dance song thumped a little too loudly in the background. The standard topics of weather, work, and any pending holidays were all covered. A well-practised script, timed to last a standard haircut. Then the mirror was presented to show the back of the head. The haircut shared only a passing resemblance to what Amos actually asked for, but he nodded in polite approval anyway. He was not here to judge the skill level of the barber. He had what he came for.

Three Tangos, two exits.

Chapter 31

Amos turned his collar up, stuffed his hands into his pockets, and headed south on Allison Street. Halfway along the street, at the end of the row of shops, a delivery van turned down a narrow alley and stopped in the car park at the rear of the buildings. Amos ducked down the alley and doubled back, heading north on Allison Street again. Beside each of the fire exits that flanked the car park was a steep stone staircase that sat at a right angle from the buildings. These aging staircases led to the flats above the shops. He pressed his back into the steps beside the barbershop and ducked low. He edged his way along and peered over the step. A puff of smoke, accompanied by a thick familiar stench, rose from an unseen smoker at the open fire exit at the other side of the staircase. A loud but muffled voice shouted from deep inside the building. The words were alien but the voice was distinctive. It was the deep slurry tones of the large receptionist. The smoker shouted a reply and flicked what was left of his marijuana stuffed smoke to the ground, adding to the pile already scattered round. The heavy door slammed closed, and the heavy bass of the music died.

Amos stayed hunched behind the staircase for a few minutes before slowly standing, keeping a careful watch at the fire exit door. Cautiously, he stepped from the cover of the staircase and placed a hand on the black iron handrail. A loud clunk sounded from the fire exit's push bar, and the heavy door swung open. Amos dived back to his hiding spot and shuffled quickly to the corner where the staircase met the building. He pressed his back against the wall and held his breath. The deep, lazy voice of the fat receptionist boomed in the silence of the car park as he trundled up the stairs. A second pair of footsteps, lighter than the fat man's, shuffled up behind him. The footsteps stopped, and three loud thuds echoed in the empty car park. A voice from the other side of the door called out something in Lithuanian, 'Tai aš.' The deep, lazy voice shouted in reply. Heavy clunks rang out from behind the door. The fat man and the voice behind the door mumbled something incoherent before the door slammed shut and both voices disappeared.

Amos didn't move.

Three minutes later, heavy clunks rang out again, and the deep, lazy voice boomed in the car park again. Heavy footsteps thumped down the stairs and vanished back inside the barbershop.

Amos held his breath and listened.

Nothing.

Slowly, he slipped from the corner and dashed up the stairs, careful to keep his footsteps light. At the top of the stone staircase, he pressed his back against the wall beside the door, hiding from the spyhole. A small rectangle of unpainted wood marked the place where a door handle once was. It had been removed, and the door could only be opened from the inside. He thumped three times on the door, just as the fat man had done. The voice from the other side shouted the same Lithuanian phrase it had before.

'Tai aš,' Amos replied, deepening his voice a little. The heavy clunks sounded, and the door opened six inches, and the guard peered one eye through the opening. As quick as he could, Amos lunged from beside the wall, spinning to face the door, and smashed his heel into where the handle once was. The door crashed back, and he rushed through the door to finish the job, but the impact from the door, which mashed into the guard's face, had sent him hurtling into the wall behind him. The collision left the man unconscious. Amos kneeled beside the guard and pressed two fingers into his neck. His pulse was strong, and he was still breathing.

One Tango down.

He then stood and made his way down the dark and dingy hallway. A malodourous cocktail of dampness and sweat hung heavy in the air. Bare floorboard groaned under each footstep down the narrow hallway. He quickly counted three doors. One on each side of him and one facing him head-on at the end of the small rectangular hallway. The door to his left opened, and a half-naked man, no more than twenty-six, stepped out and froze when the pair locked eyes. The instincts of the battle-hardened soldier took control, and he thrust his open hand forward, catching the stranger's Adam's apple in the crescent between his index finger and thumb. The stranger collapsed against the doorway and choked uncontrollably. Amos lunged forward and thrust his knee into the choking man's jaw.

Two Tangos down.

The half-naked stranger was unconscious but alive. Amos stepped over the limp body and pushed open the door. The hinges whined in a weak protest. The room's cocktail had the same mixture of damp and sweat as the hallway but introduced an acidic, vinegary undertone. Thick, heavy curtains choked all but a thin sliver of light from the room's only window. The sliver fell on a bed at the far end of the dark room, and a small dim lamp beside the bed was the room's only light source. Under the lamp, a small round tin tray, like the lid of a biscuit tin, held a blackened spoon, a lighter, and a grubby hypodermic needle. From the farthest corner of the bed, cowering under a dirty blanket, a small, fragile voice said, 'Who, who, who are you?' The girl pulled the blanket close, protecting what was left of her dignity. Even in the dim light of the room, he could see the girl's eyes. The large blue rings had shrunk the black centre to the size of a pinhole.

'I'm not going to hurt you,' Amos replied, holding his hands flat as though he were greeting a nervous puppy for the first time. 'I'm looking for a girl called Sandy. Do you know her?'

The girl nodded nervously. 'Yes. I... I'm Sandy.'

'Hi, Sandy. My name is Amos.'

Chapter 32

Amos had ushered the now fully dressed and fragile girl out of the flat and back along the empty car park. Once through the lane, they doubled back and headed towards the front of the barbershop. He slowly guided her across the street towards the café, where the car had been parked. The fat receptionist crashed through the door of the barbershop and yelled something that Amos didn't understand. He ran after them as fast as his girth would allow, which, if Amos was alone, would not have been a problem. But the girl's dazed and fragile condition made their escape cumbersome and slow.

'Get in the car!' Amos yelled, as he turned back and marched towards the receptionist. The heavy man shouted some more and waved his hand as he stamped onto the road. Amos strode confidently towards the inevitable battle until the glint of the razor blade in the man's hand made him rethink his strategy. *The only thing more dangerous than an expert with a blade is an idiot with a blade.* The razor swung wildly back and forth as the man's pace slowed. The two met toe to toe at the white lines painted in the middle of the road. Amos raised his hands in a defensive position.

With each wild swing, the fat receptionist shuffled forward, and Amos slipped back, dodging the blade by inches. The shouting became less and less as the fat man's breathing got heavier and heavier. Every swing was slower than the last and with even less control. The Lithuanian lashed out again, bringing his right arm across his body. Amos pounced and grabbed the wrist of the razor-wielding hand, pushing the fat man off balance.

Amos's hammering fist landed on the receptionist's face and sent him tumbling to the ground. Blood gushed from his nose as the blade flew from his hand and scraped along the ground. A few kicks to the man's protruding stomach ensured that the fight was well and truly over. But the two younger, fitter, and stronger Lithuanians emerging from the shop seemed to have other ideas. Amos dashed back to the car and drove off, leaving the small crew to attend to their downed comrade.

Sandy sat quivering in the passenger seat of the borrowed Ford. Amos slammed his foot on the brake and turned a sharp left, then right, then left again. The corners were taken randomly, with no destination in mind. He needed to put distance between them and the barbershop, and he didn't want anyone to be able to report which way they went with any accuracy.

He took a few more random corners before slowing down and thinking about where to go next.

'Are you OK?' he finally asked the girl. 'Are you hurt?'

'No, I'm OK,' Sandy replied slowly. 'Who are you, anyway?'

'My name is Amos, remember? I'm looking for my daughter, Mary.'

'I don't know any Mary.'

'Then why are both of your names on the list?'

'List? What... what list? And who... who are you?' The words trickled out of her mouth, and her eyes closed. Her head flopped to one side as she lost control of her bladder. The thick ammonia smell overpowered the apple and cinnamon-scented air freshener that hung from the rear-view mirror.

'Sandy?!' he shouted. 'Sandy, are you OK? Stay with

me, Sandy.' With his free hand, he pushed back her head and checked her eyes. He did not know what he was expecting to see or what to do if he did see anything. But it seemed like the right thing to do. Her breathing, although shallow, was steady, and there was no vomit. Not yet, anyway. He grabbed at her wrist while keeping one eye fixed on the road ahead. Her pulse was slow but steady. He let her sleep and drove on aimlessly.

***

With the adrenaline rush gone, Amos recalled the mind map. The crossed-out picture of Onion was no longer crossed out, and the sleeping Sandy was now connected to him. A line then led from Sandy to a picture of the fat, angry receptionist with the word "Lithuanians" underneath. A question mark, which branched from Rachel, was now added with the words "Police Mole" under it. Still, nothing made sense. Yet something was now scratching at the back of his mind. He missed something. Someone said something, and he missed it, but what? His attention was being inexplicably drawn to the gorilla named George now. The shadow returned. It loomed in the distance, promising an answer again, but this time, it didn't move. It didn't venture forward and slowly reveal what was missing. It loitered in the deepest, darkest corner of his mind, clutching a vital piece of the puzzle. The harder he pushed towards it, the deeper it plunged into the mirk. *Let it breathe.*

The Ford's built-in Bluetooth system blasted the incoming phone call through the overly loud speakers and snapped him back to the present. The display read *Gerry.*

'Hey, Buttercup,' Gerry's voice boomed inside the car.

'Hold on, Gerry,' he said, fumbling for the volume control.

'Everything OK, mate?'

'Aye, just turning the volume down a bit. That's better.'

'Good,' Gerry said. 'Well, mate, I knew Allison Street sounded familiar for some reason. It was in the news a few years ago. A Lithuanian gang was suspected of running a sex ring in there. It made a big splash in the papers, but it never went to court.'

'What? Why not?' Amos asked incredulously.

'It's still an active investigation but get this; I did a little digging in the police records.'

'How did you manage that if it's still an active case?'

'Ask no questions and hear no lies, young Grasshopper,' Gerry said in comical accent. 'Even though it's classed as an active investigation, there's been no movement on it, and the lead investigator doesn't actually investigate anymore.'

'What do you mean?' he asked.

'The Officer in Charge was a DCI Fraser Graham. He has since been promoted to Superintendent Fraser Graham.'

'And the case didn't get passed to someone else?'

'Nope. Looks like this one fell through the cracks.'

'I don't buy it. Something stinks there, Gerry.'

'Yip.'

'What does Rachel say about it?'

'Nothing yet, she hasn't checked back in. What did you find at Allison Street?'

He looked at the spaced-out girl asleep in the

passenger seat. 'Evidence for Superintendent Graham's forgotten case.' He said, then filled Gerry in on the incident at the barbers. 'I'm going to get this girl somewhere safe and see if I can get any more intel. I'll let you know what I find. Oh, and Gerry?'

'Yeah?'

'Let me know as soon as Rachel checks in. I've got a bad feeling.'

'OK. Stay safe, Buttercup.' With that, Gerry was gone and the only noise in the car was the ridiculously loud engine, and the snores of the sleeping girl.

Chapter 33

Alexandria McDonald, known to her friends as Sandy, cowered in the same corner booth seat, under the same window, in the same café that Amos used before. The same smell of fried food billowed from the serving hatch behind the serving counter. The same small plump lady slid a large plate loaded with sausage, eggs, toast, beans, and bacon in front of Sandy and laid a coffee in front of them both. 'Back again?' she asked Amos with a tired smile. 'Aren't you having anything to eat?'

'No, just a coffee for me. Thanks,' he replied.

'What about you, honey? You need anything else?' Sandy flashed a glance at the lady and shook her head nervously. 'OK, honey, if you need anything, you let me know, OK?' she said, with exaggerated kindness, obviously sensing the girl's fragility.

'That's great, thanks,' Amos said, before sipping cautiously from his mug. The woman smiled at him and the frightened girl sat opposite before shuffling back behind the counter. Sandy's eyes flicked back and forth between Amos and the plate. 'Please,' he said, nudging the plate closer. 'It's all yours. I already ate.' She stared at the food, hugging herself, and rocked back and forth in what he could only imagine was either a defensive or self-soothing habit. Maybe a bit of both. 'I'm not going to hurt you,' he whispered. 'I only want to help.' Slowly, she reached for the plate and pulled it close. Amos smiled as warmly as he could, rested one arm on the back of the booth, and lifted his coffee. She began to nibble warily at the toast like a mouse gnawing at food scraps while keeping a keen eye out for the cat it knows lurks close by.

'What do you want with me?' Sandy mumbled. Crumbs fell from her mouth as she spoke.

'I'm looking for my daughter, Sandy, that's all.'

'This Mary lassie, you mean?'

He swallowed a mouthful of coffee and nodded. 'Yes, Sandy, Mary. She was kidnapped yesterday, and now her name is on a list with fifteen other people, including yours. I need to know why.' Sandy edged forward in her seat and stuffed a sausage into her mouth, her cheeks bulging like a hamster. Amos pulled his phone from his pocket.

'Do you recognise any of the names on this list?' He slid the phone across the table. Sandy glanced quickly at the screen.

'Nope,' she said quickly.

'Take a good look for Chrissake! It's important!' he snapped.

'I said I don't know any of those names,' Sandy growled. 'Look, mate, thanks for the food 'n' that, but I'm not a grass.' Sandy hugged herself tight again and retreated to the corner, rocking back and forth again, her eyes fixed on the river.

Sophia's voice chastised him in his mind. *Easy, Amos! She's a scared little girl. You can't treat her like one of your soldiers. Try to listen and understand her.'*

'I'm sorry, Sandy. I didn't mean to snap.' He slid the phone back into his pocket. 'You must be scared. What were you doing in that flat?'

A single tear slid half-way down her cheek before she wiped it away and sniffed hard. Her gaze was still fixed on the river, and on the boats sailing slowly past. It was only then that he noticed the girl's sharp cheekbones, her sunken eyes and greyed skin. Her clothes hung loosely from her thin arms as her long bony fingers reached for the toast again.

'Sandy,' he said, softening his voice. 'What did they do to you in that flat?'

'What do you care?' she sniffled, wiping another tear.

Sophia's voice spoke softly from beyond the grave again; *just be honest with her.*

'My little girl, Mary, she's around your age. I haven't been the best father, I'll admit, but I'm trying. And I would do time with a smile on my face if anyone hurts her.'

'Aye, well my dad's dead,' the girl spat.

'Really? I'm so sorry. How did he die, if you don't mind me asking?'

This seemed to take the girl by surprise as she turned to face him again. 'Cancer,' she said, as her rocking slowed. 'I was ten when he died.'

'I'm so sorry, Sandy. My wife passed away yesterday.' He winced at this admission. This level of openness was reserved for family and the closest of friends only. As uncomfortable as it was to lay himself bare to a stranger like this, it seemed to be working. The fragile girl sitting opposite had now stopped rocking completely, and her eyes were now fixed on him.

'How did she die?'

'Same as your dad, cancer.'

'Sorry.'

'Thank you. That's nice of you to say,' he said, then cupped his coffee in both hands and stared into the dark liquid, hiding his face from the broken girl's probing eyes. 'Sophia, my wife, was a very smart woman. intuitive and kind. I see the world in black and white, right and wrong, good and bad. It's probably why I joined the army, to be honest. I craved the structure and the discipline. I needed the rules and regulations, the straight lines, and strict routines. It made sense to me and brought order to a chaotic world.

'Sophia, though, she saw the grey. She saw the good in everyone and knew how to help it flourish in them. She understood people and made everyone around her feel better about themselves. A wonderfully warm woman who had decoded the subtlety and nuance of life and translated it to me.' He caught the lump in his throat and swallowed hard. 'She understood Mary in a way I never could. Or maybe I just didn't want to. I drove my daughter away because I was a pig-headed, stubborn idiot who tried to run my family like an army unit. And I lost everything.' A single, salty droplet splashed into his coffee cup. He dried his cheek with his sleeve. A deep, forced breath dried his eyes as he squared his shoulders and cleared his throat.

'My dad wasn't in the army.' Sandy said this in a voice so soft that it was almost a whisper. Amos, caught off guard by her words, gave her his complete and undivided attention. 'He was a long-distance truck driver. He worked nights, mostly. He used to come home at around six in the morning, but he'd stay up to make our breakfast and send us out to school before going to bed. He made the best scrambled eggs.

'Then, when I got home, he'd help me with my homework before heading back to work. Before he left, though, he'd say, "Goodnight, love you, see you in the morning, bye." Every time.' Sandy pulled her coffee close and seemed to hold onto it as tightly as she held the memory she was now reliving. 'He was the kindest man I ever knew.'

'He sounds like a wonderful father.'

'He was the best. And I hate him for leaving. I mean, I know it's not his fault, and he didn't choose to go, but...'

A heavy silence fell on them both.

'I know what you mean,' Amos said, breaking the sombre quiet. 'I've been angry with my wife since she left too.' These words caught him off guard. He either hadn't realised this truth or didn't want to admit it.

'Well, at least you have your daughter. I bet things between you aren't as bad as you think. All girls have a special place in their hearts for their fathers, trust me.'

'That's the thing though, Sandy, my daughter has been taken by her psychopath of a boyfriend and I'm trying to get her back. Now, for some reason, her name is on a list with yours and fourteen others. I was hoping you could help me figure out what that list was and maybe help me find her.'

'Let me see the list again,' she said. Amos scrambled for his phone and handed it to her gingerly. Sandy sipped her coffee with one hand and scrolled on the phone with the other. He had been watching her for almost a full minute before he realised that he was holding his breath. 'OK, I overheard the fat guy from the shop mention one of the girl's names. He said she had been shipped already, but I don't know where she is or who the other girls are.'

'Shipped? What do you mean shipped?'

'I mean shipped overseas. I wasn't in that flat because I wanted to be. I was their property. I was being drugged and pimped out. You know what this list is, don't you?' she asked. Amos tensed and shook his head. 'It's a shopping list,' she continued. 'They traffic girls all over the world. And it looks like your daughter is next.'

Chapter 34

Boydie watched from his office window as people shuffled around on the streets below, like ants scurrying from this place to that, busying themselves with jobs, and shopping, and housework, and family. Lying to themselves that their meaningless jobs are somehow important, and that their dull and joyless lives are anything more than a collection of mindless chores designed to keep them distracted from the truth.

That they are all slaves.

Slaves to their iPhones, to their mortgages, to their children, to their husbands and wives. Slaves to the rules and expectations of the powerful, and never daring to stray from the path set out for them. Idiots with no imagination or drive to achieve their true potential.

They are nothing more prey to life's true predators: the alphas, the ruthless elite with the brains and balls to do what is necessary to get things done. And he, Boydie, was one such predator. He had an advantage over the sheep.

He was only thirteen the night the police crowded around him in a small, dirty living room in Govan, a little after midnight. His mother lay lifeless in the bath with a needle stabbed between her toes, and his father was handcuffed in the bedroom. After a quick investigation and rushed trial, his father was convicted of manslaughter and sentenced to twelve years in prison.

Boydie, now an orphan, was forced into the care system and spent the next two years being bounced from home to home until a brutal street fight saw him take up residence in Her Majesty's Young Offenders Institution,

Polmont. It was during a visit to the youth counsellor during his stay at the juvenile detention centre that his advantage, his *gift* was revealed to him.

***

'Ah, Mr Boyd, please take a seat.' The counsellor smiled and pointed to the only empty chair in the small office, instructing the teen to sit. The counsellor was perched bolt upright at the edge of his seat, typing enthusiastically at the laptop. His dark, wiry, unkempt hair accented his slender features, and his thin nose looked barely capable of holding the rimless glasses balanced on top of it.

The cold room was lit by a buzzing fluorescent light set into the soft ceiling tiles. The bare brick wall of the adjacent building filled the view from the only window and choked all the natural light into the small office. A modest desk tucked into the corner of the room held only a laptop, a desk tidy and a small pile of manilla folders — patient files, Boydie guessed. On the brass desktop name plate, engraved in bold black lettering, was the name *James Stevens PHD*. Boydie stepped forward, slid back the folding chair that was tucked under the desk opposite Stevens, and sat as instructed. 'Just let me finish what I'm doing here,' Stevens said. He finished typing with an overexaggerated flourish, then turned to Boydie and smiled. 'Mr Boyd, nice to see you again. How have you been since our last session?'

'Fine, and it's Boydie,' Boydie said.

'Sorry, yes, Boydie,' Stevens said, holding his hands up apologetically. 'Now, where did we get to on our last discussion?' He pulled a folder from the top of the pile and scrolled his finger down the first page. 'Ah, yes, we talked about how to control your anger. Have you been practising the techniques we discussed?'

'Yes. they don't work,' Boydie replied coldly.

'Really? I'm sorry to hear that. Why do you think they don't work?'

'You tell me, you're the doctor. I'm just a stupid, maladjusted youth with anger issues.'

'Oh, you are far from stupid, Boydie. In fact, I would rate you as one of the most intelligent young men I've come across in a long time.' This comment made Boydie's chest swell, and a self-satisfied grin spread across his face. 'That is what makes these sessions a little frustrating for me, in fact,' continued Stevens. 'You are clearly a bright young man with incredible potential, but your anger is holding you back. I would like to help you control that anger and focus your energy on something more productive.'

'Like what?'

'Only you can answer that question, I'm afraid. What makes you feel excited? What drives you to excel? What's your passion?'

Boydie shrugged his shoulders and grunted.

'That's OK; that is why we're here. To discover the real you and focus that intellect on something positive and productive.'

'I'm here because of a court order. If I hadn't put that wee guy in hospital, I wouldn't be here at all.'

'Yes, that was an unfortunate incident, but I believe the surgery was a success, and the young lad will be able to walk again after some physical therapy. How does that make you feel?'

'It doesn't,' Boydie said coldly.

'What do you mean?' Stevens asked, clasping his

hands and sitting back in his chair.

'I mean I don't feel anything, I'm not his carer. The chances of me ever seeing him again are pretty low, so it makes no difference to me if the guy can run 100 metres in twelve seconds or if he struggles to wipe his own arse?'

'So, I take it you don't feel any remorse for what happened?' Stevens asked, with one eyebrow raised in a quizzical look.

'Remorse? He chose to go out drinking that night. He chose to start a fight. I warned him to walk away, but he decided to try and play the hard man in front of his buddies. Jim, we are nothing more than the sum total of the decisions we make. I mean, deep down, I might be the nicest guy in the world, but if I choose to act like a prick, then I'm a prick.

'That wee guy chose to be a prick that night, and now he has to live with the consequences of that decision. The fact that he ended up in the hospital needing surgery and rehab was not my doing; it was his. He had the option to choose a different path that night. And if he had, his night would have ended very differently. Why should I feel sorry for the choices someone else made?'

'See! That's the intellect I'm talking about! That level of insight is far beyond the grasp of the average fifteen-year-old boy. But there was one detail you missed during your analysis.'

'Really? What's that?'

'He's not sitting in a twelve-by-twelve room in Polmont every night. *That* was your doing. *That* was your choice. You could've made your point and stopped, but you didn't. And that is what I want to help you with. Now, can you remember the breathing exercises we covered last week?'

Before Boydie could answer, the office door exploded inward, and two boys fell to the floor grappling. They rolled on the floor, grabbing at each other's faces and punching wildly. Stevens bounced from his chair and tried to pry the two boys apart. The two-man brawl had now become a three-way fight, and it wasn't clear to Boydie who the winner was going to be. Stevens shouted for help before a stray hand punched him in the face, knocking his rimless glasses from his nose.

The three struggled for a few minutes before Stevens's backup arrived. Three heavy-set guards wearing stab-proof vests scrambled through the door and pried the trio apart. The two boys were subdued and handcuffed, while Stevens retrieved his glasses from the floor. All six then stumbled into the hallway. One boy was dragged left, while the other was dragged right. Both still shouting and promising violence to the other.

'Sorry, Boydie. Give me a minute,' Stevens said, as he fixed his glasses and closed the door, leaving Boydie alone in the small office.

Boydie sat in silence for a moment, listening carefully to the footsteps in the hallway grow quiet. He bounced from his chair and rushed to the pile of folders on the desk. Quickly, he ruffled through the papers, scanning the pages until he saw what he would later refer to as his *gift*. On the third page, scribbled at the bottom in bold black pen were the words *Possible narcissistic psychopathic traits?* The words were underlined and circled. Boydie noted this, then quickly took his seat.

Once Stevens had returned and the session was over, Boydie headed straight for the library. He requested all the psychology books the library had in its limited resources and was permitted one hour supervised internet access. The information online was vast and overwhelming, but he was determined. He had done what Stevens wanted; he had found his passion. He grabbed a pen and paper and jotted down notes from the article on screen:

- ***Narcissistic personality disorder.*** *Sufferers are characterised by strong personality traits, such as an over exaggerated sense of self-importance. They're people who tend to have conflicting relationships and a deep and excessive need for attention*
- ***Psychopathic personality.*** *The most distinctive trait of psychopaths is a lack of empathy. They're people who are manipulative, feel no remorse, and can't establish real emotional bonds*

A big tick in both boxes, he thought.

- *Narcissistic Psychopaths often have a history of childhood abuse, neglect, or trauma.*

The cigarette burns on his legs, given to him by his alcoholic father. The dislocated shoulder he had got from his mother for his eighth birthday. The weekends spent locked in an empty flat while his "parents" went on drug-fuelled benders. The drug dealer who kept his parents stash well stocked as long as Boydie kept quiet and did as he was told on the late-night visits to his room.

How could he not be damaged by this? How could anyone go through that and walk away intact? The memories fanned the flames in his stomach, which he thought had gone extinct since his mother's death. Since he laid her head down in the grimy bath and pierced the needle into the only usable vein she had left. Since the moment his latex glove-covered fingers pressed the plunger on the same syringe his father used not ten minutes before. Since her eyes rolled upwards, and he watched her pupils disappear.

A clean first kill.

A justified first kill.

But the lack of any emotions about that night had confused and frustrated him for so long. He hadn't expected to feel shame or guilt; they deserved it, but he expected something. This, however, answered all his questions. This explained why he felt so indifferent. It wasn't his fault. It was his mother's. She was supposed to protect him. She was supposed to care for him. But she failed, and he punished her for that. His chest felt suddenly light. A weight he hadn't realised he was carrying was suddenly lifted. Questions that had tortured him since that day had been answered. He felt righteous. He felt vindicated. He felt good. A smile crept across his face.

'Hey Boydie,' a boy called from the library door, 'you coming? They're starting the film in five minutes.'

'Aye, I'm almost finished. What movie are they playing tonight?'

'Scarface,' the boy replied.

***

The vibrating phone on his desk snapped Boydie back to the present. He watched the slaves below, scurrying back and forth like obedient little worker ants, for a moment longer, then turned his attention to the phone. 'Hello,' he hissed over the phone.

'Boydie, it's me,' the voice said.

'Ah, PC Plod, what have you got for me?'

'Don't call me that,' Plod snapped angrily, 'I hate that.'

'I know you do. Now, for the second time, what have you got for me? Have you dealt with that bitch cop yet?'

'She's been instructed to shut down her investigation and hand in all her notes. as well as any evidence that has been collected. If she has the phone, we will have it by tomorrow morning.'

'Good.' Boydie said this and slithered back to the window to watch his prey again. 'I need everything to be in place for this final meeting. Once the others sign on the dotted line, we will be Scotland's biggest conglomerate and control ninety percent of all drugs and women coming in and out of the country. And with Scotland's top cop on the payroll...' Boydie breathed deep and let the silence make his point for him.

'We'll be very rich men,' Plod said.

'Money? Is that all you want?'

'Of course, what else is there?

'That's the problem with you people; you think too small. A king does not rule with wealth alone. Power and fear — that is how you command true respect. Money is just a tool. Once you have the money, you get the power. Fear is much harder to achieve,' Boydie said, as he glided back behind his desk.

'Is that how you see yourself? A king?' Plod asked.

'There you go, thinking too small again. I'm trying to teach you to be a king while I am the emperor who allows you to rule over a small patch in my vast empire. Don't you get it? This deal is just the start! One day, I am going to control the biggest organised crime syndicate in the United Kingdom and then, with my connections, Europe. I will control everything from drugs to trafficking to prostitution and I need to know you are up to the task.' The fine Italian leather of the custom-made chair groaned under Boydie's weight.

'Your connections? I think you put a bit too much faith in The Order, Brother Boyd.'

'The Order? Haven't you listened to a word I've said? I am more than the Freemasons! My reach goes beyond that bunch of tired old men in robes passing each other government contracts and tips on rigged horse races and complaining about how the Catholics have ruined the country. Now, you better get up to speed quick, Plod, or I'll have you replaced the same way I replaced your predecessor.'

'Don't threaten me, Boydie. You need me, remember? You need me to keep the police off your back. I'm the one who got McGuire's investigation shut down, and I'm the one who got your buddy released from custody. Don't think you can treat me like one of your lackeys! I am a senior member of Police Scotland, dammit! And stop calling me Plod!' the voice demanded.

'Then do your damn job and bring me that phone!' With that, Boydie hung up the phone and tossed it onto the custom-made replica desk. 'Idiot!' he hissed, then periscoped his head up to look out the window once more. The sun had almost set, and the streets were all but bare. All the ants had scurried back to their nests to bury their heads in their phones to distract them from the truth of their meaningless lives. The drunks would be out soon, fighting with each other in the streets. The corner of his mouth curled up. He missed the days of street fighting,

but he had bigger plans now.
Much bigger.

Chapter 35

The heavy bedroom door pushed slowly open and shook Mary from her half-sleep. She had struggled to stay awake but couldn't sleep either, and she had been tossing and turning for the past hour or so. She scrambled to the head of the bed, pulled her knees close, and held her breath. The smell of coffee wafted into the room, followed by the six-foot-two, muscle bound man. George cautiously carried the source of the smell over to the bed. Mary breathed out slowly and relaxed her knees back down. 'Hey, George,' she sighed.

'Hi Mary,' he replied softly. Carefully, he turned the cup in his hands and offered Mary the handle. 'Two sugars with a little milk, just how you like it. How are you feeling?'

'Smashing, George! Living the dream, mate!' she snapped sarcastically. 'How do you think I'm feeling?'

George looked at the floor and shuffled uncomfortably. 'I know, stupid question, I suppose. I was just—' his voice trailed off, not quite knowing how to finish the sentence. 'Look, Mary, all he wants is the phone. If you give him what he wants, I'm sure he'll let you go and you can move on with your life.'

'You think I'm that stupid? Do you honestly think he's just going to let me go? And anyway, I don't have the phone; my dad does. Isn't there a tracker on the phone?'

'Yes, but the signal has been compromised. It's showing up in twenty-six different locations at the same time.'

Mary smiled and sipped the coffee. It tasted good.

'Uncle Gerry,' she said, 'Aye, you're never finding that phone,' she chuckled, and took another gulp of coffee. She felt the hot liquid slip down her throat and warm her stomach. She focused on this sensation, it felt good. 'Why do you do it George?'

'Do what, Mary?'

'Why do you stay with Boydie? You're not like him. You're not a bad guy, deep down. You have a gentleness to you. Boydie is literally a psychopath.'

'No man chooses evil because it is evil; he only mistakes it for happiness.'

'What are you talking about?' she snapped.

'It's a quote from a philosopher, I forget which one. Probably one of the stoics, Epictetus, maybe.'

Mary waved this away and interrupted, 'What does it mean?'

'Boydie isn't the way he is because he's an evil man.' The bed springs groaned under George's massive bulk as he lowered himself onto the bed. 'He believes he's doing a good thing. He is following his dream and is willing to do whatever it takes to achieve his goal. Given his background, it's actually quite inspiring. He came from a broken home and built an empire. I'm lucky to be by his side.'

'Better to reign in Hell than serve in Heaven?'

'Paradise Lost? I'm impressed.' He smiled.

'No idea, I saw it on Facebook.' Mary took another long slow sip from her mug. 'But you're not like him. I mean, he's killed people, I've seen him do it.'

'Me too, which makes us just as bad.'

'I never killed anyone. Neither did you,' Mary protested.

'The only thing necessary for the triumph of evil is for

good men to do nothing.'

'Another pearl of wisdom from one of your stoics? Do you spend all of your spare time looking up useless quotes, hoping it'll one day come in handy to impress some stupid girl?'

'No, it's not one of the stoics, and it's not to impress *some stupid girl.*' George's broad muscular shoulders slumped, and his eyes fell to his own hands. The once strong, powerful silverback now looked lost, weak and vulnerable like an infant pining for its lost mother.

'George, don't,' she pleaded, as she reached over and gently touched his hands. 'We can't, you know that. It was a mistake the first time. If Boydie ever found out, he'd kill us both.'

'I know,' he said, holding her small hand in his. They both savoured the touch for a long moment before Mary pulled back and finished her coffee with one last long swig. George stood and took the cup from her, then placed it on the dressing table at the foot of the bed.

'Is my dad OK?' Mary asked, breaking the long silence.

'Aye. He's strong, Mary. Stronger than Boydie gives him credit for,' George said, as he sat back down on the bed.

'He's the toughest man I know,' Mary said, turning her gaze to her own hands. 'We haven't been getting along too well recently. My mum said we were too much alike.' The mention of her mother swelled the lump in her throat. Mary swallowed it and continued. 'He never really understood me, you know? He didn't get my humour or understand my mental health stuff. He thought my depression was a weakness.'

'You are not weak.'

'I know, but you have to see it from his perspective. He's from a different generation and a different time, and he's a soldier to boot. Weakness meant death for a lot of men.'

'Sounds a lot like toxic masculinity to me.'

'You're wrong!' Mary snapped back, a little harder than she expected. 'Out there, in the field, you have to be tough. You need that resilience and that strength, especially when you have people looking to you for answers. You can't show fear. Fear costs people's lives.' She paused and felt the weight of her own words press down on her. It was as though they were being said to her for the first time. 'He had to be that way,' she finally whispered. 'It was that or people died. Having that responsibility weighs on you. It changes you.' Her words dripped slowly from her mouth. 'Maybe I didn't understand him either. Maybe I could've been a bit more patient too.'

'You OK?' George asked. Mary snapped herself out of her daze and stared, once again, into his soft eyes. The air between them thickened, and Mary's pulse quickened. An unseen force pulled her closer to him. The long, slow kiss quickened her heart and set her skin alight. Passion, danger, and excitement set her nerves on fire. The kiss lingered on her lips and tongue as they parted. Her eyes stayed closed, savouring every last moment. Finally, Mary opened her eyes and saw George staring deep into her very soul. It was as though he saw her very essence. Their eyes stayed locked for the longest moment before Mary bounced from the bed and walked to the en-suite bathroom, stealing one last long glance at the gentle ape before closing the door behind her.

Once she had done what she needed to do, Mary

washed her hands and splashed cold water on her face. She stood slumped over, resting her hands on the sink, and stared at her reflection in the mirror on the wall. 'What is wrong with you?' she snarled at the stranger staring back at her with a piercing and contemptuous glare. *The first half-decent guy you fall for, and he's the cousin of your current, maniac boyfriend.* Mary wiped away a tear that had begun to make its way down her cheek. 'I miss my mum,' she whispered to the mirror. 'She'd know exactly what to do.' But as Mary said the words out loud, an old memory replayed in her mind, and her mother's voice spoke softly, "Don't worry, baby, it's an accident, and accidents happen. It's only a problem if it can't be fixed." These words had always soothed Mary as a child, and they worked just as well today as they did back then. She pulled as much air into her lungs as she possibly could, held it, and then let it out slowly, just the way her dad had shown her. *Control your breathing, and you control your heart.*

Her brow furrowed, and her resolve steeled. She knew what she had to do.

With a new sense of purpose and determination, Mary stood tall and resolute, took another deep breath, and breathed out sharp. She snapped her shoulders back, clenched her jaw, and swallowed the lump of fear that had begun to make its way up her oesophagus. She was going to do it. No question in her mind. This was not only her best shot at getting out of here, but it was the right thing to do.

She marshalled her courage, marched for the door, and yanked it open. 'OK, George, here's what we're going to do,' she barked, with the familiar tone that she heard come from her father countless times and loathed it every time. The fact that it was now coming from her mouth not only shocked her, but it also surprised her at how empowered she had felt by it. She allowed herself a moment to smirk before she continued. 'We're going to...' her leg wobbled beneath her as she grabbed at the bed frame for support.

'Oh, it worked a bit quicker than I was told,' George said, as he darted forward and helped stabilise her.

'What?' Mary slurred; her words dripped clumsily from her mouth.

'He said it would take fifteen minutes. I'm sorry, Mary; I had no choice.'

Mary glared incredulously at the gorilla, then at the coffee mug, then back to George. 'You drugged... George, I can't.'

'I know, I feel really bad, but I couldn't afford you making a scene. I won't let them hurt you, Mary, I promise.'

'No... you don't under... I...' Mary staggered forward and collapsed onto the bed. She opened her mouth again to force the words out, but the sound that escaped was guttural and panicked. Darkness swept in from her peripherals until the whole world went black.

'I'm so sorry, Mary,' George whispered as he effortlessly scooped her up from the bed and carefully carried her through the bedroom door.

Chapter 36

The hard gravel of the café's car park crunched loudly under Amos's pacing feet. 'Pick up the phone, Gerry.' The phone rang again in his ear. No answer. He ended the call and dialled another number. This time, the call was answered within three rings. 'Hello, Amos,' McGuire said softly.

'Rachel, I can't get a hold of Gerry. Have you spoken to him?'

'No, not since I checked in a couple of hours ago. Is everything OK?'

'No, Rachel, everything is not OK!' he snapped, as he paced the parking lot. 'Things are pretty damn far from OK!'

'Jesus, calm down. What happened?' The softness had gone from her voice and was replaced with a strange mixture of defensiveness and concern.

'Mary has been kidnapped by sex traffickers.'

'What? No, Mr B a drug dealer.'

'Well, apparently, he's added drugging young girls and selling them as sex slaves to his repertoire.'

'Amos, that doesn't make any sense.'

'Doesn't it? Why? I mean, who knows what this maniac is capable of?' Amos concentrated hard, trying to keep images he would rather not have in his head out of his head — images that would no doubt send him into a complete panic. That was the last thing he needed now.

'Listen, Amos, sex trafficking is exclusively run by a Lithuanian gang that go by the name "The Vilinius", also known as "The Russians".

'Why are they called "The Russians" if they're

189

Lithuanian?'

'Does it matter? Now, if Mr B were to start trafficking young girls, it would start a turf war with The Russians, and he wouldn't want that. He hasn't got the manpower.'

'Well, he has. And Mary's name is on a list of girls he's shipping overseas.' The gravel crunched louder as his pace quickened.

'How did you find this out?' McGuire asked. He spent the next few minutes filling her in on his conversation with Onion, the barbershop, and the sex ring in the flat above. He told her about the girl he rescued and the list of names. He did not tell her about the episode in the car, which he was still telling himself was nothing more than a panic attack. A panic attack was a battle of mind and body, and he could control his body if he controlled his breathing. It was a battle he could win. He couldn't control it if it was the other thing, and he needed to stay in control. He needed to remain focused and not worry about the other thing right now. Mary needed him now more than ever.

'OK, Amos, I can make a few phone calls. A friend of mine works on the task force looking into sex trafficking. Maybe he can give us an idea of where these girls are held before they're shipped abroad.'

'No,' he said, as he stopped pacing and stood still. 'If the police could have stopped them, then they would have done it by now. I know someone who will know. I'll get the intel myself.' A steely calm settled over his mind. A vicious resolve he hadn't felt since Baghdad. It was a feeling beyond anger. A feeling beyond fear and hatred. It was a strange serenity that could only be discovered by having a single purpose in life and the knowledge that you will succeed in the pursuit of that goal because failing is simply not an option. Give a soldier a mission and a purpose, and you turn him into a one-man army.

Amos was more than a soldier.

He was more than a Royal Engineer.

He was a father.

'Amos,' McGuire said, 'Don't do anything silly. Leave this to the police.'

'Keep trying Gerry,' he said, his voice was cold and monotone. 'Make sure he's OK. I'll check back in later.' He ended the call and pocketed the phone.

The bell above the café door dinged loudly as he marched back in. Without saying a word, he settled the bill, then ushered the frail girl out of the booth and into the car. He fired up the engine and spun the car around before she clicked her seatbelt into place. The car's modified engine spat and banged as the tyres hit concrete and shot along the road.

The girl sat nervously in the passenger seat, clearly sensing the tension in the car. He caught the girl's frightened posture from the corner of his eye and felt a pang of guilt stir in the pit of his stomach, but he stamped it out instantly. *I know the poor girl has been through a lot, and she's probably terrified. I don't blame her. But I can't afford emotion right now. I need to stay focused.* he turned his attention back to the road ahead and drove in silence. He needed to think. He needed a plan of action.

Amos parked the car outside the unkept garden in Govan and glanced at the house, confident that Onion would be gone by now and that this was as safe a place as any for the girl for now but told her to get out as quickly as possible. Back to her mother's perhaps, or another relative. Anywhere but here. 'You have a second chance,' he said. 'Don't blow it.'

***

The car park behind the barbershop was a little more than half full now. *People are home from work now*, Amos guessed. He parked in the far corner so he could keep watch over the back door of the shop while giving himself some cover behind another car. Darkness had crept in enough for the streetlights to have kicked in. The door to the barbers swung open, and the fat man limped upstairs to the flat above, followed by the two younger, fitter men. Amos ducked down and watched carefully as the door to the flat closed behind them.

He waited.

Nobody else entered, and nobody left. Amos reached across and emptied the glove box, stashing its contents into his jacket pocket, then did the same with the contents of the car's boot. Quickly and quietly, he darted across the car park and bolted up the stairs. He didn't knock this time or call out any passphrases. This time, he simply aimed for the same patch of unpainted wood where the door handle had been removed and smashed his heel into it. The door, already weakened by the breach earlier, caved in easily.

Tango one, the one who cut Amos's hair earlier that day, rushed towards him, screaming something undecipherable. The space in the doorway allowed for a clean swing of the baseball bat, which connected with the Tango's head, knocking him out cold instantly.

One Tango down.

The second Tango, the other thinner worker, scrambled from the bathroom and bounced carefully forward, fists raised in an experienced boxer's stance. The narrow hallway left no room to swing, so Amos dropped the bat and raised his hands but kept them open. The boxer jabbed, but Amos slipped and palmed it away. The boxer tried the jab again but followed with a right cross. Amos blocked the jab again but had to duck backwards from the heavy right hand, knocking him off balance. The boxer saw this advantage and lunged forward with the heavy right-hand hook. Amos quickly regained his balance and readied himself. He flung his arm up, blocked the hook, and drove his fist into the boxer's nose. The nose cracked loudly under the impact, which stunned him. This gave Amos enough time to grab the boxer's neck and drag him down while driving his knee into the boxer's ribs. Another loud crack, this time from the boxer's ribs, echoed through the hall, and Tango two hit the floor. A stamp to the face rendered him unconscious.

Two Tangos down.

The fat receptionist had been watching this interaction and fled to the kitchen. He reappeared with a meat cleaver and charged forwards. Amos tucked his hand into his jacket pocket and allowed the fat man to get just outside of arms reach before whipping out the pistol that was stashed in the car's glove box and aimed it between the charging man's eyes. The fat man grinded to a halt, struggling to manage his own momentum.

'Put the knife down,' Amos said coldly. The meat cleaver clattered to the floor, and the fat man raised his hands. Amos flicked the gun and instructed the man into the kitchen, but the portly Lithuanian stared back in defiance and did not move. Amos swung, and the butt of the pistol split the fat man's eyebrow. The man staggered back, and Amos pushed him through the doorway and shouted, 'Sit!' pointing to one of the wooden dining chairs tucked under a small table in the corner of the room. The man ambled over, glancing angrily between the chair and the gun that was aimed squarely at his head. Amos pulled a zip tie from his pocket as the man flopped down onto the chair. Pressing the gun to the now-sweating man's head, Amos instructed him to cuff himself. The fat man obliged, then wiped at the blood streaking its way down his rotund features. Amos pulled the other chair from under the table and positioned himself in front of his prisoner.

'Where are the other girls?' Amos asked. The Lithuanian barked something that he was sure was not meant to be flattering, then spat. Amos calmly wiped the phlegm from his face and swung again. The butt of the pistol collided with the man's lip this time, cutting it deep and sending his head reeling backwards. 'Where are the girls?!' Amos shouted again. The Lithuanian licked the blood from his lips and laughed a deep, evil belly laugh until he coughed.

'You no shoot,' he growled. 'You no have the drąsa.'

You're right,' Amos said, clicking the pistol's safety catch back into position, then slipping it back into his jacket pocket. The man grinned a toothy and confident grin, then rocked awkwardly to his feet. Amos rose with him and pushed him back down. The man landed hard back into the chair as Amos fixed his eyes on him and pulled the Smith & Wesson tactical knife from his pocket. Without saying a word, and without breaking eye contact with his prisoner, he flicked the blade free from its handle. Fear flashed across the prisoner's face for the first time, and Amos saw his flabby neck quiver as he swallowed hard. Amos flipped the knife in his hand and threw himself back down onto the small wooden chair, driving the blade into the man's flabby leg, a few inches above the knee cap. The chubby leg swallowed almost the full length of the blade before it hit bone and stopped.

The screaming finally died down after a couple of minutes. Amos let the man feel the pain in its entirety. He let the sensation completely engulf the mobster before asking his question again. 'Where are the other girls being held?!' he screamed.

The fat man suffered three more strategically placed incisions before offering any information of value, a feat Amos was both impressed by and disappointed in, but the information almost knocked the wind from his lungs. 'What did you say?!' Amos shouted. The mobster wearily repeated himself, then his eyes rolled into the back of their sockets, and his head lolled backwards. 'Are you sure?' he demanded and shook the Lithuanian, trying to rouse him.

No use. Shock had fully set in, and the man was unconscious. 'Shit!' he spat, and bolted, leaving the fat man to bleed out.

He fumbled for his phone as he scrambled down the stairs. He quickly searched for Gerry's number and dialled. No answer. 'Come on, Gerry, pick up.' He dialled again but got the same result. On the eighth ring, the answer machine kicked in. 'Gerry, it's Amos. Phone me. Now!' He hung up and dialled another number.

'Hi, Amos,' McGuire said.

'Rachel, have you spoken to Gerry?' His voice was rushed and panicked.

'What's wrong?'

'Have you talked to Gerry?' he demanded again.

'No, why?'

'Gerry's in trouble.'

'What?! How? Are you sure?'

'Yes. We need to go back to Edinburgh.'

'OK, I'm on my way, I'll meet you at the scrapyard.'

Amos bolted for the car, slammed himself into the bucket seat and gunned the engine. The loud engine spat and cracked, as the tyres screeched against the tarmac.

Chapter 37

In the weeks after Mary's fifteenth birthday and that unpleasant dinner with her boyfriend, William, Mary had barely spoken to Amos. She refused to acknowledge his presence whenever he walked into the room, and any interaction between them was done through Sophia. He didn't like putting his wife in the middle like that, but he had little choice at the moment. His once close and loving relationship with his daughter had become fractured and tense because of some... some... boy. Some silly passing infatuation she had for a teenage reprobate had driven a wedge between them. *There was something not right about him. You did the right thing.* This thought was of little consolation to him when he was being ignored at the breakfast table. It didn't fortify his resolve when he reached to give Mary a goodnight kiss — the same goodnight kiss he had given her every night for the past fifteen years — and she turned her head away. And it didn't make him feel any better when Father's Day came and went without so much as a card or a hug. *The girl holds a grudge just as long as her mother can.*

He had seen something in the boy. What that exact thing was, he couldn't explain or point out, but it was there. His gut had told him something was off, and he trusted his gut. He'd seen boys like him in his army days. Boys who joined up with no other desire than to hurt people. He had seen the same look in their eyes as he saw in William's at the restaurant that night. The same forced smile that didn't reach his eyes. And the "accident" with the water? That was deliberate. He was trying to change the subject, create a distraction, and dodge the issue. *I'm right; the boy isn't right. And if the silent treatment for a few weeks is the price for keeping Mary safe, then so be it.*

The phone rang on the desk of his office. He put the schematic of the building he was set to demolish in a few weeks' time aside and answered.

'Hello?'

'Hello, I'm looking to speak with a Mr Fisher,' a young voice said.

'Speaking.'

'Mr Fisher of Fisher Demolitions?'

'That's correct, how may I help?' he replied curtly.

'Good afternoon, Mr Fisher. My name is Frank Lopez. I have been asked to contact you to get a quote for a demolition job,' the voice asked nervously.

'No problem, what company are you calling from?' he asked, not entirely confident the call was not a prank call. He had had them before from teenagers asking him to blow up their school or the stadium of whatever football team opposed their favourite team. He had been asked to blow up Ibrox football stadium three times this year alone.

'Lopez Construction Limited,' Frank said, his tone rising at the end of the answer, making it sound more like a question than a statement.

'Lopez Construction? You sound a bit young to have your own construction business.'

'It's my dad's company,' the boy on the phone said. 'He's just starting out and doesn't have a secretary yet, so I'm helping him out.'

'OK, Frank Lopez,' he said, still not entirely convinced. 'So, what is your dad demolishing? And what kind of demolition is he looking for exactly?' he asked, ready to hang up if the young voice named a football stadium.

'OK, Mr Fisher, my dad asked me to tell you that he is pulling down an abandoned factory on the east side of Glasgow. He said a structural survey has already been carried out, which discovered some asbestos, but this has been removed. He is looking for a demolition plan for an explosive demolition. He was hoping to pull it down conventionally, with excavators and stuff, but the client has changed the deadline, and he needs to accelerate his plans. Does that make any sense to you?'

Frank Lopez had rhymed this off as though he were reading from a script, but he said enough of the right words to remove at least some of the doubts in Amos's mind. 'Yes, son, it makes sense. Tell your dad I can meet him on site tomorrow afternoon and make a preliminary assessment. Then, I will write up a full proposal and submit a plan by the end of next week.'

'Actually, he asked if you could go tonight, around seven,' Frank stammered, clearly nervous.

'Tonight? No, I'm sorry. That's not enough notice.'

'He is going to Inverness tomorrow morning and needs this done as quickly as possible. Glasgow City Council has said that he needs this proposal submitted by Friday in order to meet the deadline. Please, Mr Fisher, this is my dad's first big project and the first time he's asked for my help. Isn't there anything you can do?' The boy's pleading voice tugged on something deep inside of Amos. Maybe it was the pathetic tone of the nervous Frank, trying desperately not to let his father down. Or maybe he was projecting his own issues with his daughter onto the young boy and his father, and Amos felt he could help the pair in a way he was not able to do for

199

himself and Mary. Maybe he could get some brownie points with the fates and earn his way back into his daughter's heart. Whatever the reason, after a few silent moments of intense internal deliberation and despite the small and almost imperceptible alarm sounding at the back of his head, Amos agreed. A grateful Frank Lopez thanked him on behalf of his absent father and confirmed the site location.

Amos ended the call, slid the phone back onto the desk, and stared at its blank screen. The alarm bell in his mind was quiet, but consistent. There was a desperation in the boy's voice. Was it nerves? Or inexperience? Maybe both? Was he afraid of simply letting his father down? This was Mr Lopez's Senior's first big job after all. There must be a lot riding on the contract being a success. A contract like that could make or break a new company. Amos knew that all too well. But the bell continued to ring.

He swiped his hand through the air as though to physically wave the alarm in his head away. How dangerous could it be? This was Glasgow, not Baghdad, after all.

At six fifty-five, Amos pulled into the address that Frank Lopez had given him. A row of hedge bushes had been left unkept and had now engulfed the eight-foot mesh fencing that lined the factory's entrance. Two lifeless saplings stood guard at the end of a narrow road that opened onto a wide, open, and abandoned car park, which was in the process of being repossessed by the surrounding flora and fauna. The huge grey, lifeless factory building loomed at the north side of the car park like a headstone on a grave and dominated the small industrial estate. The front door of the decrepit building was buckled and held in place by a single rusted hinge. Large windows lined the face of the factory and would probably have let ample natural light into the offices, which so often lay at the front of these old factories. The two windows that flanked the broken door had been smashed and now looked more like the empty eye sockets of a decaying skull than the entrance to the foyer of a busy factory.

He rolled his Audi into the space directly in front of the skull. The empty, windowless sockets watched him as he opened the door and stepped out of the car. He cast his eye over the face of the building and wondered what mess might be awaiting him inside. He bent back into his car and lifted the camera and folder from the passenger seat. He stopped when he stood and was met with the penetrating stare of a fox, which skulked from the factory door. The scavenger's beady eyes seemed to pierce into him.

It held his gaze.

Waiting.

Unafraid.

The fox sprinted for the bush when the first blow sent Amos to the floor. Pain shot from the base of his spine and down through his legs, and he collapsed face down onto the concrete steps. He rolled as quickly as he could to find the source of the impact, but was interrupted by a kick to the abdomen. This forced all the air from his lungs as another foot kicked his back. A frantic flurry of kicks from two attackers landed faster than he could react to them, and all he could do was curl himself into a ball to minimise the damage. This seemed to work, and the frequency of the kicks began to slow.

Amos took advantage of the lull. He exploded from

his ball and kicked the legs from under the attacker in front of him. The body landed with a grunt. The voice sounded young and male. He scrambled to get a look at the attackers face, but it was covered by a neck bandana, the type made popular during the COVID pandemic.

Shit.

Amos rolled onto his back to get a look at the second attacker, but a bandana was covering his face with a skull design. This one was taller and heavier than the first. He had a baseball bat raised high above his head and was bringing it down hard. Amos rolled towards him, and the bat hit nothing but the ground. Amos kicked his leg out and swept the legs from under Skull Face. The heavy guy fell on his side, the baseball bat clattered on the ground, and rolled away. Amos jumped to his feet and buried his boot in Skull Face's stomach. The groan from Skull Face sounded just as young as the first attacker. He knelt over the squirming boy and yanked the bandana from his face while the boy struggled for breath on the ground. Amos clenched his fist as tight as he could and readied to swing but paused. 'William?' he gasped.

'George,' William coughed, 'Help.'

A fist caught Amos's ear and knocked him to the ground. Dazed and confused, and with a loud ringing in his left ear, he fell to his back and stared blankly at the sky. William and George, now back on their feet, took up positions on either side of the defenceless Amos.

'Surprised, old man?' William spat, then buried a boot into Amos's ribs. The blow knocked the wind out of his lungs. 'What did you expect? Huh?' He bent down, leaning in so close that Amos could feel the spit landing on his cheek. 'You brought this on yourself when you told Mary to stay away from me.' A second kick cracked the two ribs that had been weakened by the first. 'Well, she's mine now, dickhead.' William's heel slammed into Amos's stomach. 'You saw something at that dinner, though, didn't you, old man? You saw what everyone else missed. You saw the darkness in me; I could tell. Well, you were right.' This kick landed on Amos's cheek, snapping his head back. 'My darkness is a gift, and I'm going to use it to become the most powerful man in Scotland.' William disappeared from view, then reappeared with something resting over his shoulder.' But you won't be around to see it.' William took the bat from his shoulder and gripped it tight in both hands. 'Hey, Mr Fisher, say hello to my little friend.' He screamed and brought it down hard.

Chapter 38

Panic had washed Amos's body with adrenaline, which, if he was in a fight, would be highly advantageous. But as he was crawling along the M8 Motorway at half its seventy-mile-an-hour speed limit due to heavy traffic, all it did was send his mind racing with a million different terrifying scenarios. The Lithuanian had only given a single name before he lapsed into unconsciousness. But that name sent shockwaves through Amos's spine and started the alarm in his head screaming.

The name the man gave was Damir Volkov.

Damir Volkov, the giant greasy Russian that had given the trio sanctuary and breakfast that morning, was involved with the sex trafficking Lithuanians and, in turn, Mr B.

His internal warning system had failed him, and now *he* had failed his best friend. He dragged his friend into the line of fire and left him alone with the enemy. He left him with a wolf, dressed in sheep's clothing, who had fooled them all. *You idiot, Amos! How could you be so stupid?* Gerry was never a fighter; he wasn't built the same way Amos was. Gerry was all brains and no brawn, always had been. He was emotionally and intellectually strong, but he never had the physical or mental strength to hold up in battle. And now, because of him, his friend was in trouble.

He dialled Gerry's number again. It went straight to the answer machine.

Shit.

He felt his chest heave fast and heavy as he gulped so much air in and out that the windscreen was steaming up from the inside. The steering wheel had become slippery with the sweat from his hands. His heart was pounding faster and faster in his chest, and his mind jumped from one thought to another at lightning speed. *Is Gerry still alive? Is he being tortured? Is Mary still alive? This is all my fault. I should have just gone to the police. If I had, though, he would have killed her for sure. He might kill her anyway.* Uncontrolled panic swept up from the pit of his stomach and filled his chest. It worked its way up his throat, flooded his mouth with saliva, and filled his ears with the sound of blood rushing through his veins. It was now working its way to his eyes. He felt his cheeks flush, and pressure built behind his eyes.

Control your breathing and you control your heart. Control your heart and you control your mind.

He focused hard on his breath, blocking all other senses out, and concentrated on nothing but the air coming in through his nose. The pressure behind his eyes eased. He counted each breath, consciously slowing it down. The saliva flowed down his throat as he drew a long slow breath and held it. As he let the air slip through the small slit in his mouth, his heart slowed and his mind quietened.

Good. Stay in control. Mary and Gerry need you.

He pawed at the car's Bluetooth controls, found McGuire's number on the screen, and dialled.

'Amos, what's happening? Have you spoken to Gerry? Is he OK?' McGuire's voice boomed with controlled panic over the speakers.

'No,' Amos replied. 'His phone is going straight to voicemail, and I'm still twenty minutes away, stuck behind some stupid old tart doing half the speed limit on the outside lane of the M8. Either overtake or get out of the overtaking lane!' He shouted the last part at the elderly lady driving the BMW in front of him, even though she couldn't hear him. He flashed his lights, hoping she would get the point and either speed up or, preferably, get out of his way.

The response was the exact opposite. The old lady caught him in her rear-view mirror, flipped him the middle finger, and carried on with her speed unchanged.

'I know,' McGuire said. 'I'm three cars behind you. You need to calm down, Amos.'

He glanced in his rear-view mirror and saw the same small, dark Kia Picanto he saw parked outside the warehouses at the boatyard where he and McGuire first met.

'Good. Are you armed?' he asked, ignoring her plea for him to calm down.

'What? No, of course I'm not armed.'

'What do you mean you're not armed? These people aren't playing games here, Rachel. They're dangerous, and we need to be prepared.' His tone now incredulous. He was amazed that she had not come prepared, despite being told what the dangers were. *She would never make a good soldier.*

'The Strathclyde Police don't just let you walk out with a gun. It would require a detailed report of what type of incident I needed it for and submit a risk assessment. They would also want to know where I was going and why. All in all, it would be about three miles of red tape, all of which I would need to get signed off by my superior, and that would send alarm bells ringing, and the wrong people would find out!' McGuire yelled.

'OK, calm down,' he conceded. 'What did you bring, then?'

'I brought a taser and my mace spray.' She said this, calming her voice somewhat.

'Oh, I didn't know you had your mace spray. That tips the odds in our favour.'

'Amos, I know you are stressed and scared, but sarcasm doesn't help.'

'You're right, I am scared. I'm scared because you brought a can of hairspray to a gunfight!' he yelled. 'Never mind; you can have my gun. I'll take the baseball bat.'

'Where the hell did you get a gun?!' McGuire yelled incredulously.

'Never mind. Can you shoot?'

'I am an Authorised Firearms Officer with the Strathclyde Police. Yes, I can shoot.'

'That'll have to do I suppose,' he said before returning his attention to the BMW. 'Move, you old fart!'

'Amos, I found out a few details about Mr B. His name is Billy Boyd, no middle name.'

'Billy Boyd? Why does that name sound familiar?' The shadow that promised answers returned in the corner of his mind. He focused hard on it, but it shrunk back the more he tried. *Let it breathe.*

'He's extremely dangerous, although we haven't managed to pin anything concrete on him, which means he's smart too. He spent some time in the Polmont juvenile detention facility when he was fifteen for grievous bodily harm. While he was there, he had a psychological evaluation and was preliminary assessed for possible narcissistic psychopathic traits, but was released before this could be properly diagnosed or any treatment plan was put in place.'

'What do you mean he was released? Wasn't there any

follow-up?'

'Social work tried to, but he disappeared as soon as he was released.'

'What do you mean disappeared? How can a fifteen-year-old kid just disappear?' he screamed at the dashboard.

'There was a strong suspicion that he had taken up residence with a…' There was a pause, and he could hear the shuffling of paper. 'Sandra Brown; his aunt on his mother's side. It was believed that Sandra and her only son, George, took the boy in and hid him from the social workers. After that, he seems to have slipped through the net and been forgotten about by the system. Apparently, there was a big shakeup at the department of corrections at the time; stuff like that happened more than a few times.'

'That's a joke! Complete incompetence!'

'I know,' McGuire said solemnly.

'Never mind,' Amos said, swiping his hand as though wiping his indignation for the decade-old incompetence from his mind. 'None of that matters right now. We need to focus on getting Gerry out safe.' As he said those words, the BMW indicated and shuffled into the middle lane. 'Finally! OK, the stupid old tart has moved. We'll stop on the main road before turning onto the dirt road that leads to the scrapyard. There, we can regroup and come up with a plan of attack. Try to keep up.' Without waiting for a confirmation, Amos ended the call and pushed the accelerator hard to the floor. For the first time, he was glad to hear the overly loud engine roar into life as the Ford lurched forward and chewed up the road.

Hold on, mate; I'm coming. I just hope I'm not too late.

Chapter 39

Amos stopped the car at the gap in the trees that served as an entrance to the scrapyard's long dirt track. He pulled the pistol from the glove compartment and performed the necessary checks. He then stepped out of the car, pulled the back door open, and lifted the baseball bat from the seat. McGuire pulled in behind him as he slammed the heavy door closed. He eyed her as she slipped out of her small car. Her pencil skirt made the task more difficult than it needed to be, and the heels struggled to find any stability on the gravel. She clumsily waddled to him, trying hard to stand tall and walk with authority, but failing.

'OK, what's the plan?' She said, forcing calm and confidence with her voice because her body language was clearly failing to deliver the message. He watched her with a raised eyebrow and shook his head.

'The plan,' he started, 'is to save Gerry. We don't know how many Tangos there are, where they are, or what kind of weaponry they have.'

'Tangos?' McGuire asked.

'Targets, enemies,' he clarified.

'Ah, you mean suspects.'

'Tangos, suspects, whatever. The bad guys, OK?' Amos snapped, annoyed at the pointless interaction.

'OK, sorry. So, how do you want to do this?'

'I wish we had some intel. Even if we had a pair of eyes to give us numbers. What I wouldn't give for an intelligence drone and a thermal imaging camera right about now.'

'I couldn't manage those from the office, but what

about these?' McGuire said this before stumbling to the boot of her small Kia. She pulled out a large, deep black briefcase and handed it to him. Kneeling down, he opened the case and saw four Sepura SC20 TETRA police issue radios, each with in-ear earpiece and inline mic.

'That's a good start. It's better than nothing, I suppose. At least we can communicate better,' he said and looked up to see McGuire holding a pair of Steiner tactical binoculars. 'Now we're talking.' Amos said it with a smile. A plan was forming in his mind. It was only half of a plan, granted, but the plan allowed him to keep McGuire out of danger as much as possible. He bounced to his feet and held his hand out. 'Give me your pepper spray.'

'What? Why?' McGuire demanded.

'I'm going in alone.'

'Are you hell!' The words seemed to have rushed from her mouth without her consent as she rocked from the shock of saying them. 'I, eh, I mean, no, Amos. You'll need backup, and I am the commanding officer on the scene.'

'Nice try, but I'm not in the army anymore, and you are definitely not my CO. Look, I need you to get a good vantage point where you can see over the fence and into the yard. I need you to be my eyes and watch my back while I sneak in and get Gerry out. Got it?'

'That's it? That's your big plan?' McGuire spat, not trying to hide her indignation of the "plan".

'You have any better ideas? I'm open to suggestions.'

McGuire glared at him silently for a long moment, then opened her mouth to speak, then closed it without a word. 'No,' she finally admitted.

'Good. Now, how do you expect to climb a tree wearing those?' Amos asked, pointing her pencil skirt and hight heels.

'You think some radios and some pepper spray were all I brought? I never go anywhere without the right outfit for the job.' She said this as she reached into the boot again and pulled a small suitcase from the back. Without a word of warning, McGuire kicked off her high heels and unbuttoned her shirt. Amos spun, suddenly very interested in the flora and fauna on the opposite side of the road.

'Jesus, Rachel! A bit of warning next time,' he said.

'What? Oh, Amos, don't be a prude. I'm wearing—' she began, and then remembered she wasn't wearing any underwear. A strategic choice or armour for her battle at the office. 'In fact, aye, just keep looking over there.'

A few minutes passed before she gave him the OK to turn around. She had discarded the pencil skirt, high heels, and fitted blouse and was now dressed in black combat trousers, a polo shirt with the word "Police" emblazoned on her left breast, and a pair of black tactical boots to complete the look.

'Do you always travel with a change of clothes in your boot?' he asked.

'Proper previous planning prevents piss poor performance,' McGuire said. The confidence in her voice was not forced this time, and her body language reiterated what her tone implied. *Clothes really do make the man... or woman*, he thought. 'Here,' she said, tossing him two things. 'The mace and the taser. Now, you'll only get one shot out of the taser, so use it wisely.' Amos nodded a thanks.

They left their cars at the side of the road and made

their way down the dirt road on foot, sticking as tight to the tree line as possible. Once the gates of the scrapyard were in sight, they ducked off the road and stumbled their way through the trees. A felled tree, lying at an angle on its taller and stronger neighbour, had given McGuire a relatively easy climb to a vantage point where she could see eighty percent of the scrapyard, unobstructed. Once she was settled on a thick and sturdy branch, she performed another radio check. Amos confirmed with a 'Loud and clear. What do you see?'

'Not much,' McGuire said, panning the binoculars around the yard. 'Wait, OK, I see one Tango on the gate holding what looks like a Russian made AK47.'

'How do you know what a Russian made AK47 looks like?' Amos asked, more than a little surprised.

'I play a lot of Call of Duty.'

'OK,' he said, not entirely sure what she meant, but he didn't think that this was the time to expand his pop culture knowledge. He shook his head and asked, 'What else? Can you see where they're holding Gerry?'

'Not yet,' McGuire said and scanned some more. 'There are a few Tangos at the large cabin on the north side of the yard.'

'How many? Can you see?'

'There's one on the door and another going in and out.'

'Do they have weapons?'

'The floater has an AK but the guy on the door doesn't seem to be armed, from what I see.'

'OK,' he said, gathering his thoughts and calming his mind. 'Four Tangos, possibly all armed.'

'Four?' McGuire asked. 'I only see three.'

'You're forgetting Volkov; he's in there somewhere.

If they've got the big cabin guarded, then I'm guessing that's where Gerry is. Rachel, if this goes sideways, get out of here and do whatever you can to save Mary, please.'

'OK, I promise.'

Without another word, Amos checked the safety of the gun and slipped it into his cargo trousers. He then went to the other pockets to make sure he had everything he needed. Then he flung the baseball bat over his shoulder and skulked through the trees towards the first Tango.

He reached the point where the tree line met the tall stone pillar of the yard entrance and stepped gingerly out of the bush when the radio in his ear burst to life. 'Amos!' McGuire shouted in a whisper. 'The security camera.' He looked up at the camera on the opposite pillar and pointed straight at the intercom.

'Shit!' he spat, then began to circle the perimeter, looking for another way in.

After almost twenty minutes of stumbling over undergrowth and pushing through heavy bushes, he discovered an opening at the far corner of the yard where a tree had snagged the barbed wire fence and pulled it from the ground. The hole looked just about big enough for him to force his way through. A pile of tyres had been stacked three feet from the gap, offering cover from prying eyes. This was a good entry point. He could slip inside and use the tyres as cover as he surveyed the yard. Then he could stealthily move from cover to cover and take out the Tangos one by one, quickly and quietly. Getting into the north cabin may be a bit tricky, and he may need some sort of distraction.

His thoughts were interrupted by the only thing that could destroy his plan of attack.

The large, lean Rottweiler ambled slowly from behind a discarded car seat where it had clearly been sleeping, stretched, and lazily walked past on the other side of the tyre wall. The animal did not notice the armed stranger lurking in the trees beyond the fence. Amos stood stone and held his breath.

Shit.

New plan.

Twenty minutes later, Amos had stumbled his way back to the tree where McGuire was hiding. She clambered her way down, and he explained his new plan.

'I don't like this; it's too risky,' she said.

'I don't like it either, but we don't have much of a choice, do we?'

'We could... I mean... there's always—' She paused for a long moment before heaving a heavy sigh. 'No. No, we don't,' she finally conceded. Amos passed her the baseball bat and disappeared back into the tree line as she quickly made her way back up the long dirt road.

Amos moved quickly this time, and the route back to the gap in the fence at the far side of the scrapyard took him less than fifteen minutes. He felt naked without the bat, even though he still had the pistol, taser, and mace. 'OK, Rachel, I'm in position. Are you ready?' he whispered into the mic clipped to his jacket.

'Not really.' The radio crackled so loudly in his ear that he worried that it might not only give away his position but any element of surprise and therefore jeopardise the mission and their lives. His hand snatched the radio clipped to his belt and adjusted the volume to something more akin to a whisper than a roar.

'What do you mean, not really? How long does it take?' he snapped in a hushed and harassed tone.

'I'm in position, but I don't like the plan. I know we don't have any alternatives; I just wish we had some backup.'

'Aye, me too, but we're all Gerry and Mary have. Now, are you ready?'

A loud sigh crackled in his earpiece, then McGuire finally said, 'OK. I'm ready.'

'Good. Now, light it.'

Back out on the main road, McGuire rolled the small, dark Kia slowly down the dirt road. She aimed it at the tall, corrugated gate of the scrapyard and used a belt to secure the steering wheel in place as best she could. She kicked open the driver's side door, then awkwardly jammed the baseball bat into the accelerator pedal. The small car lunged forward, and she jumped from the car, hitting the ground hard and rolling into the bush. She ambled to her feet and found she had escaped with only a few cuts and scrapes to her hands and arms. She would be limping for a while and would no doubt be stuck wearing trousers to cover the bruises on her legs. Apart from these minor injuries, she was unhurt.

Dusting herself off, she looked up just in time to see the small dark car hit the gate with enough force to buckle it enough to bury its bonnet almost entirely underneath it. The car whined loudly against the buckled fence as the rag stuffed into its fuel tank burned slowly. McGuire could hear panicked shouts and angry barks from beyond the fence. She ducked down and darted as quickly as her limp would allow into the trees and back to the perch she found before, scouring the yard for any sign of Amos. What she saw, though, was two armed Tangos rush their way to the gate to help the third already stationed there. But before either man reached the gate, the burning rag reached the fuel tank. The explosion took the entrance almost to the ground, blew the gate clean from the stone pillars at each side, and knocked the Tango stationed at the gate flat. The guard did not get back up. Whether he was dead or just unconscious was anyone's guess, and McGuire was not entirely sure which she would have preferred. 'OK, Amos, one Tango down. I can see two armed Tangos running towards the gate to help him. You're up.' She drew a deep breath. 'Good luck,' she added.

By the time the car exploded, Amos was already under the fence and had taken up position behind the tyre wall. He watched the two Tangos with AK47s scramble from the cabin on the north side of the yard and darted behind an old, rusted Ford Transit with no tyres or doors. Pressing his back against the van, he shuffled his way to the back and edged his head around the corner. The coast was clear. His heart pounded in his chest, and that familiar rush of adrenaline surged through his whole body. Adrenaline could be useful, but if left unchecked, it could cost the mission. He had seen it happen many times with young soldiers. A couple of deep breaths and a shake of his arms seemed to ease the tension in his body and keep his mind focused. With his body and mind ready, he hunched his head and shoulders, then quickly and silently made his way towards the gate, ducking between various stacks of car parts and junk. He stopped behind a pile of twisted and bent exhaust pipes twenty feet from where the downed AK47 was lying. He stole another glance around the yard. The two AK47s that rushed from the cabin had helped their unconscious comrade to a seated position, but they could not rouse him. One of the AKs made his way towards the reception cabin, thirty yards away on the opposite side from where he was hiding, and disappeared inside. This was his chance. He grabbed a small length of bent pipe from the pile and quietly rushed the AK still trying to rouse the unconscious man. The AK looked up just in time to see the length of pipe come crashing down on his head. The Tango fell to the ground with a thud.

Two Tangos down.

Without stopping, he dived back behind the pile of pipes, hoping to use the same strategy on the second AK when he came to investigate his two comrades. He kept his eyes trained on the reception door, waiting for Tango three to appear.

Then he heard it.

The deep, throaty growl came from behind him. Amos spun to see the bared teeth of the lean, angry Rottweiler. The dog exploded forward, and Amos swung the pipe. The dog's powerful jaws clamped down on the pipe and ripped it clean from his hands. Amos rocked back and kicked the beast with both feet as hard as he could. The kick knocked the dog back, and it struggled to find its feet in the wet mud. Amos scrambled in his pocket. The angry dog ducked its head low and stared unblinkingly at its prey. With its ears tucked back and teeth bared, the animal barked its vicious and dangerous warning before lunging a second time. The powerful jaws snapped inches from his face before the Rottweiler whimpered loudly and dropped to the floor. Amos held the trigger of the taser a second longer before letting go, making sure to stop before the animal stopped breathing. The dog lay still on the muddy ground, its muscles still twitching from the fifteen hundred volts.

Amos stood and took the barbs from the poor dog's

chest. Then McGuire's voice crackled in his ear: 'Amos, duck!' He ducked his head instinctively as three loud cracks sent three bullets whooshing past his head. He dived back behind the pile of pipes while the voice of the third Tango coming from the reception cabin shouted something he could not understand. *Damn, Amos, get your head in the game! That weapon has a ninety-nine percent accuracy up to three hundred metres. You're lucky to be alive!* he scolded himself. Luckily, this meant that the Tango using it was untrained. He crawled his way to the other side of the pile of pipes while the untrained Tango showered the ground with bullets. Amos snuck his head around the corner of the pile to see the AK advance confidently towards where Amos was. He waited. The AK wasn't ducking for cover or reserving ammo.

A few more steps.

Bullets ricocheted off the pipes, buried themselves in the ground, and shot high into the trees. The Tango took one more step towards the pile where Amos was hiding and pulled the trigger again, but only got a quiet click in return. He shook the gun in frustration and fumbled with the magazine. Amos pounced from his spot and lunged forward, swinging the pipe with everything he had and connecting with the last AK's head.

Three Tangos down.

With the element of surprise gone, he made his way directly for the large cabin, scanning the yard with his pistol as he went. 'Rachel, all three Tangos down. I'm making my way to the cabin.'

'OK, Amos. Just be careful.'

'I will. Oh, and Rachel.'

'Yes?'

'Thanks, you saved my life back there.'

He sidled up to the open door of the large cabin. He quickly edged his head around the door frame, stealing a quick glance inside. The room was dark and empty. He swung the pistol through the door, panning to his blind spot first, then stepped softly through the door and scanned back around the rest of the room.

Nothing.

Then he heard muffled moans emanating from behind him. Amos swung; his pistol was trained at chest height. He stepped slowly forward and pushed the door open. Inside, a bruised and bleeding Gerry was strapped to a chair with a giant Slavic hand pressed tightly against his mouth and an even bigger blade against his throat.

'Put da gun down,' Volkov said. His already giant frame seemed even bigger now, towering behind Gerry.

Amos didn't move.

'Put da gun down, or I kill him and then I kill you.' Volkov slid the knife, slicing the skin on Gerry's throat and letting the blood drip down. Gerry winced and moaned.

'OK, OK,' Amos blurted, and held his hands aloft. He lowered slowly and put the gun on the floor.

'Good. Now kick it to me,' Volkov said, in a low, threatening tone. Amos half-heartedly shoved the pistol with his foot, and it came to rest halfway between them. 'I did not want to do this. Gerry is Bratishka, you know? He is like my brother. I owe him a lot for what he has done for me. I love him like family.'

'Is this how you treat all your relatives, Damir?'

'No. But dis is business. And nothing gets in the way of business.'

'You mean you sex trafficking business for Mr B?

'I do not vork for Mr B!' Volkov spat. 'Ve are business partners, ushering in a new era. No longer will rival gangs fight over turf. No more senseless killings over who has the right to sell what and where. I built this business from nothing, and joining with Mr B will create something much bigger. Ve vill share netvorks and resources and be more rich than ever before.'

'You mean you sold out to Mr B, like a little bitch, because you were scared of him?' Amos said.

This infuriated the giant Russian. He took the knife from Gerry's throat, pointed it at Amos, and shouted, 'I am afraid of no man! I am Pakhan! All men fear me.'

'If you say so, Pac-Man. Well, I am Amos Fisher, and I do not fear you.' He stepped forward with his arms raised and beckoned the Russian closer. 'Let's go, fat man. You and me!' he shouted.

Volkov flipped the large knife in his hand so the point was facing down and slammed it into the wall behind him. The knife handle protruded from the wall like a strange hunting trophy, and the giant Russian stepped out from behind the chair where Gerry was bound. 'OK, little man, let's go.'

Amos circled left, forcing the Russian to turn his back to where the gun lay on the floor, hoping to keep it out of his sight and therefore out of his mind. The Russian swung a heavy right hand, but Amos ducked under it and stepped through, and the two men swapped places. Amos kicked at the back of the giant's knee, and the leg collapsed under him. With the large man now on one knee, Amos pivoted and volleyed in the kidney; a blow that would have crumbled any other man. Volkov, however, did not seem to notice. He sprang to his feet with surprising agility, spun and lunged forward. Amos darted left and swung a powerful kick to Volkov's stomach. The man's own mass and momentum had added power and heft to this blow and sent him to his knees once more. He spun just in time for Amos to land a flurry of punches on his face. Amos finished this devastating combo with an uppercut that sent Volkov rocking back. Amos felt the momentum was on his side, so he only took a second to regain his breath and pushed forward, driving the power from his legs up through his hips and twisting his shoulders, focusing all his power into one final hook that would lay his opponent flat.

Or so he thought.

Volkov grabbed the fist mid-flight. The force of the impact sent a painful shudder up Amos's arm and into his shoulder. The Russian's huge, greasy hand clamped down hard on the fist. Volkov rose slowly from his knees and wiped the blood from his mouth with his free hand.

'My turn,' he growled, and swung a hand so large, one could be forgiven for mistaking it as a shovel. It landed across Amos's cheek and sent him to the floor. He bounced back up as quickly as he could, but Volkov clamped his two shovel-sized hands around his throat, lifted him clean off the floor, and slammed him against the wall. The giant held him tight to the wall, and Amos could feel the huge finger dig deeper into his throat. He felt his windpipe closing, and his vision began to blur.

'I did not want it to come to this, Mr Fisher,' Volkov said while squeezing the life from him. 'I like you, truly I do. And I will take no joy in killing Gerry. But... is business.' Just before Amos lost consciousness, he scrambled inside his pocket and found what he was looking for. He whipped the can from his pocket and emptied the mace into the giant Russian's eyes. Volkov screamed in pain and his hands shot to his eyes. Amos dropped to the floor, coughing.

Both men stood defenceless for what seemed like minutes before Volkov's screaming promise to kill him jolted Amos into action. Through teary eyes, Amos stumbled across the floor, picked up the pistol from the floor, and turned to the wounded Russian.

'Hey, friend,' Volkov pleaded, seeing the gun pointed at his head. 'Is only business.'

Amos glanced at Gerry, taking in his swollen face and bloodied mouth. 'No. You hurt my friend. It's personal,' he said, then squeezed the trigger.

Volkov dropped to the floor.

The room went silent.

Amos stared as blood pooled around the lifeless body on the floor. He breathed deep, enjoying the feeling of air in his lungs again and allowing his heart rate to settle again.

'Hey, Buttercup... you done? I mean, I like being tied up and stuff, but I can't feel my fingers.'

Chapter 40

Amos helped Gerry along the long dirt road and into the back seat of the blue Ford Focus, where McGuire was already waiting. 'Jesus Gerry, are you OK?' she gasped, as Amos plumped himself into the driver's seat.

'Never been, urgh, better, Rachel. Why do you ask?' Gerry groaned sarcastically.

'What did they do to you?' she asked, ignoring the quip. Amos turned around to properly assess the full extent of his friend's injuries for the first time. Gerry's left eye was swollen and almost completely closed; his nose had been broken, and the swelling of his mouth did nothing to hide the teeth he was now missing. Bruises were beginning to form on his cheeks, and deep cuts littered both arms.

'Oh, you know, the standard six hour beating before the waterboarding started. And when they got bored with that, the cutting started. The full five-star treatment, really. But it's OK; I'll get my own back. Just wait till they see the review I'm going to leave them on Yelp.' Gerry said, then started to laugh, but a coughing fit brought chest pains and an end to the hilarity.

'Good to see you've still got your sense of humour,' Amos mused.

'If you don't laugh, then you're just letting the bastards win,' Gerry said between coughs.

'OK, someone is going to have to explain this to me,' McGuire interjected. 'I thought you said we could trust this Volkov guy? And if he was working for Mr B, then why did he help us to begin with? Why not just hand us straight over?'

'Damir didn't know what we were doing. He offered to help us because he and I are... I mean, *were* good friends. He didn't know until I broke through the security on Mr B's site on the dark web.'

'What?' Amos said. 'You got in? What did you find? Do you know where Mary is?'

'Hold on, Buttercup, I'm getting there. Remember I told you there was something familiar about the coding on the security protocols?'

'Yes,' he replied, a little unsure where his friend was going with this.

'That's because I wrote it.'

'What?' Amos and McGuire said in unison, both amazed and confused.

'Well not just me. I helped create the protocols about five or six years ago for a school project.'

'A school project?' Amos asked, utterly lost now.

'Yes. I helped Mary write it for a coding competition when she was at high school. It's evolved a good bit since then and is a lot more sophisticated, but the base code is there and unmistakable.'

Amos stared at him blankly. Just like the doctor's, Gerry's words floated in front of him without taking hold. They were separate entities that existed, unconnected to one another.

'Are you saying Mary wrote the code for Mr B, I mean Billy Boyd's website?' McGuire asked, clearly sensing Amos's struggle. Those words he understood. She had come to his rescue, and he was silently thankful.

'Billy Boyd? Is that this maniac's name? Thank God we don't need to call him Mr B anymore. He sounded like a crappy Bond villain. But yes, Mary not only wrote the security protocols, but she also pretty much built the entire network. It's really impressive. I mean, I know we were talking about an insidious underground criminal network here, but that girl did a damn fine job. Leaps and bounds ahead of whatever your lot is capable of,' Gerry said, nodding at McGuire.

'I don't understand,' Amos said. 'Are you saying Mary built a website so this Billy Boyd could traffic girls in and out of the country and sell them for sex? I can't believe she would be a part of something like that.'

'Well, it looks like the network was built a few years ago, but the first log about the trafficking dates back only a couple of months.'

'Wait,' McGuire said. 'That's around the time Mary reached out to me. That must have been why. She found out that Boyd was selling girls and drew the line.'

'But she knew about the drugs,' Amos said. He was more disappointed in himself than anything else. 'Not only did she know, but she also helped create an untraceable criminal empire online.'

'It's a different world than the one we grew up in, mate,' Gerry said. 'Kids don't have the same opportunities we did. When we were younger, we could walk out of a job on Friday and have another one by Monday. The internet and technology have taken over. There aren't a lot of jobs available, so kids have to create their own. That's why being a YouTuber is an actual career path these days. Mary simply saw a gap in the market and filled it. I mean, fair enough, she did it illegally, but she made money. And I can see her point, to be honest. I mean, people who waste their lives on drugs do so of their own accord. It's their choice. But these girls don't want to be sold as sex slaves. She's done you proud on that one, mate.'

'Actually, there may be another reason she reached out to me,' McGuire said. 'It's not really my place to tell you this, Amos, but under the circumstances, I think you should know.' McGuire took a long, slow blink, *probably gathering courage*, Amos thought.

'Spit it out Rachel, we don't have time for dramatics,' he snapped.

'I got Mary's medical report. She's pregnant.'

The words did not hang in the air. They did not sound muffled and distant. They had real substance and meaning. And they hit hard enough to knock the wind from his lungs. He stared at her incredulously. He stared ahead in silence for the longest moment as the weight of the situation pressed down on top of him. His mind raced with a thousand questions all at once, each with their own voice shouting over one another, fighting for dominance in his thoughts.

Calm down Amos. This changes nothing. Stay focused and get her... them back!

'OK, Gerry, any idea where she is?' he finally asked.

'Actually, mate, I do.'

Chapter 41

The drive to Parkhead was not as quiet as it was the first time Amos took McGuire home. The car was a buzz with excited chatter and theories about timelines and who could be involved. She told them about Billy Boyd's connections to the Freemasons and the implications that could have. She filled them in on DCI Clarke's revelation about Superintendent Graham being Boyd's inside man and the reason Boyd has managed to stay one step ahead of the police. She spoke about Boyd's known associates, which included one George Brown. George was an amateur bodybuilder who was banned from competing for life after coming in second place at a competition and assaulting the winner with the trophy. She went on to tell them that George was also admitted to the hospital after overdosing on anabolic steroids, which caused a myocardial infarction, which had stopped his heart for a little over a minute before doctors could revive him.

Gerry spoke mostly in technical jargon that lost both Amos and McGuire. He rambled on and on about how good a teacher he was and that Mary was one of his finest students. He had boasted at Mary's technological prowess for single-handedly building Boyd's entire online empire and that she had, so efficiently, bulletproofed it from any outside attempts to infiltrate or hack the network. The only reason he, Gerry, was able to hack in was because he taught her to always leave a back door open for emergencies. And once he realised who wrote the code, he had a good idea of where to look.

Once inside, Gerry told them he was able to access a list of all transactions made within the three major hubs in Scotland, as well as the names of local sellers. This allowed Boyd to track the buying trends in real time and allocate supply to where the highest demand was. It also listed the names and locations of all the girls being held, as well as which girls were being sold abroad. This is where Amos focused hard.

'There is a shipment due to depart tonight,' Gerry said. 'It's set to leave from the Clyde Boatyard in Clydebank. From there, it will dock in Belfast, then Liverpool, before making its final stop in Amsterdam. Once there, the girls can be shipped all over Europe with no way of tracking them.'

'Great,' McGuire chirped confidently. 'With all that intel, we have him dead to rights. I can call it in and have Boyd arrested, and Mary will be safe.'

'Not so fast there, Buttercup. Like I said, Mary did a fantastic job of covering her tracks. Mr Boyd's name is nowhere near any of this. All the major players in this have been assigned code names. At the top of the food chain, the Colonel of the outfit is "B", who we know is Billy Boyd; no points for creativity on that moniker. Next in command, we have three majors: number one, "The Pakhan", who we now know is Damir Volkov, headed up the eastern European arm of the operation, selling and trafficking girls in and out of the country.

Number two, "Plod", he is B's man inside the police. He feeds any information back to the organisation and torpedoes any investigations and so on.'

'Superintendent Graham,' McGuire offered.

'Right,' Gerry agreed. 'And last, but not least, we have "The Red Hand." There hasn't been any movement on this account yet. It looks like this is a new faction of the gang, and no transactions have taken place yet. From what I can gather, this "Red Hand" will be Boyd's arms dealer. He'll be selling weapons and shipping them in and out of the country.'

'The Red Hand? Is that a Northern Ireland connection there?' Amos asked.

'Possibly. They could be looking to restart the troubles in Ireland, for all we know.'

'Wait! What?' McGuire shouted. 'Weapons? This just became a whole new thing.'

'My thoughts exactly. Now, we could hand this over to the police, but *if* you make any arrests and *if* you manage to make one of the small-time dealers talk, which I highly doubt you could, it would be far too late. Mary will have been shipped out of the country or worse.'

'He's right,' Amos added. 'We've got to deal with this ourselves. We don't have time to get the police involved, *and* we don't know who we could trust anyway. Graham may be one of many.'

'So, what's the plan then?' she asked.

'I'm taking you home, then I go get my daughter,' he replied sternly.

'What?' McGuire screamed 'No! Not a chance, Amos. You're going to need help. You can't do this alone. Tell him Gerry.'

Gerry looked at her with his one good eye and swallowed the blood collecting in his mouth. 'Normally, I'd agree with you one hundred percent. I would not let him go it alone under any circumstances. But I've been strapped to a chair for the past eight hours and tortured within an inch of my life. At this point, I'm more likely to get him killed.'

'Then tell him not to go. He can't do this by himself.'

Gerry laughed, then groaned at the pain it caused.

'Aw, Buttercup, Amos Fisher is the most stubborn, pig-headed, single-minded arsehole you will ever meet. If he has made his mind up, there is absolutely nothing you or I can do to stop him. There has only ever been one person on this planet who has ever managed it, and that wonderful woman passed away yesterday morning.'

Amos's hands gripped tighter on the wheel, turning his knuckles white. He gave a low guttural grunt and swallowed hard, pushing the lump back down his throat.

'So, did you find out what was on the phone, and can we use it to nail this prick?' Amos growled.

'Oh, aye, the phone,' Gerry said, clearly picking up on his friend's need to change the subject. 'I almost forgot about that. As far as I can tell, the phone is the key, or at least part of the key. The laptop detailed large amounts of cash flow coming and going from various offshore bank accounts but did not have any specific details about which accounts. I'm guessing that the file vault on the phone has the details of the transactions and, hopefully, the names of all the top players. I'm telling you, guys, crack that file vault, and you can put Mr Boyd and his bigoted, catholic hating, silly handshaking, shower of inbred wanker pals in prison.'

'Got something against the Freemasons, Mr O'Hara?' McGuire asked in a somewhat surprised tone and was clearly taken aback by the outburst.

'I'm a gay Catholic. What do you think, lady?' Gerry replied with as much sarcasm as his swollen face and missing teeth would permit.

'How do I open the vault, Gerry?' Amos asked, deliberately breaking the tension in the car.

'Right, aye, well, the vault works on a basic RFID system, or radio frequency identification. This refers to a wireless system comprised of two basic components, the tag and reader.'

Amos interrupted, 'Gerry! Let's pretend that I didn't spend ten years in the army intelligence division and explain it like you would to a standard Tommy.'

'Tommy?' McGuire asked.

'Standard infantry soldier,' Gerry explained. 'Not exactly the sharpest knives in the drawer. Probably a term frowned upon in your modern-day armed forces, but we're old soldiers.' Gerry turned back to Amos and continued. 'Basically, one phone is the key, and the other is the lock. Get both phones in close proximity, and the vault opens. Simple.'

'Well, other than the fact that I need to get the personal mobile phone from a murderous psychopath, it's a doddle. How do you expect me to get the phone, Gerry? Ask politely?'

'Hey, the execution is your bit; I've done the hard work for you already.'

'Gee, thanks,' Amos said sarcastically.

'No problem, Buttercup,' Gerry replied sincerely.

Amos pulled the car into the same empty spot across from the school he had used the first time he dropped McGuire off. The time on the Ford's dashboard showed 10 pm. The school had been abandoned long ago, and the playground lay deserted. McGuire stepped out of the car first and helped Gerry to his feet. He rolled the passenger window down and called out, 'Rachel.'

'Yes?' she replied, holding Gerry steady.

'I need the phone.'

McGuire nodded. 'I'll be back in a minute.'

Gerry draped his arm around her shoulders and the two shuffled awkwardly inside.

Quiet settled in the car for the first time since his "episode" at the petrol station. He could not deny it any longer. The attacks were getting more frequent. He had managed to lie to himself quite convincingly while Sophia was ill, but now that she was gone, he was going to have to face the truth sooner or later. He just had to get Mary back first. Then he would do what his late wife had begged him so many times to do and go for the scans. The scans he had avoided for so long because he knew what they would tell him. He knew they would have nothing good to say. He could feel the truth lingering in the distance. He could feel its maniacal eyes watching his every move and hear its blood-curdling breath whisper undeniable facts.

Not yet. Not while he still had a job to do. Not while he still had a child, and now a grandchild to save. His thoughts drifted toward the baby. He longed to see it born. He ached to see it grow and shower it with the love and affection he struggled to show his own daughter. That thought stabbed him hard. Guilt flooded him now. *I'm sorry, Peanut. I didn't know how to love you, and that was my fault. I learned to listen too late, and I'm sorry.*

'Here you go.'

He snapped his head around to see McGuire handing him the phone through the open window. Shaking off his daze, he reached out and took the phone, then stashed it in his jacket pocket.

'Are you OK?' she asked.

'Aye,' he lied, 'I'm fine. Thanks for that,' he said, patting the pocket where the phone now sat.

'No problem. You sure you're OK?'

'Aye, I'm fine. Just take care of Gerry. I'll be back

once I've got Mary, then we'll figure out our next move.'

McGuire nodded and hobbled back towards her house. Amos watched her limp and thought of Gerry and the torture he had endured because of him. No more. This ends now. He jammed the Ford into gear and slammed his foot hard on the accelerator. Anger had taken over now. It was driving his every thought and emotion. Rage turned the wheel sharply and gunned the accelerator once more as the loud and obnoxious Ford barrelled along the road.

Chapter 42

Amos found himself parked outside the gate of the Clyde Boatyard for the second time. This was the same boatyard where McGuire arranged to meet him when he knew her simply as "Beth". The abandoned windowless and tyreless car sat unmoved in the empty car park opposite the boatyard gate. The closest streetlight was too far away to cast any useable light on the yard's entrance, and the road was unused at this time of night. He parked in the darkest corner of the car park, opposite the vandalised car shell, stashed the phone in the glove compartment, and checked the ammo of the pistol. Half a clip and one in the chamber — *it'll have to do*. He was hoping not to use any of the rounds anyway. Stealth was the plan.

The dirt road, which was lit only by the soft glow of the full moon, was difficult by foot, but the dark offered perfect cover. He kept low and shuffled along the main access road as quickly as possible. He stopped at the last warehouse, which overlooked the marina, and tucked himself inside the open door, which was hanging by a single hinge. From this foxhole, he could survey the whole marina and the approaching road without being seen.

The boat was already docked, and he could see three Tangos busying themselves on deck, shouting instructions to each other in a language he couldn't understand. There was no sign of any girls. Was he too late? *Had they already been loaded, and the crew were making their final preparations to ship off?*

No sooner had he asked himself these questions when a heavy box truck rumbled along the dirt road and slowed to a stop between his foxhole and the docked ship. The passenger door swung open, and a bald, stocky man stepped from the van, calling instructions back to the driver. Baldy then slammed the door, walked around the front of the cabin, and headed for the docked boat. Amos crouched forward and readied himself.

Wait for it.

A moment later, he heard the driver's door slam. Amos watched and waited. He listened hard as the sound of incoherent mumblings grew closer. A small, dark figure then emerged from the far corner of the truck. The red glow from the Tango's cigarette did little to expose his features in the dark. With another exasperated grumble, the cigarette man threw his smoke to the ground and stamped it out with his heel. Then, Cigarette Man looked straight at him.

Amos froze. He held his breath.

Cigarette Man blew the last of the smoke from his lungs, then turned to face the docked boat, turning his back to the foxhole and Amos. Amos took this opportunity and sprang silently from his hiding spot. Cigarette Man shouted something in Latvian, or Russian, or another eastern European language to his comrades on the ship as they edged back towards the truck's roller shutter. He looked at the sky and gave another quiet groan to himself.

This is when Amos struck.

A rear naked choke hold, if done correctly, will knock the average adult male out in under twelve seconds, and Cigarette Man was no exception. His body went limp with three seconds to spare. However, letting go at this point would ensure he regained consciousness just as quickly. Amos held on for a few minutes longer. This would keep the cigarette-smoking Tango sleeping for a lot longer, but there was a danger of permanent damage.

He didn't care. His daughter was inside the truck, and this prick helped put her there. He stopped himself before the Tango stopped breathing completely, although he was unsure the arsehole deserved to live. Amos quickly stole a glance at the ship. No alert had been raised, and the men shuffled on deck just as before.

Good.

He sidled to the roller shutter door and hoisted himself onto the rear foot shelf. 'Mary,' he started, as he twisted the T-handle and yanked the roller shutter upwards. 'It's me; are you in—' The roller shutter just cleared his head when something hard shot from the darkness of the truck's cargo hold and smashed into his nose. Amos tumbled backwards onto the ground and tasted blood in his mouth. Dazed and in pain, he blinked the glaze from his eyes just in time to see the same hard something crashing down onto his head again.

And for the third time, everything went black.

Chapter 43

Ice water hit his face with the force of a nine-millimetre parabellum round hitting an army-issued body armour at point blank range. This was a sensation Amos was all too familiar with, although it happened only once in his entire military career.

Amos and a team of Royal Marines, were securing a small village three miles outside Al-Fallujah. The building, which was to be converted into weapons storage for the forward post, had not been cleared by the Marines properly. He had stepped into the small room at the back and was shot in the chest by a panicked woman trying to protect her daughter. Although the broken ribs and the bruising healed, the experience has stayed with him ever since. One frightened mother, armed with nothing more than a 9mm pistol she didn't know how to use, was prepared to lay her life on the line, taking on a patrol of highly trained Royal Marines and a Royal Engineer, to protect her child.

You can beat me. You can torture me. You can take everything I have and leave me for dead with nothing but my thoughts to console me as death nears. But lay one finger on my child, and I will not stop until I see the life drain from your eyes. And there is nothing you can do to stop me.

The ice water stole whatever air was in his lungs and left him gasping. He frantically searched around the dark space for a clue as to where he was and who was holding the icy water. But his bleary eyes saw nothing beyond the circle of light cast around his chair by the pendulum light hanging from the high ceiling. He tried to spin but found his hands were tied behind his back and his legs were tied to the chair. Another rope, lashed around his chest, secured him to the back of the chair and held him in place. He pulled at the restraints, but his hands didn't budge. The sound of his grunts reverberated in the large, empty space.

'Calm down there, Mr Fisher; you'll do yourself an injury.' The thick Northern Irish accent echoed from behind. Amos strained his neck to find the source, but was unsuccessful. 'I hear you've been giving my friend a bit of a bother now.' The voice moved slowly to the right, circling him like a predator enjoying the hunt.

'Who are you?' Amos asked, blinking the last of the cold water from his eyes and straining at the shadow that now stood in front of him.

'Ah, come now, Mr Fisher, let's not play funny buggers. You know exactly who I am.'

'The Red Hand?'

The voice in the darkness scoffed. 'Aye,' he finally said. 'A bit of a stupid name, to be honest. It makes me sound like some kind of Bond villain. I blame all these stupid superhero movies for filling this generation's heads with stupid ideas like secret identities and stuff. But, aye, Amos, I'm the Red Hand.'

'Look, I don't know who you are, and I don't care. I just want my daughter back. That's all.'

'Now, that's not entirely true now, is it Amos?'

'What?'

'I said it before, you know exactly who I am. We've met before.' The Irishman stepped forward into the halo of light surrounding Amos's seat. He stood six foot tall and wore a faded brown leather jacket which hung open, exposing a blue checked shirt and blue jeans. 'In fact,' he continued. 'You gave me this scar.' The figure bent close and drew his finger along his face where a deep angry scar stretched from the inside corner of his left eye, along his cheek towards his ear. 'That was a while ago, I'll grant you, but surely you haven't forgotten me, Captain Fisher?' he said, stepping back into the gloom.

'Sean O'Neil?' Amos gasped.

'Ah, so you haven't forgotten me after all? Good lad.'

'I thought you were dead. The IRA bombed your car back in ninety-six?' This revelation almost stole as much air from him as the cold water had.

'Aye, they tried, but the stupid Fenian bastards blew up the wrong guy. I tell you, Amos, you want a job done right, don't ask a Catholic to do it.'

'Last time we met, you were smuggling guns for the Ulster Volunteer Forces. Now, almost thirty years later, you're doing the same thing, taking orders from Billy Boyd?'

'I was a soldier in the UVF!' O'Neil screamed and lunged out of the shadows, slamming his fist into Amos's cheek and snapping his head to the right. He spit the blood gathering in his mouth onto the floor and turned back to the Irishman. 'And I still am,' O'Neil continued in a softer tone. 'The fighting never stopped, Captain Fisher. The Good Friday agreement changed nothing. And I take orders from no one. I'm just serving the cause in a different way now.'

'By being a bitch to a two-bit drug dealer who's too young to even understand your "cause"?' This quip earned him another punch. This time, it split his lip.

'Brother Boyd understands the cause very well, actually. This partnership is worth a lot of money, and it will help us finally bring about a United Ireland.'

'You're insane, O'Neil, but I honestly couldn't care. Just give me my daughter, and you can do whatever you want.'

'What are you talking about? I have no idea where your daughter is.'

'She's one of the girls on the truck. You can do what you want with the others, I just want Mary.'

'There weren't any girls on the truck. Only weapons. And you're going nowhere until we settle this little score.' O'Neil traced his finger along his scar again. 'You gave me this little beauty last time we met. Do you remember?'

'I remember you had a teenage girl strapped to a bed, and she was screaming at you to stop. I remember you and your shit eating pal taking turns, you sick bastard.'

'She was a casualty of war! The little Catholic whore.' O'Neil stepped closer and kneeled so that he was staring Amos dead in the eyes. 'And then you shot me in the face,' he whispered.

'And the only reason you're not dead is because your rapist pal blindsided me as I was pulling the trigger,' Amos barked as he lunged forward; his forehead connected perfectly with the Irishman's nose, sending him reeling backwards.

'Argh, you bastard!' O'Neil shouted. Amos pulled frantically at the ropes, but there was no give. Then he heard it. The distinct sound of metal sliding against metal and the click signifying a round had entered the chamber. Amos stopped and looked up to see the pistol emerge in black and come to a stop in front of his eyes. 'Now, you die, Captain Fisher.'

'Wait!' A voice boomed from somewhere in the darkness.

'What? Who's there?' the Irishman called.

'We need him alive, for now,' the voice said.

'Plod? Is that you?'

The voice gave an irritated sigh. 'I hate that name.'

'Would you rather I called you—'

The voice interrupted, 'Don't use my real name in front of witnesses.'

'What does it matter, dead men tell no tales.'

'I don't care. No names.'

'Whatever you say, Plod.'

'Graham!' Amos called. 'Graham, you don't need to do this. You can walk away from all of this. Just give me back my daughter. I won't tell anyone you're involved.' The pistol dropped from his face as the Irishman looked into the void behind his shoulder and shrugged.

'Can I kill him now?' O'Neil asked.

'Do you have the phone?' the voice replied. 'Or the girl?'

'No, he didn't have the phone on him,' the Irishman replied. 'The girl? Have you lost the girl?'

'Wait.' Amos panicked. 'Are you talking about Mary? You don't have her? Where is my daughter, Graham?'

'Where is the phone?' Plod asked.

'Somewhere safe. Give me my daughter, and you'll get your phone.'

'That's not how this is going to work, Mr Fisher. You give us the phone, and we'll make it quick. Mess me around, and Mr O'Neil here will take his time killing you and your daughter.'

'Touch my daughter, you wanker and—'

The butt of O'Neil's pistol smashing into his temple interrupted Amos's threat to the policeman. He blinked and focused on the Irishman just as the second blow broke his nose. O'Neil disappeared into the darkness for a moment, then reappeared without his gun or jacket, and the sleeves of his checked shirt were now rolled up to his elbows. 'I believe the man asked you a question,' he said, then drove his fist hard into Amos's gut. Amos fought to catch his breath.

'That the best you've got,' he finally grunted. The Irishman pulled his hand back, readying for another blow, when the sound of an electronic ringing shrilled through the large open space.

'Speak,' he heard Graham say from behind him. 'Yes.'

Amos watched as the Irishman stopped his swing and stared over him into the darkness, and waited.

'I see,' Graham continued. 'One hour.'

'Well?' O'Neil asked. 'Who was that?'

'It's the girl. She has the phone and wants to meet. Bring Mr Fisher.'

Amos recoiled. The phone was in the glove box of the car, which was parked outside the boatyard. How could Mary have it? How did she get away from that psychopath? Where is she now?

'Why?' O'Neil asked.

'Leverage.'

'Let's go,' Graham ordered. O'Neil loosened the ropes around Amos's chest and feet, then yanked him from the chair.

'Walk,' O'Neil said, pushing Amos towards the open door at the far corner of the room. The cold night air bit at his wet skin. He looked left and right to get his bearings. To his surprise, he saw the boat still docked in the marina. He was still in the boatyard and had just been led out of the same building he was using as cover to spy on the truck when it arrived. That means that the car should still be parked in the car park outside the boatyard's entrance, and whoever was on that phone was lying.

Mary, if that was you, I hope you know what you're doing.

The Irishman shoved him again, pushing Amos towards the now empty box van that was still parked between the abandoned warehouse and the docked boat. The roller door was fully open, and a guard, the same one who knocked him out, stood waiting on the rear foothold. The guard reached down and grabbed the shoulder of Amos's jacket. This steadied him as he stepped onto the back of the truck, and then the guard threw him inside. With his hands still tied behind his back, Amos had no way to soften his landing and fell hard on his face. Pain radiated from his nose and down through his whole body. The roller shutter came down, entombing him in darkness again.

The thick, distinctive odour of fermented fruit mixed with motor oil, which seemed to ooze from the truck floor, stirred a distant memory in him. It was the smell of gun oil left behind by the weapons that occupied the space that Amos now found himself in. He used the corner of the cargo hold to scramble to a semi-comfortable seated position. It wasn't exactly his comfortable leather armchair from his study at home, but at least his broken nose wasn't pressed into the floor anymore.

He closed his eyes and pictured the evidence wall in his mind once more. A picture of the giant Russian, Damir Volkov, with the note "Human Trafficker" had been added and crossed out. A picture of Sean O'Neil had been added with the note "Arms Dealer" underneath.

Another card with Superintendent Graham had been added with the note "Police Informant," although this had no picture attached to it, just a faceless shape. He turned his attention to the centre of the diagram, where the other pictureless card of Billy Boyd hung.

The shadow of an answer loomed again in the back of his mind. Something about the name was significant. Someone had said something he'd missed. Something important. The thought niggled at him. He focused hard. His mind fought back. He could feel the pressure and exhaustion assaulting his cognition. The thought that was planted was now being suffocated and drowned, but he could not let up. He had given his mind the time and space to work on the problem, and it had come up with nothing. He needed the answer that loomed in the shadows of his damaged brain. *It's there*; he could feel it. His mind flashed to George again. *What was it he said when he broke into my house? "Hey, old man. Remember me?"* This meant something and he missed it. But what? If he could just focus a little harder. He needed answers, and time was rapidly running out. He was locked in the back of a van, being escorted to God knows where. To be killed at the hands of a psychopath.

Wait.

A psychopath.

That's it.

The smile. The stare. The drink.

The figure stepped from the shadows and into the forefront of his mind. A grin spread across his face. *I know who you are, Billy Boyd. It might have taken me a while, but given enough time, I can still solve any problem.* He finally tacked a face onto the blank card with the name Billy Boyd.

All that was left now was to figure out who the girl on the other end of the phone call with Graham was and how she had the phone. He had just set his mind on working that mystery out when the truck banked right, sending him rocking and something on the floor sliding. The sound snapped him out of his thoughts. He leaned forward and strained his eyes in the darkness. The truck banked, which sent it sliding again. Amos pounced to his knees and shuffled towards the sound. He shuffled forward, struggling to keep his balance with the swaying of the truck. The thing touched his knees. Amos stopped and swivelled onto his bum. His hands searched blindly for the object. Finally, his fingers nestled into the familiar ridges of the Smith & Wesson tactical blade. O'Neil found the pistol, but somehow missed the knife. He must be slipping in his advanced years. *Old age doesn't come by itself*, Amos thought and allowed himself a grin. He flipped the blade free from the handle and tried to cut the rope from his wrists, but the angle was too awkward. He did not have the mobility of his youth and lacked the dexterity required. *Old age doesn't come by itself,* he thought again, but this time without the grin.

Chapter 44

Three months after the attack in the car park of the abandoned factory, the first episode happened. Being a patient had not felt natural to Amos. Phrases like "take it easy" and "don't strain yourself" did not sit well with the old soldier. A soldier's instinct was to keep moving. It was drilled deep into their psyches until it became second nature. Staying still, especially in combat, invites death or worse. Momentum meant survival. Every good soldier knew this, and Amos was a very good soldier.

He had pushed himself past what the doctors advised and achieved more than they expected, quicker than they expected. He even threw himself headfirst back into his work. As the doctors explained, however, the combination of the intense physical strain he put himself through and the level of stress he put his mind through when working on the complex calculations his work required was all too much. The first seizure happened while he was working alone in his study. Sandy, the golden retriever, was curled on the rug, basking in the warmth of the midday sun pouring through the patio windows. Amos scribbled furiously at his desk. The numbers weren't flowing like they used to. Numbers were easy; they were logical. Two plus two always equals four, no matter what. That was why he liked them. Numbers did not add differently, changing their answers depending on their mood, or divide in a new way because they watched a documentary, and now they're vegan. Numbers were emotionless and consistent.

At least, they were.

Now they seemed aloof and awkward. They did not

speak to him as easily as they used to. Fog clouded his mind, and thoughts became muggy, thick, and sticky. They shuddered, jumped, and sometimes stopped completely. *Mind over matter, Sapper! Push through.* He concentrated hard on the numbers on the page. His brain was tired, but this was a fight he had to win.

There was no way for Amos to know how long he had been lying on the floor when Sandy's wet tongue licked at his face. The last thing he remembered was sitting at his desk, staring at a page of numbers. He pushed the dog away and lay motionless on the floor, gathering his thoughts and getting his bearings. He was still in his office. The sun was still shining, although its intensity had faded, and the glow was turning from bright yellow to a more orange hue. The dog returned, licking his face once more and whining with concern. 'I'm OK, Sandy. I'm OK,' Amos spluttered, as he pushed the dog away again and struggled to his feet. He reached for the desk, gripping on for balance as he shimmied along to his chair. His legs were weak, and he could taste copper in his mouth. As Amos let his mind go blank and tried to relax, he heard the door connecting the kitchen and garage swing closed.

'Amos, you home?' Sophia called.

'In here,' he replied hoarsely. The study door eased open, and his wife's soft features peeked in.

'You OK? You don't sound well.'

He explained what had happened and, despite his protests, Sophia immediately called the doctor and booked an appointment.

Amos was expecting a dark room with a light box hung on the wall with sheets of X-ray film slid into clips along its upper edge. He expected grainy black-and-white images showing very little detail and a tired old man spouting indecipherable jargon. He was wrong. The room was bright, crisp, and sterile, with two small potted plants decorating the corners of the long windowsill. The computer screen that displayed his scan was mounted onto a tall arm that hinged in the centre and swivelled left and right. And the doctor was a young, attractive woman with impossibly white teeth and thick brown hair that hung loose at her shoulders. She oozed a charismatic charm and energy that instantly disarmed him and made him feel a little more comfortable than he usually did in hospitals. The image on the screen was nothing like the black-and-white, rudimentary scans he had seen when he was still in uniform. These images were ultra-high-definition, ultra-high-resolution, three-dimensional models that allowed the doctor to peel Amos's brain apart layer by layer. This was revolutionary. It was amazing. It was fascinating. He was lost in the wonder of the technology when he realised that both the doctor and his wife were speaking to him.

'Amos,' Sophia called in a worried tone that told him that this was not the first time she tried to get his attention.

'Yes?' he replied, trying to focus on her words.

'Did you hear what the doctor said?'

'Sorry, doctor, I was distracted. You were saying?'

The young doctor smiled and nodded to Sophia. 'I was saying, Mr Fisher, that the head trauma you suffered to your right hemisphere has also created small tumours, known as gliomas, within the hippocampus and amygdala. Often, a person with this condition develops a form of temporal lobe epilepsy.' She may not have been a tired old man, but her words were just as alien. The word "tumour" had sent his brain into a downward spiral, and he became lost. Sophia, clearly picking up on his confusion, stepped in. 'Tumours? You mean like cancer?'

'It's not that simple. These growths don't seem to be malignant, which is good, but we need to monitor them very closely. Each seizure could cause even more damage and cause the tumours to become cancerous.'

'So, what does that mean, exactly?' she asked. 'Will he have more of these seizures? Are they life threatening?'

'If the condition is monitored properly and we can manage the number of stressors in Mr Fisher's life, we can try to minimise the risk of further episodes.'

'What kind of stressors?' Sophia asked while Amos watched the two go back and forth, passionately exchanging words like two characters from a telenovela. Amos couldn't speak Spanish, and he couldn't understand these two ladies either.

'So,' Sophia said, patting his hands and bringing him into the moment. 'If we reduce the amount of stress in his life, regulate his diet, and make sure he doesn't get any more blows to the head, the seizures should be manageable?'

'Exactly,' the young attractive doctor said.

'Great,' Sophia smiled. 'Shouldn't be too hard, eh, Amos?'

'It's very important we reduce the stress in your life as much as possible, Mr Fisher.' The doctor continued, her tone becoming much more serious. 'Any further seizures could create more damage to the brain. This could lead to increased memory loss and mood swings and, in some cases, prove fatal.

The doctor's words hit Amos like raindrops on an

umbrella. He could hear their pitter-patter but was kept dry beneath his protective shield. Sophia's sharp gasp was his first clue that the doctor's words were not welcome ones. He reached for his wife's hand and searched her eyes for some meaning. He saw only fear. Sophia patted the back of his hand, and he could see her choke back her tears. He smiled his best, reassuring smile.

'It's OK. Everything is going to be fine,' he said, without really knowing if that was true. Truth didn't matter in that moment; only Sophia did, and she needed him to be strong. So, he was strong.

Chapter 45

The box truck ground to a stop, and Amos was sent tumbling into the truck's bulkhead. His cheek hit the wall, and pain from his nose, which had just dulled, exploded through his face again. Amos grimaced and choked back a groan. The truck rocked left to right, then two loud bangs echoed as the cabin doors were slammed shut. Amos pressed his back against the bulkhead, pushed himself to his feet, and focused on the roller shutter.

The shutter did not open.

Amos held his breath and listened. Three voices began, low and muffled, muttering back and forth at the roller shutter. He strained to hear, but he could not make out what the hushed voices said. He edged closer, closing his eyes and robbing himself of sight in an attempt to heighten his other senses. The voices grew louder but were still indecipherable. He sidled closer again and crouched low.

'What do you mean—' he heard one voice say before it dropped to a mumble again. A second voice replied, but he couldn't make any words out.

'I was told—' the third voice shouted, but Amos couldn't hear the rest.

'Sick of his shit!' voice one shouted. Voice two mumbled another low and lengthy reply before Amos heard voice one and three grumble incoherently.

A minute later, another loud bang shook the truck, and the engine coughed back to life. The truck lurched forward, and Amos found himself pressed nose first into the floor again. The truck trundled on, turning left and right at seemingly random intervals. Amos closed his eyes and tried to map Glasgow out in his mind, but he could not begin to guess where exactly he was or who was now driving. He was too tired to think. Voices one and three, who Amos had guessed were O'Neil and Graham, sounded pissed. But voice two sounded calm and collected. His tone, although distorted through the truck's walls, sounded vaguely familiar.

Fifteen minutes later, the heavy truck slowed gently to a stop. The truck swayed again as the driver stepped from the cabin and slammed the door closed. Heavy footsteps trudged the length of the cargo hold and stopped at the shutter door. Amos stood and readied himself. He heard the handle pivot and the metal bolt slide from its catch. The shutter door rolled noisily upwards, revealing a single dark figure.

The dim glow of a nearby streetlight cast an awkward shadow on the figure. Amos stared, incredulous. His mind was barely able to process what he was seeing. He felt his heart skip a beat, or maybe it beat twice as fast; he couldn't tell. Tiredness drained him now, and exhaustion had robbed him of his keen wit. He was beginning to feel the familiar fog creeping from the peripherals, suffocating his reasoning, but he didn't care.

It can't be you; it's impossible, Amos thought, but did not fight the confusion. He relished the mirage and willed it to stay. 'Sophia?' He said it in a hushed whisper, as though anything louder would chase the image away. He felt his eyes swell, and this time he did not fight it. As he blinked his vision clear, a single droplet slipped down his cheek.

'Dad! Dad, it's me. It's Mary.'

Amos stumbled forward. 'Sophia,' he said, his voice breaking. 'Sophia, please don't go! I can't do this without you. I need you, please.'

'Dad!' Mary cried. 'George, help me! Something's wrong.' George Brown appeared at Mary's side and effortlessly hoisted her into the truck, then climbed in after. Amos didn't notice the gorilla-sized man standing at his daughter's side. He was transfixed by the vision of his dead wife standing in front of him.

Mary rushed to her father and grabbed him tight, while George loosened the ropes from Amos's wrists. 'Dad, it's Mary!' she yelled fearfully.

The words seemed to blow the fog from his mind, bringing him sharply into the moment. He stared hard as his wife's face melted into his daughter's. 'Mary?' he sighed, as he held her face to inspect it more closely. 'Mary!' He threw his arms around her and held her as tightly as he could for the longest moment.

Finally, he held her at arm's length. 'Peanut, are you OK? Are you hurt?'

Mary sighed a heavy, grateful sigh and said 'No, Dad, I'm fine.' A nervous laugh caught her words.

'My God, Peanut, I'm so... so... so... sooo—'

'Dad!' Mary cried, she lunged forward, trying to catch her father as he began to drop to the floor. George sprang and grabbed him from behind, lowering him softly. Mary and George then stood and helplessly watched Amos have a seizure on the floor of the box truck.

Chapter 46

After thirty minutes, Amos was awake but groggy. The seizure had only lasted a few minutes, although it seemed a lot longer to Mary. Her mother had secretly told her about Amos's tumours. He had refused to tell Mary himself and did not want to put that kind of burden on his daughter. *Dad was clever, but mum was wise.* Where her father excelled in intellect, confidence, and leadership, he lacked compassion, empathy, and, sometimes, common sense. It seemed he spent so much time and energy developing his mind, body, and personality becoming a good soldier that his social and personal skills were left largely undeveloped. A choice her father never seemed to regret. She had admired it in him when she was a little girl. Her brave soldier dad was her world. Fearless. Strong. Powerful.

But as she began to grow older, and the pressures of the modern world crushed down on her as a young and impressionable teen, she began to feel lost. Images of impossibly beautiful people were paraded endlessly on Instagram, Facebook, and a plethora of other platforms designed to let glamorous people boast about their glamorous lives. The ever-changing social landscapes made it difficult for her to get to know the person she was becoming and instead thrust her this way and that, showing her the person society said she should be.

When the pressure became too much, she retreated into herself and shut down. Sophia, naturally, detected this change in Mary and consoled and comforted her. Her mother was always warm and caring. Ready to forgive anything. But Mary only ever found disappointment in her father's eyes. And she hated him for that.

Watching her father now, resting against the truck's headboard, she did not feel hatred. The terror she felt when she watched her father convulse had also passed, although the trembling hands remained, so maybe the fear had not fully gone away. Sympathy, regret, and pity were now settling in. She shook her head and rubbed her eyes with the palms of her hands, as though to wipe these emotions away. She could not let her father see pity in her eyes. He would hate that.

She kneeled by his side and took his hands. 'You OK, Dad?'

Amos looked deep into his daughter's eyes. She saw no judgement or shame, only the swell of a tear, which he quickly disposed of. 'I'm fine, Peanut. Are you OK? Did they hurt you?' he said, searching her face and arms.

'I'm OK, Dad, honestly.'

Finished with his inspection, his attention turned to the large man. 'OK, asshole, let her go. I've got the phone, not her. You don't need her anymore.'

'No, Dad, you don't understand,' Mary said as she stood and took George's hand. 'This is George, he helped me escape. He a good guy.'

'A good guy?' Amos spat as he struggled to his feet. 'Mary, this... this... goddamn ape kidnapped you, knocked me out, gave you to that maniac, and he killed my dog!' he yelled as he began to lunge forward, but Mary held him back.

'I know, Dad, but he also got me out. He brought me back. He saved me.'

'Why? Huh? Out of the goodness of his heart?' Amos lunged forward again, but Mary held him fast. She knew the only reason she could was that he was still weak from the seizure.

'Mr Fisher,' George started as he raised his hands in a surrendering gesture. 'I regret our encounter yesterday. It was not my intention to hurt you or your dog. My colleague, well, ex-colleague now, and I were sent to retrieve both the phone and your daughter. We failed spectacularly and left a bigger mess than we intended. And for that, I humbly apologise. The uncomfortable truth of the matter is that I am in love with your daughter. And when I learned that Mr B, I mean Boydie, was planning on shipping her abroad with the other girls, I stepped in. I could not allow Mary to be harmed. I know asking for your forgiveness would be an exercise in futility, and you would be justified in denying it. So, I will not ask. I will simply offer my sincerest apology and accept your condemnation.'

Mary felt the muscles in her father's chest soften and saw his fists unclench. He looked at George, then at her, then back at Geroge. 'You got her out?' he finally asked.

'Yes, Dad, he did. And he's put himself on Boydie's shit list doing it, so cut him a bit of slack, please.'

'Watch your language Peanut,' he chastised her out of habit.

'Sorry, Dad,' she replied, for the same reason, before they both realised the absurdity of the exchange. They laughed a laugh that seemed to vent all their tension, nerves, and fear in one go, then hugged each other as tight as they could for as long as they could.

Despite their tensions and despite their troubles, in her father's arms was where Mary had felt the safest. *I guess I'm still a little bit of a daddy's girl,* she thought, although she knew she probably would never admit it to him.

After a long moment, Amos held his daughter at arm's

length and turned to George, as though a thought had just urgently struck him. 'What about O'Neil and Graham?'

'Who?'

'The two guys that were in the truck? The ones bringing me to Boydie?'

'Ah, Plod and the Red Hand? I made a phone call and told them to bring you here. I told them that plans had changed and that Boydie wanted to meet them at his office,' George said.

'Right, so if you go back, you're dead?'

'Pretty much.'

'OK then. Well, now that you're safe,' Amos said, turning back to Mary, 'we can take what we know to the police.'

'No, Dad, the police are on Boydie's pay roll!' Mary cried.

'Not all of them. I've been working with the same policewoman you were working with.'

'Beth?' Mary said, surprised.

'Actually, her name is Rachel McGuire. She's held up somewhere safe with your Uncle Gerry. Let's go get your phone and regroup with them. Then, we'll plan our next move.'

Amos and Mary sat, holding each other's hands in the passenger seats of the box truck, while George drove. Mary could see something playing on her father's mind, and she knew from experience that, without prompting, it would stay there and fester.

'What's wrong?' she asked, leaning close and touching the back of his hand softly. He shifted in his seat and took a deep breath.

'I'm so sorry, Peanut. I was never a good father to you. I tried to treat you like a soldier, and you're not. You are my daughter and you deserved better.'

'No, Dad, you weren't a bad father. You did the best you could. I know I sometimes didn't live up to your expectations, and I was difficult. Don't blame yourself.'

'My expectations? My only expectation of you was to be happy.'

'Dad, I know you saw my depression as a weakness. I saw your disappointment, but it's OK. I understand now that that's just who you are. You never suffered from it, so you can't know what it's like.'

'Oh, baby girl, no! I'm so sorry you felt that way. I was never disappointed with you. I was angry at myself. I saw your issues as my fault. I thought I had let you down and that I should've been stronger for you. Oh, Peanut, you could never let me down.'

'I guess we both could've tried a little harder to understand each other better,' Mary said, shifting her eyes away from his.

'Your mum used to say the same thing to me all the time.' A sombre silence settled on them at the mention of Sophia.

A few moments later, the truck grumbled to a stop outside the gates of the Clyde Boatyard. They all stepped from the truck and walked to the Ford Focus parked in the dark corner of the empty car park. Amos fished the keys from his pocket and pressed the button. The car's lights flashed twice, indicating it was now unlocked. Amos climbed into the driver's seat, and Mary slipped into the passenger's side while George clambered his huge frame into the cramped back seat. Once inside, they sat in silence. Mary heaved a heavy sigh and let the tension slip from her shoulders. The end was in sight. This nightmare was almost over.

'The phone's in there, Peanut,' Amos said, gesturing to the glove box. Mary pulled the handle and let the door fall open. She fished the phone out and put her thumb on the screen. The biometric scanner opened the phone instantly, and it lit up the car.

The familiar yellow square with the white ghost at its centre flashed and notified her that she had a Snapchat message. Absent-mindedly, she opened the app and gasped.

'What is it?' Amos urged. 'What's wrong?'

Mary turned the phone to show her father. On the screen was a picture of Gerry and McGuire tied up, back-to-back, on two chairs. Blood-spotted white rags dangled from their mouths, and they both had fresh cuts and bruises. An address was superimposed at the bottom, and beneath the picture was the caption:

Bring the phone or they both die.
One hour.
No cops.

Chapter 47

'It's a trap,' George said from the back seat after a long silence.

'Obviously,' Amos replied sternly. He still wasn't completely convinced of the gorilla's sudden change of allegiance. He stared through the windscreen into the darkness. His eyes scanned left, then right, then down, then to the right again, but what he was looking for was not outside the car. 'They must have been watching Rachel's flat,' he said, after a long pause. 'What an idiot!'

'It's not your fault, Dad.'

'It is my fault, Mary. I should've known better. That's twice I've put your Uncle Gerry in danger because of a stupid mistake.' Amos heard the leather grip of the steering wheel groan under his tightening grip. 'Where are they?' Amos hissed through gritted teeth.

'Dad, maybe we should go to the police.'

'Where are they?' he repeated, this time with a growl.

'Boydie has a place he uses for these kinds of things. It's an old farm just outside of Clarkston,' George offered.

'These kinds of things?' he asked. 'Does he torture and kill people a lot?'

'It's the nature of the business, Dad.'

'How could you be involved with a guy like that?' Amos snapped.

'The people who end up at the farm have made their choices.' Mary said. 'They chose not to pay their bills, double-cross Boydie, or whatever. They knew the dangers and made their choices.'

'The girls he's trafficking don't have a choice!' he said.

'I know, Dad,' Mary snapped back. She looked away from him and sighed. 'That's why I decided to get out. He crossed the line.'

'That's where your line is? Drug dealing and murder are OK, but sex trafficking is too far?'

'Hurting innocent people. That is where my line is.'

The pain in her reply was obvious. 'OK, Peanut. I'm sorry.'

'So, what's the plan, Mr Fisher?' George asked.

'Plan? An old soldier with health issues, an ex-bodybuilder with anger issues, and a pregnant girl with Daddy issues, armed with nothing more than harsh words and good intentions, take on an unknown number of wackos armed to the teeth with God knows what. No back-up. No plan. No hope.' Amos stared into the darkness again and reviewed his options. 'And I don't have a choice.'

'Pregnant?' George gasped. 'Does Boydie know?'

Mary shied away. 'No. I don't think so anyway. And I want to keep it that way. I don't want that bastard anywhere near my baby. It's my wean, not his!'

'That changes things a bit, then.'

'Yes, it does,' Amos interrupted. 'The plan is I get Mary safe and then I go and save my friends.'

'Not a chance!' Mary cried. 'You can't do this alone. Plus, Boydie wants all three of us there. If we don't go, he'll kill Uncle Gerry.'

'He's going to kill him anyway. Me too, so I need you safe.'

'If I may interject, Mr Fisher, I may have a plan.'

Amos and Mary twisted in their seats and looked at

the large man.

The address Mary gave was thirty minutes from the boatyard where the car was parked. That gave the trio a thirty-minute window to gather any supplies they could and get into position. It was a tighter schedule than Amos would have liked, but then again, he'd rather not be doing this at all. He'd much rather be sitting in his comfortable leather chair in his study with his dog, Sandy, basking in the sunshine in his bed by the big windows while his wife brought him coffee.

But that was impossible.

That comfort had been ripped from his hands by an unjust God, if there even was a God, which he doubted, and a psychopathic crime boss.

They took inventory of the weapons and tools they had and reviewed the plan suggested by George. It lacked finesse, proper previous planning, and, other than insider knowledge of the farm's layout, had very little usable intel. Those same warning cries Amos had heard in the deepest recesses of his mind started shouting again. They were not muffled and distant this time, though. They were loud and clear. Everything felt wrong. The voices shouted that George's intel would be outdated now, that the enemy would be expecting his involvement, and that they would be counting on his knowledge and adjusting accordingly. They would also be outnumbered and outgunned. The voices shouted all of this and more. Each warning sounded louder than the last, and none were willing to surrender ground for the sake of clarity of thought.

His instincts were clear. This was a bad idea.

Yet, amongst the rabble and the chaos of warnings and shouting in his mind, Amos heard a whisper. The whisper seemed to seep through the cracks in the wall of noise in his head. The whisper carried with it a glimmer of hope. *Was there something to the ape's plan? You know if we just...* He shook his head as the chorus continued its discordant chanting.

But it might work. If you think about it long enough, you could find the answer.

The crack in the wall widened. The whisper grew louder. The chanting hoard softened.

Amos turned to the man who had killed his dog, kidnapped his daughter, left him unconscious, and then brought his daughter back to him.

'OK, George, run me through your plan again.'

Chapter 48

British springtime was two days old, but the trees that scattered the farm were still bare. The long skeletal fingers of their branches reached out ominously in every direction. Desperate and decaying corpses futilely grasping for survival, hoping to stretch life out for one more day before winter chokes all life from their veins again. Survival was never an option. Death is inevitable. But spring brought the promise of resurrection. Soon the temperature would rise, the trees would blossom, and the lands surrounding the farm would become a hive of activity and life.

Soon, but not now.

It was a little before 5 am, and, although twilight threatened the horizon, the moon was still the only light source on the vast and empty fields that surrounded the farm. It cast long shadows that played on the eyes. It created movement where there was none and gave the illusion of stillness everywhere else. The cold air was still and lifeless. Amos's breath hung motionless. From his position at the top of the single-lane country road, and with the help of the field glasses he salvaged from DI Rachel McGuire's car before crashing it into the scrapyard gates, he scoped out the farm. Unlike the surrounding fields, it was brightly lit by a series of floodlights. The whole compound shone like a beacon at the centre of a sea of darkness. The farmhouse was a two-storey sandstone building that looked like it was built in the early 1900s. It faced east and looked over the only approaching road. From the second-storey window, you could see a car coming from a mile away. No stealthy entry. The three outbuildings stretched west and formed a U-shape behind it. An oversized garage, probably built to house a tractor or another type of farming equipment, he guessed, was at the westernmost end of the complex. The two large doors of the garage were locked in their open positions but revealed only darkness inside. At the centre of the structure was a large courtyard, which was partially hidden by the farmhouse itself. Fifty yards east of the main buildings was a huge barn, which was probably once used to house livestock. He scoped his field glasses back and forth but saw little movement.

'The barn,' George said, 'That's where he'll be keeping them. It's where he does all the dirty work.'

'No,' Amos replied coldly, 'The courtyard is the kill box. Gerry and McGuire will be held in the garage at the far end of the compound. One Tango will be with the hostages, which covers the west side; two with rifles on the upper floor of the outbuilding to the north; and another two in the farmhouse to the east. Boydie will come out alone to lure me into a false sense of security.'

'How do you know that?' Mary asked.

'Because that's what I would do. He might be an egotistical sociopath, but he's not an idiot.' Amos lowered the glasses and tossed them into the back seat of the Ford. The heavy door closed with a reassuring thunk as his hand followed the soft, slow curve of the roof and slid down the frame of the windshield, finally coming to rest on the headlight. He stared at the car for a long moment in silence. He had seen the thing as grotesque when he first laid eyes on its overly flamboyant spoiler, its bulky body kit, and the unnecessarily loud double exhaust pipes. But now, at the end, even he had to admit it was a pretty spectacular car. It was fast, reliable, and satisfyingly responsive.

He wasn't sure why he was suddenly so sentimental, especially about a car. Maybe the car had awakened and realised some kind of juvenile, boy racer fantasy that most men seem to have stirring somewhere deep down inside them. The only differences between men and boys are the size of their shoes and the price of their toys. Or maybe it was the knowledge of his impending murder that made him appreciate the things around him a bit more. Maybe a little bit of both. Either way, he looked at the Ford now as though he were saying his final goodbyes to an old friend.

He did a final equipment check, then slipped into the driver's seat and fired up the Ford for the last time. The full beams of the bright LED headlights lit up the single-track dirt road and large swathes of the surrounding fields as the tyres spun wildly, spraying up dry dirt behind them. The roar of the car's modified engine thundered across the open fields like a lion, scattering the nocturnal wildlife back to their hides. The Ford's suspension rattled as the car chewed up the dirt road at tremendous pace. *One last hurrah in a magnificent machine.*

Twenty yards from the farmhouse's front door, he pulled on the handbrake and yanked the wheel hard left. The car skidded and travelled the last fifteen feet sideways, kicking dirt and dust over the face of the house. He slapped the handbrake back down and stamped on the accelerator again. The engine roared again, and the car lunged forward another twenty yards before he pulled the handbrake again and spun the car right, one hundred and thirty degrees, and gunned the accelerator once more. The car raced into the large courtyard of the farm and did three full doughnuts before finally coming to a rest at the south end of the compound. The car had thrown dirt all over the farmhouse, and the three outbuildings and a huge plume of dust covered the courtyard. He stepped from the car and scanned the buildings for any armed men, but the floodlights placed in the corners of the courtyard blinded his sight from what lay behind them. The ground sloped gently towards an open-faced structure with a fence and feeding trough, which lay at the south end of the courtyard. *Probably some sort of feeding pen.* A wide rain gutter ran the length of the pen. Finally, he turned his back to the farmhouse and faced the large garage.

Amos was now a sitting duck.

A cough echoed from the darkness inside the open garage door as a tall, angular silhouette snaked slowly out. The lanky figure waved a hand in front of his face in a futile attempt to fan away the dust cloud.

'Was that really necessary?' the figure hissed.

'Hello, William,' Amos said coldly. 'It's been a while.'

'Ah, so you do remember me,' William Boyd said, as he slithered from the cloud and came to a stop twenty feet from where Amos stood.

'You've lost weight. You were a lot chubbier when we went for dinner. What was that, six years ago?'

'Eight. I must admit, Amos, you've managed to impress and annoy me at the same time. Most men would have either given up by now or had the decency to just fucking die.' Boydie spat the last few words with all the venom and anger of a viper lunging for the kill.

'I would say I'm sorry to disappoint, but...' Amos let the silence finish his sentence for him.'

'Tell me something, Amos. That night at the restaurant, the night of Mary's birthday, you saw something in me, didn't you?'

'Yes. I couldn't put my finger on it at the time, but given enough time, I can figure anything out.'

'I'm curious, old man, what was it? What did I do that let you see what so many others didn't?' The dust cloud had settled now, and Amos could see Boydie's dark, beady predator eyes stare at him, tracking his every move. The air grew thick, and a few drops of light rain began to patter onto the two men.

'You really want to know?'

'I wouldn't be asking otherwise.' Boydie rubbed his hands, his long sinewy fingers intertwining as he did. His slick tongue flicked across his lips as though ready to devour Amos's words.

'Your smile,' Amos said, then let the quiet of the morning settle.

'My smile?'

'Your smile was wrong. You showing your top *and* bottom teeth, but the smile didn't reach your eyes.'

'I showed my teeth?'

'Psychopaths and sociopaths don't feel genuine happiness, so they try to emulate what they see other people do, but they get it wrong. That's why your smile was off, and it didn't reach your eyes. It's hard to show an emotion you've never felt.'

'That's it? A smile?'

'There were other signs too. I've been around a lot of kids like you. Sick little bastards who just wanted to hurt people. I know the type. And you are a sick bastard.'

'Well!' Boydie shouted, clapping his hands. The noise ricocheted off the surrounding buildings and echoed loudly before trailing off into silence. 'You've got me there, Mr Fisher.' His voice turned sharp and angry when he called Amos by his title.

'I guess I have you and George to thank for putting me in the hospital?'

'Hah!' Another clap bounced around the courtyard. 'Yes, you do. But you have to admit, you had it coming.'

'How?'

'You tried to take Mary away from me!' Amos could see saliva spraying from Boydie's mouth as he yelled this. 'She was mine, and you tried to take her from me. That couldn't go unpunished. You must have known it was coming, Amos. You saw what I was; you were the only one who ever did. Well, you and Plod. Plod saw my "condition" for what it really was. A gift.'

'You call not being able to feel basic emotions, a gift?'

'Of course! I'm not burdened with the inane trivial worries that everyone else is. I have clarity of vision and the drive to see that dream come to fruition. I am a visionary with the balls to get what needs done, done. I'm not one of those feeble ants scurrying around for scraps. I am destined for something more. Something greater.' The rain grew from a few spatters to a light but steady downpour.

'Is that why you're running guns in Ireland? You leading the revolution and uniting Ireland under one red hand?'

'What do I care about Ireland? Or its petty bullshit? Two factions of idiots are arguing about whose version of the Lord's Prayer is better. It's pathetic.'

'Think you've oversimplified the scenario a bit there, William.'

'I don't care! The gun running is a means to an end. Drug dealing is a means to an end. The girls are just a means to an end,' Boydie spat, overemphasising each word as though they were a sentence unto themselves. 'Power is what really matters. And once I finalise this deal with O'Neil, I will be one of the richest and most powerful men in Scotland.' His voice grew raspy and lowered to a growl. 'Now, Mr Fisher, give me the phone.'

'Let my friends go first.'

'THAT'S NOT HOW THIS IS GOING TO WORK!' Boydie screamed. 'Give me the phone or they die!' With that, he clicked his fingers. From the darkness of the garage behind him, a stocky man dressed in black pushed Gerry and McGuire into the beams of the floodlights. Their hands were strapped together at the wrists with zip ties. A thick rope tied around their heads held the rags, which were stuffed into their mouths, in place. Gerry stumbled and fell as the stocky goon pushed him again. McGuire, hampered by her bindings, helped him to his feet. The air grew thick.

Amos half turned his head and nodded slightly.

A deafening crack rang out in the courtyard, amplified by the stone walls surrounding them.

William Boyd ducked reflexively.

Amos Fisher stood still.

The stocky man dressed in black dropped to his knees, then fell face down into the dirt. Boydie watched on as a pool of blood spread into the dirt under his man. 'Shoot this prick!' he screamed at the upper floors of the outbuildings.

No shots were fired.

'Thank you, George,' Amos said, holding the hidden earpiece tight in his ear.

'No problem, Mr Fisher,' George's voice crackled in his ear.

'You talk too much, William. You like the sound of

your own voice. And people who talk too much are easily distracted.'

'Fine. I'll do it myself,' Boydie said as he whipped a pistol from his jacket.

'I wouldn't do that if I were you,' Mary said, as she stepped from the gloom of the garage behind him. The rifle she took from the unconscious snipers she tased in the outbuilding looked bulky but steady in her arms as she aimed it straight at his chest. 'Drop it.' Her words were stern and cold. *That's my girl*, Amos thought proudly. George stepped from the outbuilding, leaving four unconscious snipers in his wake, took up position beside Mary, and pointed his rifle. Boydie's eyes narrowed, and he growled at his cousin. He then opened his hand and let his gun clatter to the floor.

'That it?' Boydie snapped, turning his attention back to Amos. 'You gonna kill me now? Or hand me over to the cops? Huh?'

'Nope,' Amos said as he unzipped his jacket and pulled the wire from his ear. 'You kidnapped my daughter, hurt my friends, smashed up my home, and killed my dog. I'm going to kick your fucking head in.' At that moment, the heavens opened, and a thick, heavy rain came lashing down.

An evil grin spread across Boydie's face. 'Let's do this, old man. To the death.' The two men crouched and began to circle each other. Each one sizing the other up. Amos's deep-tread boots would offer him better grip than Boydie's leather dress shoes. *Failure to prepare*, he thought. The circle tightened until they were within arm's reach. Boydie feigned a lunge, and Amos snapped back. They danced around for a few seconds more before Boydie finally exploded from his coiled stance. His right hand swung wildly, but Amos ducked and drove his left elbow into Boydie's ribs. The momentum of both men moving in opposite directions added power to the blow, and Amos felt a rib crack. The dusty ground had drunk all the rain it could and choked up the rest, turning the hard ground into slippery mud. Amos's right foot landed hard and slid, throwing him off balance. He had just regained his footing and was mid-pivot when Boydie's shoulder crunched into his side and lifted him off his feet. The two men landed hard in the mud and slid. Before Amos had a chance to regroup from the tackle, Boydie had thrown him onto his back and straddled his hips, pinning his legs to the floor. Fists began to rain down. Amos instinctively raised his arms to his head to block the blows. The punches flew hard and fast. Some were deflected by his raised arms, while others hooked around, landing on his ear and head.

'Boydie!' Mary cried and fired a shot into the air. William Boyd flinched, then glanced at Mary. Amos quickly scrambled into his pocket and found the Smith & Wesson SWBG2TS tactical knife that Sophia had given him for his 50th birthday. The blade snicked open, and he drove it deep into Boydie's thigh, twisting the blade to inflict maximum damage. Boydie wrenched back in pain, and Amos curled up and landed a straight left into Boydie's already cracked rib. Amos shoved him hard, freed his legs, and scrambled back to his feet. Boydie bounced off the floor with surprising speed and pulled the blade from his thigh. Blood poured from his wound. Leaving the blade in his leg may have been a mistake. Boydie regrouped, and the two men began to circle each other again. They moved around until they had swapped sides, Amos with his back to the garage, and Boydie with his to the opening of the courtyard. In a half crouch, Boydie readied himself for another rush forward when another deafening crack echoed off the stone walls.

Amos ducked instinctively.

Boydie did not move.

William Boyd stood still for what seemed like the longest moment, his eyes glazed, before falling forward onto the pieces of his skull and brains that had exploded onto the floor in front of him.

A new figure occupied the space where Boydie stood a moment before. 'Mr Fisher, where is the phone?' the familiar voice boomed.

'Graham?' Amos said, raising his hands against the lights and torrential downpour.

'That's not Graham!' McGuire yelled, as Mary was working the rag free from Gerry's mouth. 'That's DCI Clarke!'

'I don't have time for this. Where is the phone?' As Clarke yelled, two armed men dressed in black followed behind him and pointed automatic rifles at Amos. Another two rushed from the garage and aimed their weapons at the others, who instantly raised their hands.

'It's somewhere safe,' Amos yelled over the loud torrential rain.

'I'm not playing, Mr Fisher. Give me the phone or you and your friends will be dead quicker than a gay Jew at a Nazi rally.'

'I'm telling you the truth, I don't have it here, but I can take you to it.'

'I don't believe you,' Clarke said, then pointed his gun at Mary. The shot seemed louder and slower than the others that had been fired in the confined courtyard. The echo seemed to ricochet endlessly between the four buildings.

'I'll ask one last time, Mr Fisher. Where is the phone?'

Before Amos could answer or even register what had happened, a voice boomed, 'Put the weapons down on the ground and put your hands in the air.' A spotlight brighter than the floodlights blinded him from above. It was only then that he heard the thunder of the helicopter blades and felt the rush of wind pushing him down, and the voice repeated the instructions. Loud sirens and screeching tyres sounded as countless cars ground to a halt in front of the farmhouse. The four armed men did as instructed and laid their weapons down. Clarke, however, fired a shot at the spotlight, forcing the helicopter to veer backward. He then began sprinting towards the garage, away from the sirens, barging past Amos as he went. Amos regained his footing and started after him. Clarke was ten feet from the garage door when Amos lunged and brought him to the ground. Clarke scrambled to his back, swinging his gun as he turned. Amos grabbed the hand mid-swing, and a shot zipped past his ear. He twisted the gun from Clarke's hand, tossed it in the mud, and grabbed for his head. The sound of DCI Clarke's head hitting the ground again and again was drowned out by the rain, the helicopter, and the hoard of officers now flooding the courtyard. By the time the officers had managed to drag Amos away, Clarke was dead. His blood pooled in the mud around him, and his eyes glazed over.

In a panic, Amos pushed the two men that had dragged him from Clarke's corpse away and was frantically searching for Mary. She sat in the mud, and as George lay splayed in the mud, a dark red patch soaked his stomach.

George Brown had died once before, but this time was

different. This time, it was final. His head lay cradled on her lap as his breathing slowed. His once broad, strong frame felt weak and limp in her arms now. Her hand pressed tighter into his wound to try and stem the flow, but it was no use. The thick blood oozed, mixed with heavy rain, and washed into the gutter. With the last of his strength, he raised his hand and wiped away her tears, and he smiled.

He was ready now.

Ready to die.

For her.

Chapter 49

Amos, Mary, Gerry, and McGuire sat in the boxy, windowless room, staring blankly at the one-way mirror on the wall. The bright fluorescent strip light on the low ceiling accented each cut, bruise, and scrape on all of their faces. Amos had questions to ask, things to say, and apologies to make, but he was spent. He suspected, by their silence and empty looks, that the others felt the same.

The dull hum of the light fixture filled the silence and somehow enhanced it. Four coffees sat untouched on the metal table in front of them. Amos finally reached for Mary's hand and intertwined his fingers with hers. This seemed to break her from a deep thought. She smiled at her father and clasped her hand around his. 'I love you, Peanut,' was all he could manage. Her smile spread to her eyes, and she rested her head on his shoulder.

The coffee had gone cold before the door to the interrogation room swung inward. A small, stout man with grey hair, a matching moustache, and thick, black-rimmed glasses walked into the room, slapped a manilla folder onto the table, and sat in the single chair on the other side of the table with his back to the mirror. His expensive black suit and smart shoes told Amos he wasn't with the police.

'Hello, Amos,' he said. 'It's been a while. You look good, old friend.'

'Brian?' Amos said, squinting at the well-dressed man. 'Brian Farmer, is that you?'

The man beamed. 'Jesus, Amos, I know I've put a bit of beef on, but I haven't changed that much, surely?'

'Brian, it's good to see you, mate. When did you get the caterpillar on your lip?'

'This thing?' Farmer said, stroking his grey moustache. 'I grew it a few years ago to annoy the wife. I like it. Now, to business.' Farmer opened the manilla folder. 'What the hell have you guys been up to?' This was more of an accusation than a question, and he did not wait for an answer. He slid an A4 colour picture of a dead body missing a large portion on its skull and said, 'William Boyd, AKA Mr B. Orphaned at thirteen, he spent years bouncing around foster homes before doing a short stint in Polmont, where he was primarily diagnosed with narcissistic psychopathic tendencies.' Farmer waited a beat before sliding the next picture of another corpse from the folder. 'Detective Chief Inspector James Clarke of Police Scotland. A highly decorated police officer with over twenty years' service.' Farmer left another long pause before sliding a third photo onto the table. 'Geroge Brown. A former amateur bodybuilder turned armed muscle for Mr Boyd. Anyone care to explain what happened?'

'It was me, Brian,' Amos offered. 'Just me. Nobody else.'

'You, Amos? You expect me to believe you single-handedly brought down an international drug, sex, and gun ring? That you, without the help of anyone at this table, infiltrated, what my IT specialists are calling, one of the most advanced and unhackable security systems they have ever seen? That an ex-Royal Engineer with little to no investigative or computer skills uncovered possibly the biggest case of police and political corruption in recent history? Oh, by the way, Miss Fisher, my team asked me to say that having a key and lock system over multiple devices was inspired.'

'Wait, what?' McGuire asked sitting forward in her chair.

'Yes, DI McGuire, the information discovered in the file vault has evidence of not only police corruption, ie DCI Clarke's involvement, but details certain prominent political figures too. There was evidence of everything from payoffs to underage sex scandals. The vault also detailed arms deals with Saudi, Somalian, and Ukrainian gangs. The deal you interrupted, Amos, was the trial run before the deal was to be finalised. It would have made Mr Boyd et al a lot of money.'

'Holy shit, Buttercup,' Gerry gasped.

'Holy shit indeed, Mr O'Hara. Thanks to you, though, we now have all the evidence we need to scoop up the last of the organisation and put them all in prison for a very long time. In fact, Sean O'Neil is being picked up as we speak. He was trying to flee back to Ireland when he heard about Clarke's death.'

'Why would he care about Clarke's death?' Mary asked. 'Boydie was the boss, wasn't he?'

'It looks like DI Clarke was the real brains behind the operation. As far as we can tell, Clarke spotted Mr Boyd when he was in Polmont. He obviously saw potential in the boy's condition and used him not only as the face of the criminal empire but to do all the dirty work too.'

'So, what happens now?' McGuire asked. 'What happens to us?'

'Well, DI McGuire, Special Branch will take it from here. You will return to work after a long holiday with a commendation and possibly a slightly larger office. As for the rest of you, you were never part of any of our investigation and are free to go about your lives.' With that, Farmer put the pictures back in the folder and slapped it closed.

'Wait,' Amos said. 'How did you find us?'

'The phone in your glove compartment had a tracker.'

'Aye, but Gerry scrambled that.'

'What did I tell you, Amos?' Gerry chirped. 'Always build a back door. After I cracked some of the files, and before Damir knew what I was doing, I sent all the info to Brian. I gave him the backdoor key to the scrambled signal so he could find it.'

'Now, my people are still going through all the data from the file vault. I suggest you all go home and have some rest.' Farmer pushed his chair back and stood. 'Amos,' he said, as he extended his hand. Amos shook the hand. 'Good to see you again, and my condolences for your loss.'

Farmer left the room and closed the door softly behind him.

The dull hum of the light fixture filled the room once more.

Chapter 50

Sophia's funeral took a little longer than expected to be arranged. After the whole ordeal with William Boyd, neither Amos nor Mary felt physically, mentally, or emotionally capable of rushing the task. Three weeks after her death, Amos, Mary, and a small group of close friends and family finally said their goodbyes. Amos hated it. He hated the "I'm sorry for your losses", the "How are you keepings?" and the "If there is anything I can dos." All those banal platitudes that people didn't really mean. It just seemed like the right thing to say. Each gentle touch of his arm and look of pity from others was a knife in his gut, reminding him of what he had lost. What he really wanted was to have his wife back. He wanted to not go back to a house where she wasn't. He wanted to not expect her to wake him up with a kiss like she always did and feel the pain of her loss all over again when he woke up alone in his bed. Each morning was a knife plunging into his chest. He wanted to stop lifting two cups from the cupboard when he made his morning coffee. Yesterday, he put two sugars and way too much milk into the cup, just the way she liked it, before he realised what he was doing. Another knife plunge.

Thank God he had Mary. She had stood by his side, arm in arm with him, to deflect the onslaught of well wishes from caring people. She spoke for him and thanked everyone for their kind words and offers. Mary was better at dealing with people than he was, just like her mother was. God, she looks just like her. The knife jabbed his gut again. This jab he welcomed, though. He had watched Mary intently that day and was just glad she was there.

Life seemed to go by in a haze in the weeks after the funeral. Mary had moved back into her old room, and father and daughter found solace in each other. They no longer argued about the trivial things that once strained their relationship. Amos wasn't sure if he had changed or Mary had. Maybe both.

Their life after William Boyd was, thankfully, quiet.

Then it happened.

Whether it was the stress of the previous weeks, the seizures, or the multiple head blows Amos had, the doctors couldn't be sure. All they could say for sure was that the tumours had grown. They had spread to other parts of his brain, and the seizures became more and more frequent until they caused a stroke. The doctors had said that he would probably never walk again. His speech may return, but it would take extensive rehab. They had blamed the tumours for his slow recovery, or was it his age? He wasn't sure. He couldn't concentrate on the words when they were explaining them to him. Mary had taken note of all the medication and appointment times for him. She had translated what the doctors had said and told him she would look after him. He felt guilt and relief at this. He hated being a burden on his daughter like that but was grateful for her.

In the few months since the stroke, Amos had regained partial use of his mouth, and his right hand felt like his again. He had resolved to spend most of his time in his study now, reading thriller novels. He was halfway through another Jack Reacher book when he heard the front door open and then swing closed.

'We're home, Dad,' Mary called from the hall. He folded the book over and waited to hear his new favourite sound. A few moments passed before Mary gently opened the study door, stepped in with his grandson in her arms, and sat beside him. The boy looked cosy, cocooned in his all-in-one suit. The sound of his soft gurgles filled more than just the room. Amos smiled with the working side of his mouth while the other side remained drooped. 'I spoke with Uncle Gerry today,' Mary said softly. 'He offered me a job. He said I was one of the best coders he's seen, next to him obviously, and I can work from home.' Amos beamed at her proudly and touched her arm. 'Did you see on the news that the First Minister resigned today? She said she was stepping down to spend more time with her family.' Mary smiled a knowing smile at him. Prominent political figures — that's what Farmer had said. 'We went down to the registrar office today too, didn't we?' she continued, cooing at the baby. 'Yes, we got you registered, and I finally settled on a name.' She returned her focus to her father. 'I know you probably wouldn't agree, but I named him after his father.' Amos scowled as best he could, then raised his palm in a "whatever" gesture. 'Are you hungry? You want some soup?' she asked. Amos nodded. 'Will we go and make Grandad some lunch?' Mary sang to the baby. 'Yeah? OK, let's go, George.'

The End

About The Author

I'd like to thank my family, Lindsay, Presley and Paige, for their support while writing this book. And a special thanks to Alex for all your help. You helped make this book what it is. Finally, I'd like to thank everyone at Blossom Spring Publishing for their amazing work. You have done a great job.

I am a part-time procrastinator, a full-time dreamer, and a father of two. I spend most of my free time with my head in a book and a cup of tea in my hand.

I discovered a passion for writing after watching Reacher on Amazon Prime. I mentioned to my wife that I might read one of the books. My wonderful wife then took it upon herself to pick up every Jack Reacher novel she found in every charity shop.

A love for reading was born. I then watched an interview with Lee Child where he said that his first book wasn't published until he was almost 40. Being 36 at the time myself, I decided to give writing a go.

A year and a half later, I signed my first publishing deal with Blossom Spring Publishing for my debut novel Beast and Burden.

leeadamauthour@outlook.com
Twitter (X): Lee.Adam1666750
Instagram: lee.adam1986

www.blossomspringpublishing.com

Printed in Great Britain
by Amazon

51104601R00164